Presence of

Malice

By

Kevin Paul Tracy

Daydream Industries, Inc.
www.DaydreamIndustries.com

Also by
Kevin Paul Tracy

Rogue Agenda

Published by TWB Press
  Bloodflow
  Bloodtrail

Praise for *Presence of Malice*

"A battle of sharp and captivating characters. Tracy delivers a relentless page-turner."

Nicole Disney, *Dissonance in A Minor*

"A creative thriller! The hero is wounded and fascinating, and the evil that seeps onto the pages creates a suspenseful, fascinating story. This author colors outside the lines."

Janet Lane, *Crimson Secret*

"Tracy's plot twists…into a sailor's knot. Be ready for a wild ride with surprises around every curve."

Mariko Layton, *Accidental Samurai Spy*

"A…descent into…treachery."

Mario Acevedo, *Rescue from Planet Pleasure.*

"*Presence of Malice*, where…the ugly can't get any uglier."

John Turley, *A Simple Truth*

"You've got to be kidding me. Kevin Paul Tracy has more twists in *Presence of Malice* than a bag of strawberry Twizzlers, a wild, fast-paced killer-thriller with good guys I loved to love and bad guys I loved to hate."

Terry Wright: Author, Editor, Publisher

PRESENCE OF MALICE

For Lisa

ACKNOWLEDGEMNTS

Thanks to Nicole, my oh so patient reader, for indulging my hundreds of questions, in possession of a brain so rich and fertile for picking; to Jimma for editing so thoroughly and so quickly; to Karen for one of the most striking cover designs I've seen in years.

CHAPTER 1

Paul had super powers when it came to nursing one drink while making it appear that he was chugging them as fast as his buddies. The fact was Paul hated the taste of alcohol, thought most of the hard stuff tasted like the floor of an ER trauma unit. But ask any of his acquaintances, even Brooke and Henry, his two best friends from internship, everyone'd tell you Paul could slam them back with the best of them and still walk a straight line. Only Paul rarely ever finished one drink, if that, on a night out. He just had superior acting skills, misdirection, like any good magician.

But Paul was drinking now, had been almost nonstop for twelve hours. And not just sipping, he gulped back his Long Island like it really was just iced tea. Paul was nervous – fuck, he was scared shitless! And he was mad, angrier than he'd ever been before in his life. And so far the fear had not succeeded in dousing the anger enough to send him running out of that place like a broom-pushed alley cat. Which is what he supposed he should have done – thrown away that cursed number the guy had given him on a matchbook, like they were characters out of some cheesy black and white detective movie, picked up his feet and raced his shadow out of that place and never looked back.

But Paul didn't run. And maybe the alcohol he wasn't used to shored up his anger more than his fear. Anyway, Paul stuck, like he really knew what he was doing, like he really had any business being here at all, like he really had any right to do what he was doing. And when the stranger came in, Paul knew it was *him*. He didn't know how he knew, because the man didn't look like anything special at all. The approaching roar of a very loud motorcycle, then its death, and the stranger came walking out of the afternoon brightness into the dim, smoky barroom, strode up its long length. Just a guy, middle-height in jeans and buckle-boots, red and black plaid flannel shirt, unshaven around the edges of a goatee. Only things that made him stand out were the odd, beaten, shapeless black leather fedora on his head and the heavy floor-length black canvas coat that swept about him like a shroud as he shambled.

The stranger and the bartender looked at each other, clearly knowing one another but not well enough to exchange a greeting. Then the stranger came right at Paul where he sat at the table in the corner, at the back, behind the door that opened to the restrooms and storage rooms and exit to the alley. Dim back here, the guy didn't even look Paul's way, but he walked straight up and sat down in the other chair, slumping low and breathing, smelling of exhaust and cigarettes.

"There's somethin' you should know," he said without greeting or introduction. "And know it damned good, 'cause I ain't going to repeat myself and I ain't going to be around for you to change your mind or indulge in recriminations later, understand?"

His voice was soft, his enunciation uncultured, fitting in with his bottom-rung appearance, a strong suggestion of Texas in his accent. Paul just looked at him, mouth dry in spite of – because of? – the alcohol he'd been drinking, not trusting himself to speak. The man's wavy, lobe-length hair was sandy light brown or dirty blond. Wrinkles at the corners of the dead, grey-blue eyes, more from squinting into the sun than age. His face brown, leathery.

"You pay me to do something," he went on, finally looking at Paul, square in the face. "You pay me up front. What I do, how I do it is my business and not up for discussion. But get this if you don't get anything else - I'm not a boy scout. You're not hiring a hero or calling in the cavalry, here. I'm the farthest thing from a saint or an angel. I use whatever methods I decide are necessary, and I have no scruples.

"You might as well know now that what it usually takes is rarely pretty, seldom legal and almost never civilized. If you decide later you can't stomach my methods, tough. You pull this particular trigger and there's no stopping the bullet until it hits what it's aimed at. Now if knowing all that you still want to hire me, shoot...I'm listening."

From anyone else this monologue, delivered deadpan and unselfconsciously, would have been comical.

3

But something ice-cold in Paul's loins that made his testicles retract and caused his dick to turtle told him that if he laughed at that moment he'd regret it. The guy didn't blink and he didn't lick his lips. His hands were dead-still, fingers resting on the edge of the table, not drumming, not gesturing, not wasting any movement. Looking at his chest, his stomach, he might not have been breathing at all. He had an oversized, faux-silver oval on his belt like those meant to simulate prize rodeo buckles. But those eyes, glistening with a depth of blue that should have been warm and yet somehow couldn't have been colder, regarded Paul, measuring him, waiting for his response.

Paul cleared his throat. "Will you have a drink?"

"I don't drink with folks I do business with. Blurs the lines. We ain't buddies. We got business. If after our business is done you still want to hang out, we'll see about it. For now, I'd prefer to know what I'm here for."

"Anything, right?" Paul asked, then tried to explain himself. "I mean the guy gave me your number, he said you don't care, as long as there's money in it."

"That's right. Jobs I turn down, I turn down for my own reasons. It don't have nothing to do with conscience."

"I need you to kill my partner."

The stranger didn't react, not even so much as the twitch of an eyelash. He looked at Paul. Feeling the need to justify himself, Paul explained, "He has me in a way I can't get out of. It's all twisted, how he did it, but he knew what he was doing, what he wanted to do from the very beginning. Backed me into this corner and now he laughs at me because we both know there's no way for me to get out of it. The humiliation, that's only part of it. I could live with that, almost. But I'm going to go down, now, blamed for his shit and no way out. IRS breathing down my neck and I think even they know it's him and not me, but they're going after the fish they can land and he's going to get off with nothing more than a slap on the wrist. I want to see him dead before they send me up. I want that much satisfaction, at least."

The stranger just continued to stare at him. Paul fidgeted, then filled the silence by giving his name, the name of his partner and the address of their medical offices. Still the man stared in silence, so Paul offered the addresses of a few of the places his target was known to be seen: home, club, restaurants, etc. Still the silent patience.

"Well?" Paul snapped, angry, forgetting the fear, ready for the stranger to say no.

The man in black looked at Paul just a little longer. "What's the practice worth?"

Paul blinked at the non-sequitur. "I don't know, sell it now, before the scandal breaks, maybe ten million five. After, you probably couldn't give it away. Property and equipment maybe half a million. Why?"

"I'll take the half mil."

"What!" Paul's voice echoed along the narrow tavern. Faces turned, then whipped quickly back to their own business again, not wanting to be involved in case trouble broke out. The mysterious stranger hadn't flinched, but his eyes darkened perceptibly. "What?" Paul said again in a whisper. "You've got to be kidding me!"

"We're talking about taking a man's life. The only one he has. When it's gone it's gone forever. That's serious. Are you? If so, five hundred large ought to about cover it."

As the initial alarm blunted Paul reflected that his

companion was right. The practice was doomed, no question. Paul wasn't going to need money where he was going, and he had more than that in liquid assets and could liquidate probably another five times more for lawyers' fees and such. It was only the shock of hearing it said out loud that jolted him, not so much the money itself.

"Fine," Paul said, feigning reluctance. "But there's another problem. No way I can get my hands on that kind of cash without throwing up all sorts of alarms in the Treasury Department, not to mention the IRS. Did I mention they already have a thumb on me?"

His sarcasm was lost on the stranger. "All we do, we make it traceable. Before the end of the day a lawyer is going to contact you and your lawyer. You're going to settle a malpractice suit he is preparing to file out of court for the amount discussed. All paperwork to be filed legally and traceable. Story is, you didn't want to involve insurance if you didn't have to – premiums and all that – and to keep the press out. It's done all of the time."

"Who is the patient?"

"You'll find a complete set of medical records in your office in the morning, so if anyone checks it will seem as if the patient was a particularly difficult person whom you declined for surgery because of unrealistic expectations, who continued to hound you until you finally scheduled a procedure just to appease her. Once under anesthesia all you did was give her a surface cut with a scalpel and then bandage her up. But she wasn't fooled and now is suing you."

It seemed Paul's day to gawk. It could work – he knew of just such similar situations. The man was quick, efficient and simple. "Who are you?" he asked, his voice sounding hoarse to his own ears.

The stranger took the opportunity to stand and pull the copious wings of his oil-stained canvas coat around himself. He turned, strode between the tables, booths and stools without seeming to touch anything and was gone, the rumble of his bike thundering off into the hot afternoon.

CHAPTER 2

Patricia Duffy looked on as Dr. Gerald Gannery, MD grinned his biggest grin for the camera and the photographer snapped away. There were several other people moving around behind the lights, so Patricia stood back a distance to keep out of the way. With all the bright lights in his eyes Patricia doubted that Gerry could see her here in the shadows. For now, his entire world consisted of himself and the photographer. Gerry was dressed in shirtsleeves and suspenders sitting on a desk in a studio mocked up like an office.

To test her theory, she raised her middle finger at him. He waved vaguely back and smiled, which would not have been his reaction had he seen her clearly. She would have been fired, and right now she wasn't sure that she was glad he hadn't seen her.

"Can you turn down the wattage there, Doc?" the photographer paused to ask, glancing at Gerry over the top of his camera.

"Pardon me?"

"The smile," the photographer said. "It's eating your whole face."

"Sorry," Gerry said, then continued to smile. The photographer snapped a couple of more frames, then sighed in exasperation. "I'm sorry," Gerry said again. "It's just that life is so God damned good right now."

"Okay," the photographer said, "let's wrap. I have enough for now, I think."

As Gerry jumped down off of the desk, Patricia trotted up to him and handed him his coat, which he donned without thanking her. He strode off the edge of the stage and into the darkness. She followed him and began congratulating him on a fabulous photo shoot, feeling every bit the hypocrite. He stared through her vacantly as his pupils adjusted and she got down to telling him where he was supposed to be next.

"You have two hours for lunch and then you need to be at CNBC by four to do the spot shoot for the evening news. The script is in the town car. You can memorize it on the way as you always do. Then..."

"With who?"

"What?"

"With whom am I having lunch?" Gerry's voice was exaggeratedly pleasant, which was a major danger signal to Patricia, no less virulent than the flashing red light on the control panel of a nuclear reactor warning of meltdown.

Her heart sank. "I'm sorry, sir, but Mr. Moonletter canceled and I haven't been able to..."

"When?" Gerry began walking purposely toward the exit, nodding and waving importantly to people as they went.

Patricia scampered to follow. "What?"

If anything, his voice got even more saccharin sweet. "When did Moonletter cancel?"

"This morning. But I..."

"What time?" They were outside now, crossing the causeway to their waiting car.

Patricia said nothing about the makeup he was still wearing from the photo shoot. Instead she said, "Well, nine, but I..."

"It is now quarter to one," Gerry said, pausing by the open door of the town car to show her his watch without looking at it himself.

"I know, but..."

"That's three hours and forty-five minutes exactly."

"Yes, but I..."

"And you haven't scheduled a lunch with anyone else, anyone at all in that time?" Gerry was still smiling, the predatory sneer of a tiger as he toys with his prey.

"Well there was your dry cleaning, and then your mother called for a car and I had to send one, and then..."

"Ssht!" Gerry said as people emerged from the exit they had just left behind. "Get in the car." He climbed in and she followed. The chauffer closed the door on them and got behind the wheel.

As they pulled out into traffic Patricia grew quiet. Excuses would not help her now. She felt his grip on her bare knee and winced as he dug his fingers into her flesh. When he spoke his voice was soft, reasonable, dripping with venom.

"Time, to further abuse an already overused cliché, is money, my dear Patricia," he said. "Any moment not spent furthering one's goals in life had better be spent on leisure. And lunch, Patricia!" His voice sounded genuinely disappointed, as a father with a child. "Lunch is a prime opportunity for networking. To let such a window pass unused...well, it's criminal. Don't you agree?"

She tried to breathe to clear her mind of the pain shooting up her thigh, but it was impossible. Her heart beat with fear of another tirade and in spite of her best effort to keep her lips sealed a forlorn whimper escaped them.

"Every moment wasted that could be better spent is another nail in the coffin," he growled, though still smiling for the benefit of the chauffer, speaking through clenched teeth. "And let me assure you if it happens again I will make *fucking* sure that it's your coffin and not mine." His voice verged dangerously on hysterical. Patricia felt the pain as deep as her tibia now and tears flowed from her eyes.

"Hide your face, *cunt!*" he hissed.

She turned to the window and let her shoulder-length copper hair fall to curtain her features. She bit her cheek to restrain herself from crying out. She tasted blood.

And suddenly the pressure on her leg was gone. If anything the pain intensified and she gasped, then sobbed softly to herself. She pulled her leg away from his and put her hand protectively around it, rubbing to bring the feeling back.

"Don't be such a priss," he said. "I barely squeezed. Y'know you're going to have to toughen up if you're going to be a corporate attaché. Nowadays a good blow job just won't cut it. You've got to be ruthless. How many times have I told you, 'no quarter to your friends and no mercy to your enemies.' Sun Tzu said that."

She'd read *The Art of War* looking for that quote and just as she'd suspected Sun Tzu had said nothing of the sort. However, by inadvertently directing her attention to that text, Gerry had unintentionally done her a favor. There was much in Sun Tzu's writings that she had learned.

Gannery had snatched her right out of graduate school to work for him. Her parents had mortgaged the family home twice to pay for her school. Gannery had bought that loan in exchange for four years' commitment from her. She had been bright-eyed and idealistic, fresh from the well-intentioned but abysmally naïve curriculum of an Ivy League tradition. She'd not been prepared for the ethically corrupt, morally ambiguous reality of business in practice. Now she dared not leave him, not with the fate of her family's home hanging over her head. It wasn't just her parents, but her sister, her brother, their families, and two grandmothers, all living on a small family farm.

But even that wasn't it. In truth, she was afraid to quit. She was afraid of him. She had seen the black hole in his center that would never pass for a heart. She saw the white hot liquid lava roiling just below his surface, the capacity to do great evil when crossed. She was afraid, she was weak, but she was certain taking her family's home away would be the least of his vengeance should she leave him.

He'd kill her.

"So now I have two hours of knocking around,"

Gerry was saying. "I can't go to a restaurant – I don't dare be seen out alone, as if I couldn't get a lunch meeting. I'm going to have Palmer drop you off at the Wall Street office. I want you to think about what I've said. And I want you to think about whether or not you're tough enough and smart enough to be my assistant."

They rode the rest of the way in silence. Patricia had dried her face by the time the driver pulled up to the curb outside the building that housed the medical practice her boss shared with Dr. Paul Jurgens. She thanked him quietly and climbed out. Gerry glared out the far window and did not acknowledge her departure. The car pulled into traffic. Patricia stared after it for a few moments, then walked toward the entrance of the building.

She saw a lanky stranger dressed in a dirty canvas duster and beat-up leather fedora standing by the window recess next to the entrance. He struck her as an anachronism, out of place in the city as if he'd only just stepped out of a Western. She thought he was watching her, studying her, but it was hard to tell because his eyes were shadowed by the hat's brim.

After she had stepped inside the tinted glass of the entrance she turned to look at him again. He tossed his cigarette to the pavement, bouncing, sparking like a child's firework, strode purposefully toward a motorcycle parked at the curb, started it and sped off in the direction Gerry's town car had gone.

*

Dr. Gerald Gannery, MD, wasn't really angry. But just as one must not squander an opportunity to promote oneself, one should also never squander an opportunity to instruct a subordinate in the proper performance of their duties. In point of fact he had done Patricia a favor.

Having done her such a service, it was only right that he should feel, contrary to anger, quite pleased with himself.

"Palmer," he said to the driver. "Is there any little hole in the wall café around here where I won't be seen?"

The bullet-shaped mass of Palmer's black head nodded slowly once. He maneuvered around traffic, circling blocks until he came back around to a little beat up sidewalk restaurant on Pearl just off of Wall. Gerry sighed.

"This the best you can do?"

"You don't want to be seen, Boss, right?" Palmer's basso voice carried easily over the seat.

Gannery didn't answer but sighed again and got out, hefting his briefcase after him. As he was crossing the walk to the greasy spoon someone pulled up behind him in a very loud and annoying motorcycle and killed the engine. Gannery entered the noisy and malodorous diner decorated in Formica and stainless steel and walked among the tables holding his jacket close so as not to brush up against anything or anyone.

The waitresses were dressed in very short pink checkered flare-skirts, white blouses, thin red ties, and tiny white caps reminiscent of nurses. The patrons were mostly blue-collar and either greasy or dusty, or some combination of the two. Gannery took a booth at the back as far from the huge bay windows that fronted the place as possible, used the paper napkin provided to brush at the bench, then sat himself down, holding his briefcase up as if afraid to set it down.

The motorcycle guy, some big scarecrow of a ragamuffin smelling of tobacco and exhaust, took the only other remaining booth right next to Gannery's. The doctor wrinkled his nose at the fumes and shook his head. He flagged a passing waitress.

"Could somebody come wipe this table down?"

She patted his arm cheerfully and then veritably bellowed for a harried busboy, a short, dusky, brooding fellow, who bustled over and gave Gannery's table a cursory wipe with a soiled rag. With another resigned sigh Gannery settled his briefcase down on the table and opened it.

Consulting his PDA for the number, Gannery retrieved his cell phone and dialed.

"Bloom Agency."

"Hello, Dora, this is Gerald. May I speak to Harry?"

"Whom may I say is calling?"

Gannery missed a beat. "Gerald. Dr. Gerald Gannery."

"Just a moment," Dora said and the line went blank.

The waitress came and Gannery ordered a salad and iced tea, something he thought might have a minimum of germs and incidental kitchen filth in it.

Harry came on the line. "Gerry! Buddy! How are you?"

"Fine. I was wondering how it was going with the HBO people?"

"What do you mean?"

"What do you mean what do I mean? The deal!"

"Well I haven't spoken to them since our last meeting."

"Well why the hell not?" Gannery snapped.

"Calm down, Gerry..."

"Don't tell me how to be, Harry. Why the hell haven't you talked to the HBO people?"

"Okay, Gerry. It's because you haven't fulfilled your end of the bargain yet."

Gannery hesitated.

Harry Bloom, Agent and Publicist, went on, "They are going to be watching you on CNBC tonight, of course. But until you are free to make this deal, we have nothing more to discuss with them. Have you been able to get out of your current partnership?"

"Not yet," Gerry growled. "The IRS and Justice Department are stupid! I mean, I couldn't make it too obvious or they'd smell a setup, but Jesus Christ already!"

"Gerry, why don't you just buy the guy out? Why do you have to destroy him like this?"

"I told you," Gerry said. "Because I don't have the money to buy him out. After four divorces I'm hemorrhaging cash like a clubbed seal."

"Then why not offer to let him buy you out?"

"Because he'd want to know why. And he wouldn't want to do it, but he would. As a friend. And I can't let anyone get up on me. I won't owe anyone a favor. Especially not him." He wasn't bothering to hold his voice down. No one here could possibly comprehend the implications of what he was saying, not this riff-raff.

"How so?"

"It's a long story." Gerry was uncomfortable with the tack the conversation had taken. "Look, this isn't personal, Harry, it's business."

"I'm not sure he'd agree," Harry said.

"Whose side are you on?" Gerry snapped.

"Your side. But I couldn't do what you're doing."

"Why not? You face an obstacle, you surmount it. He's an obstacle. That's all. Listen, tell the HBO folks it's all but a done deal. Tell them if they wait, they won't regret it."

"I'll see what I can do," Harry said in a doubtful tone. "But they aren't going to wait forever."

Gannery hung up as the waitress brought his order. The tea splashed as she hit the table with it and a single spot appeared on his otherwise pristine pressed white shirt. "Shit," he said. "Where's the restroom?" She pointed it out to him. He hurried across the long restaurant to the door marked *Mens* and went in. That always annoyed him about public restrooms – the word *Men* was already pluralized, and if they meant the possessive they left out the apostrophe.

The bathroom was a nightmare and he was reluctant to stand close to the sink as he dabbed at the spot on his shirt with a sopping, shredding wad of toilet paper. The water was ice cold, the hand-soap watery and smelled of dishwashing liquid. There were no towels and the hand dryer whined loudly but blew no air. He ended by shaking his hands dry. Cursing some more he returned to his booth.

The motorcycle guy was gone, thank God.

He had gotten halfway through his salad when the waitress returned.

"That guy?" She pointed to the booth where the biker had been sitting. "He took something out of your case there before he left."

Gannery lunged for his briefcase and took an instant visual inventory. Nothing seemed to be missing. "What did he take?"

"I didn't see," she said. "But he's still out there talking to that black fella." She used her pen to point outside.

Gannery looked out the window. Palmer lounged

against the front fender of the Lincoln. Next to him leaned the lanky, tanned stranger. They were chatting and chuckling together. Gannery extricated himself from the booth and charged toward the door. As he emerged into the heated air he observed that the stranger was back astride his two-wheeled monstrosity. The machine roared to life and sped away.

Marching up to Palmer, Gannery demanded, "What the fuck did he want?"

"Nothin' much," Palmer said, nonplused. "Jus' passin' the time o' day. How come?"

"Because he stole something from my briefcase!"

Palmer galvanized and stepped toward the driver's door of the town car. "Want me to chase 'im down?"

Gannery, who realized he didn't know yet what exactly had been taken, if anything, told Palmer no and marched back into the diner. Resuming his seat, he took a more thorough inventory of the contents of his briefcase and again found nothing missing.

The waitress must have been mistaken, or the man was only interested in cash and found none. But then, as Gannery started to close the case he noted the faceplate of his cell phone. Instead of showing the logo of his service provider as it usually did, there was a number displayed there. It was Harold Bloom's number.

The stranger had accessed the last-number-dialed feature of the phone to find out whom Gannery had been speaking to. Clearing the screen, Gannery placed the phone back in the briefcase and closed and latched the lid. He sat pensively for a moment, then slowly resumed his meal.

He felt a bead of sweat at his temple and felt his neck and jaw tighten. He'd been violated, and seemed only able to move his eyes back and forth. He felt angry and vulnerable at the same time, the predator as prey.

CHAPTER 3

Patricia Duffy used her key to open the door to Dr. Gannery's office. It was a room oppressive with the things the man thought spoke of power and influence. The sitting furniture was dark brown leather and the shelves and desk were cherry wood. There was a small wet bar and a series of paintings in gothic frames depicting men of stature such as Hippocrates, Alexander Fleming, and Louis Pasteur. Jonas Salk smiled benignly down upon her from over a settee and the current Surgeon General of The United States (what was the name again?) frowned down on her from behind the desk.

She walked around the desk and sat in Gannery's chair. Picking up the remote control she pressed the power button and the television in an unobtrusive corner came on. She changed the Channel to CNBC. The evening news was just starting. Putting down the remote, she wiggled the mouse to deactivate the screen saver of Gannery's computer, a scalpel cutting delicate patterns in red on a black background.

She could usually access his schedule from her desk but for some reason all this afternoon it had been locked up and she couldn't get in. It was now 5:00 and she was tired of fighting it. Gannery didn't like her using his computer when he wasn't in, but she had some appointments she needed to put into his schedule. She was about to type in the password that allowed her access to her boss's computer when she froze with her hands poised above the keyboard.

It was now clear why his scheduling database was not accessible to her. The password prompt was not there. In its place was Gannery's fully functional desktop. Her password would only have gained her access to his schedule. But here she was with full access to everything on his computer. And as intriguing and frightening as this was, it wasn't the only thing that had made her freeze.

She had lifted her hand off the mouse to type in the password, but the pointer moved across the screen anyway. Not drifting, but crossing with a purpose. A scattering of documents were opened and there were windows with progress bars indicating that several file downloading operations were currently under way. The computer rummaged and browsed through the entire contents of every file and database it had access to as if it had a mind of its own.

Or someone who'd gained access from outside did so.

She had no idea who would have authorized

access to Gannery's computer, much less remotely. She had no idea such a thing was even possible. And it wasn't Gannery himself because even now he sat in the green room at the CNBC studio waiting for his segment to be announced.

Still frozen in place she examined the exposed documents and files that were being accessed. She couldn't be sure but it appeared that the major operations were involved in downloading Gannery's entire email database, all incoming and outgoing mail. She recognized his schedule – the download of that information was even now reaching completion. There were letters, reports, personal notes, historical backlog of all websites he'd visited going back who knew how far...

Patricia knew Gannery would be livid if he knew someone was rifling through his professional life like this. She stood and traced the power cord of the computer to the surge-protecting power-strip into which it was plugged. She wrapped her hand around the plug-head...then hesitated. Backing away slowly she sat in the chair again and watched as the hacker, whoever he was, went about his business.

She picked up the phone and dialed a number.

"Y'hello!"

"Derick? Patricia from Dr. Gannery's office?"

"Hey, Patty!"

Patricia winced – she hated it when people called her Pat or Patty - but kept her voice pleasant. "Listen, I'm in the doctor's office now and it seems as if someone is accessing his computer from the outside. I'm sitting here watching them do it as we speak."

"Well, no one should be able to do that but me." Derick, their regular IT contractor, sounded livid.

"So what do I do?"

"Just a minute, let me get in..." She heard keys clacking on a keyboard several blocks away somewhere in SoHo, Derick's apartment. She imagined some hovel littered with esoteric electronics equipment setting off an eerie green glow, illuminating a pyramid of empty pop cans and a stack of empty pizza cartons. Which probably wasn't fair to Derick, she'd never seen the place.

"Hoo, shit! There he is!" Derick said in a mixture of irritation and admiration.

"So?"

"Well," Derick said thoughtfully. "I can do a lot of things, some of them not so legal. I can trace his ass, I can reflux on 'im - cram a virus right back up his own connection thread, or I can just shut 'im out. Your call."

"Trace him," Patricia said. If she knew Gannery he'd want to take his own revenge.

"Okay, but this could take a while," Derick said.

"How long?"

She could almost hear him shrug. "Depends on how good he is."

"I'll wait," she said and let the handset of the phone settle into the crook of her neck.

On the television her boss, Dr. Gerald Gannery, was smiling modestly as the interviewer touted his resume, an impressive collection of board memberships, published books and papers, obscure contributions to improvements in cosmetic surgery, *ad nauseum*.

"What an asshole!"

"Huh?" Patricia said, startled.

"This guy," Derick said over the phone. "This hacker. He's good."

"Mmm." Patricia was watching the interview.

23

"And so with the recent return of silicone to the implant market," the interviewer, whose name Patricia hadn't caught, was saying, "you expect the demand for breast augmentation to increase?"

"Exponentially," Gannery said, hefting a fake boob in his hand as if it was a water balloon. "You see, silicone has always been the most natural appearing and feeling implant. You've seen implants with a sort of edged look to them, like bags of marbles?"

The interviewer laughed as if he hoped Gannery was making a joke. Gannery laughed, too...belatedly. Patricia groaned. She'd never known Gannery to be anything but self-serving, boorish, and mean. When he tried to be amiable, friendly and...well, likable, it just didn't come off natural. He looked like a skeleton trying to convince you he was grinning by choice.

"Well," he went on, "silicone never gave that effect. Hence a more natural look and feel."

"Aha!" Derick said into her ear. "Got him!"

"Do you have an address?" She said.

"Well, I have GPS coordinates."

"Fine," Patricia said. "What are they?" She picked up a pen and jotted the numbers down on a sticky-pad.

"Just about anyone," Gannery was saying in response to a question about who could most benefit from breast implants. "Not just women, but men who want that ripped look without having to go to the gym five hours a day. We're also doing an increasing number of anterior implants for both men and women. Asses."

The interviewer blinked. "Is there anything you can tell people who might still be having second thoughts?"

"Well there are always going to be those who

refuse to do what is necessary to improve their appearance. My assistant, Patricia, for example, is put together like a ten-year-old boy. In fact, there is a lot of work she needs done. But she won't listen to me. She could be so much more attractive than she is if she'd just listen to me, let me help her. But some people are content to remain plain."

Patricia sat red-faced glaring at the screen. Derick was asking her something but all she heard was the roaring of blood rushing past her ears. Her boss was looking directly at the camera, directly at her from the television screen, sneering and all but winking at her. She felt utterly exposed, naked, horrified.

"I meant," the interviewer said, clearly also embarrassed, "what would you say to those still having second thoughts about silicone, given the previous recall?"

"Oh," Gannery said, clearly unaware that he'd said anything inappropriate. "There is nothing showing any flaws in silicone implants were the cause of the problems those women experienced, whose law suits led to the recall. They were all results of improper handling by inexperienced physicians. The FDA would not have re-approved them if there was any danger at all. Silicone is perfectly safe if implanted correctly by a qualified and experienced surgeon like myself."

"Patricia?" Derick was calling over the phone, which had fallen away from her ear.

Mechanically Patricia put it up to her ear again. "Huh?"

"I asked if you wanted me to boot him, now that we have his location."

"Boot him?"

"Kick him off. Sever his connection. Lock him out."

Patricia turned her gaze back to the computer screen, which still flickered with activity. Her jaw tensed and her teeth ground together. "No," she said through them. "Let him do whatever he wants."

"What? Are you crazy?"

"You heard me, Derick," she snapped angrily. Then she softened her voice. "We don't want him to know he's been spotted. Let us deal with him ourselves. Okay?"

CHAPTER 4

Paul slept terribly that night. It wasn't just the bed pitching and rolling all night because of his hangover, but it was the dreams that tossed and turned him, entangling him in the sheets he shared with his wife. He'd been fantasizing about various forms of revenge on Gerald Gannery, his partner, for months now, ever since he'd learned of the IRS investigation. Sometimes graphic, lurid daydreams of violence and blood that he knew, as a civilized man, he'd never actually carry out.

Then two days ago Paul allowed himself to drink enough to initiate a shouting match with that one-time best friend and now most hated of nemeses at a gathering of medical specialists to compare notes on innovations in methodologies and procedures and to...who was kidding who - mostly to drink pretentious libations, smoke politically-outlawed cigars, play golf and patronize some of the more expensive and accomplished members of the world's oldest profession. It was in the lounge of the Ritz Carlton that Paul overheard Gannery speaking to another colleague about a nephew-in-law with a small but exclusive jewelry concern in Ithaca that Gannery had bought for him and that now he planned to sell for a hefty profit, installing the young man in a larger suite here in the city. It had galled Paul, who'd been drinking all weekend, to hear Gannery speak of moving money around so whimsically in the face of the immanent failure of their own practice.

Before he knew he was going to, Paul stood between the two, confronting Gannery and verbally slandering the man with such incompetent epithets as *thief*, *traitor*, and, worst of all, *stupid idiot*! Gannery had been amused with affected surprise, looking over Paul's shoulder to share his laughter with others present, and had only raised his voice to repeatedly encourage Paul to get whatever it was out of his system and go sleep the rest off.

Marching away Paul'd felt more humiliated than he'd tried to make Gannery feel. He felt as if he should have been able to express himself with more imagination, more flare, more *umph*. Instead he'd sounded like a petulant child on a playground confronting a bully. It had been a thoroughly unsatisfying encounter and left Paul with a red face and wilting shoulders, slinking away into the lobby.

It was here that the virtual stranger approached him. Virtual because though Paul couldn't place the face he seemed to know the older man from somewhere. The man tugged Paul's sleeve hard enough to cause him to stumble briefly off course, veer and turn. The man was in his late fifties, early sixties and though dressed impeccably there was an angry sadness about him, a shabby sort of run-down aura, like a limousine that'd seen better days. The man seemed to sneer and Paul realized the man thought he was smiling.

"I know about you," the man said. "I heard Dr. Gannery speaking about you to a group of others, like he was sad that you were in the trouble you're in, like he wished there was something he could do to help you but, alas, you'd made your own bed. I've known guys like him. I could smell the insincerity on him, the glee. And maybe I can do you a favor."

The man's words resonated in Paul's gut and he ground his teeth. "Yes?"

Looking around as if for something in particular, the old man rushed over to a nearby lobby newsstand, took a matchbook from a candy carafe full of them on the counter and came back, jotting something on the cover with a silver Write Bros. pen. He handed the matchbook to Paul with only one ominous warning:

"Don't call this number unless you mean it. Unless you really, really mean it."

Paul glanced at the number. It was a New Jersey exchange. "Who is it?"

"He's a...an...well, he's a fixer, of sorts." The man seemed even more intense, angrier than when he'd first accosted Paul, as if thinking of the man at the other end of that line churned up his passion, though whether with hate or glee it was hard for Paul to tell.

"What do you mean, 'fixer'?" Paul asked irritably.

"You pay him," the man said sarcastically, as if he thought Paul were being deliberately obtuse, "and he fixes whatever you need fixing. Anything, and I mean anything. For a price."

Paul felt a revulsion he couldn't explain for the number on the matchbook, and for the man who'd given it to him. But with that revulsion there was a sort of sick attraction, a repulsive lust, a sense of dangerous power sitting in the palm of his hand in the form of an innocuous-looking series of digits scrawled on a plain white folded piece of card paper. "What do you mean to *really* mean it? I don't understand."

"You'll see," the other said. He tittered briefly like some borderline lunatic. "You'll see." And then he was gone, rushed toward the street exit as if late for an execution.

Paul found himself breathing hard, the matchbook in his hand, unsure how it'd gotten there but studying the numbers so hard that they began to rise up off the flat white surface as if eager to be dialed and used.

He'd dialed the number.

A click, but silence except for the faint hiss of a completed connection.

"Hello?" Paul had ventured.

"Hunter's Bar and Lounge, in Jersey. Know it?" The voice on the other end had been gruff, no-nonsense.

"I c-can find it," Paul'd said.

"Tomorrow. Lunch time. Say 11:30. Take the very last table by the back door. Okay?"

"Okay." And that'd been it. In fact it had seemed so simple it was almost easy for Paul to convince himself that it hadn't happened at all. Almost. But today he'd gone to the bar, taken the table as instructed and sure enough the stranger had appeared. A half-hour late, but he'd appeared. And now he'd been hired. Simple as that.

Paul pulled out of his nightmare/memory and snapped to a sitting position as if electrocuted. He trembled from head to toe, covered in a veneer of cold slime, his own sweat. He looked over at his wife's supine form, her chest rising and falling with her soft snores. His ears seemed filled with the roaring rush of his own blood and his head throbbed. He was not used to drinking, did not know how he'd managed to drive home early yesterday without killing himself or, worse yet, someone else. He recalled murmuring something to his wife about not feeling well and going straight to bed at 3:00 in the afternoon.

He looked at the bedside clock now, it was 2:54 AM, nearly twelve hours. Slipping out of bed and into his slippers Paul padded to the bathroom for a hearty morning pee and instead found himself kneeling on the floor surging with fits as vomit jetted into the toilet bowl. He stayed there for several minutes trembling, unsure if it was finished or not, then stood up and looked at himself in the mirror.

Haggard, dark raccoon circles, blanched face. This was the face of a murderer, the face of a vengeful killer. It didn't matter that he wasn't going to pull the trigger himself. He was just as much a murderer as this fixer was, or would be. It struck him for the first time that the man who'd given him the fixer's number hadn't suggested a hit. He only said the man fixed things. Killing Gerald had been Paul's idea.

"Dear, God," he whispered in horror, "what have I done?" I'm not a killer. I'm not a man who puts contracts out on people, calls hit men and coldly orders the execution of an enemy. I'm not that guy.

Except that after yesterday, he was.

31

Paul walked out into his bedroom to Gloria's side of the bed and looked down on her peaceful, beautiful face. He leaned down and kissed her head, inhaling the fragrance of her blond hair.

"Throw up?" she murmured.

"Yes," he said quietly.

"Poor dear," she said without opening her eyes. "Pepto Bismal in the hall closet. Come back to bed."

"'Kay," he said.

Moving out into the hallway he paused at the open door of the room his daughters shared. In the glow of their *"Finding Nemo"* nightlights three-year-old Emily and five-year-old Natalie reposed, the soft sound of their breathing like the susurrus of a breeze through wildflowers.

Farther down was his son's room, seven-year-old Gerald. He was sleeping cross-wise in his bed, his feet stretched out over the floor, the covers cast aside. Paul went in and lifted his boy, placing him right on the mattress. When he tried covering Gerald with the sheets and blankets the child whined petulantly and pushed them away again.

Gerald had been named after Gannery. They'd been best friends in graduate school, Paul and Gannery, when Gloria had become pregnant and given birth, and it had seemed the thing to do at the time. Now those days seemed like an entirely different lifetime, a whole other realm of reality.

Paul had kept the matchbook with the fixer's number on it for so long because he'd wanted to believe he could be just as tough, just as cold and calculating as Gannery. But now, looking down at his young son, Paul knew he wasn't like Gannery. He wasn't a murderer.

"Oh God, what have I done?" he whispered again.

He would find a way to undo this.

CHAPTER 5

Gannery looked around at the thinning rush-hour throng of Grand Central Station to see if anyone was watching him before turning to the kiosk and dialing the pay phone. He'd been looking over his shoulder a lot since the diner yesterday. He didn't know much about bugging but he thought he was relatively safe using a public line.

The line on the other end rang.

Perhaps he was overreacting in assuming that whoever was watching him was willing to go to such lengths, or even had such resources. But with the games he had set in motion against Paul, not to mention numerous other gambits he'd ventured in the past, there were people out there with not only the resources but the motivation to use them against him. The greatest challenge Gannery could face would be if any two or more of his enemies joined forces against him, but he had long since despaired of anyone being smart enough or game enough to take that initiative.

Someone on the other line picked up.

"Yeah!"

"Vinnie? Gerry."

"Hey, Doc. S'up? Long time no see. We was beginnin' t'think you weren't so proud of bein' associated with us."

"Don't be ridiculous, Vinnie," Gannery said. "I've been busy."

"But you need somethin' now, dontcha? We don't hear from ya for what, a year? Now you need somethin', we get a call. That how it is, Doc?"

"Of course not, Vinnie," Gannery said.

"Then you come on by the house and mamma'll fix ya some cacciatore and we'll talk. Like old times, right Doc?"

"I can't," Gannery said.

"Oh right," Vinnie said sarcastically. "Busy. S'whaddaya need, Doc?"

"There's a guy following me," Gannery said, looking around again. "I don't know what he wants, but this is a bad time in my life for complications."

"So you want me to find him and find out what he wants."

Gannery described the motorcyclist from the diner to Vinnie. "You can hang with me until he shows his face again, then waylay him and question him."

"Okay, Doc," Vinnie said. "'Cause it's you."

Gannery's cell phone was ringing and vibrating in his breast pocket even before he said goodbye to Vinnie and hung up the pay phone. The incoming number on the faceplate told him Paul was calling. They had barely spoken since the IRS had seized the financial records of the partnership.

Curiosity warring with caution, Gannery answered the call.

*

Paul was smartly dressed with black suit jacket and tie, sitting ramrod straight behind his desk as Gannery walked in. There came a time in every conflict, Gannery knew from experience, when one's foe, against the ropes, turned to pleading for mercy. Part of Gannery had hoped that Paul would not resort to that, the part of him that still respected and admired his old friend. But another part of him, the part that relished not just victory but the utter defeat of an opponent, was excitedly tremulous at the prospect of hearing those pleas.

So he'd come when Paul called, even though they hadn't spoken in weeks.

"Close the door, would you," Paul said, evincing no emotion.

Gannery did so but remained standing, refusing to take the guest seat until asked to do so. Old friend or no, he had no intention of diminishing his own pleasure in this moment by making things one whit easier for Paul.

But Paul didn't ask him to sit. Instead he tossed something across the desk that teetered on the edge on Gannery's side, then fell to the floor. Gannery looked at Paul curiously, then squatted to pick up a worn and bent pack of matches.

"What's this?"

"I hired a man to kill you," Paul said.

Gannery rocked back on his heels for a second. This was not exactly what he expected to hear. "A man who wears a long black coat and drives a motorcycle?" After the initial shock, he wasn't frightened. On the contrary, his senses electrified and he suddenly felt like a tiger in the jungle that could smell the hunter nearby. It was just another move in the game of chess that he'd initiated with Paul. A move he hadn't thought Paul capable of, a move no one had ever made against him before, but one that increased his excitement rather than blunted it.

Paul looking wide-eyed at Gannery, clearly surprised that Gannery had already spotted the man. "That's his number," Paul said, gesturing to the matchbook.

Gannery flipped open the matchbook and looked at the numbers. Curiosity flashed bright and hot in his brain. He couldn't resist. He reached for the phone, slid it across the desk and dialed the number. It rang four times.

Then someone picked up.

"Hello?" Gannery said.

"Let me speak to him," a voice said.

Gannery felt a thrill. "Who is this?" No answer. He held the phone out to Paul. "He wants to talk to you."

Paul blanched and showed emotion for the first time since Gannery had arrived – hesitation and terror. He took the phone in a trembling hand and put it to his ear. "Yes? Yes...yes..." Sweat sprung out on his brow. "Yes...okay..." He offered the phone to Gannery again.

Gannery took it and put it to his ear.

"As for you, Gerald, we have nothing to say to each other."

The line went dead.

Gannery replaced the earpiece to the cradle and slowly doffed his coat, draped it on the back of the seat and sat down.

"Interesting move, Paul," he said.

"He said I can't call off the hit," Paul said. "He reminded me of what he said when we first met, that there was no going back. I'm sorry, Gerry."

Gannery scowled. "Fuck you, Paul! That's your whole problem. You're a pussy. You took this step, now own it, man! Be proud of it! I didn't expect it of you. Makes me respect you a little more. But if you start whining now you're going to make me sick all over again."

Paul placed both white-knuckled fists on the desk in front of him. "Jesus, Gerry, this isn't D&D at the Student Union anymore. This is real life. This guy is going to try to kill you and I paid him to do it. Don't talk to me like I'm a piece of shit. I'm trying to do the right thing here, to stop something I should never have started. If that makes me a pussy, as you put it, then fuck you right back!"

By the end of this tirade Paul was standing, trembling with his rage.

Gannery regarded him, but wasn't really listening anymore. "This is going to make life interesting."

"Are you going to call the cops?" Paul asked.

Gannery looked at him, nonplused. "What fun is there in that?"

CHAPTER 6

Patricia had to wait until 10 AM for Radio Shack to open. Now she sat in the back of a cab, still parked at the curb, and read the directions of the GPS device she'd just purchased. She was still fumbling with inserting the batteries when the driver, a swarthy man of middle-eastern descent, threw his elbow over the back of the seat and glared at her.

"We going someplace, sister, or not?" His accent was mild, but noticeable.

"Relax," she said distractedly. "You're on the meter."

"You don't need one of those," the driver said. "Just give me the address. I know all five boroughs like the palm of my hand."

"The back," she said.

39

"Huh?"

"The back of your hand," she said. "And I don't have an address, just lat and long."

"Please," he said, holding out his hand through open the Plexiglas window and waving his fingers.

Patricia placed the small electronic device in his hand and he turned to the front. She sat forward and watched him expertly piece the thing together and activate it.

"Okay," said the driver, whose ID sheet prominently displayed with yellowing Scotch tape on the other side of the transparent divider said he was Ibrahim Al-Sadif. "It's working. What coordinates are we going to?"

She pulled out the sticky-sheet from the prior night and handed it to him. He stuck it to his dashboard, placed the GPS device on the seat next to him and pulled out into traffic. Patricia sat back, a little unnerved that she'd just surrendered a $50 piece of electronics over to a total stranger. Still, he seemed to know exactly what he was doing. And why not? He drove a cab for a living. It probably wasn't the first time he'd used such a device.

They left the city behind pretty quickly and found themselves in the seedier part of Queens. Having rarely been outside the city, Patricia could remember having crossed one of the bridges maybe once the entire three-years she'd lived in New York, if that. In Queens she was quickly lost and realized, as so many travelers often did, what an act of faith it was to place oneself in the hands of a cab driver.

They were in a neighborhood of rundown tenements, one out of every four of which, it seemed, was condemned. He made one or two wrong turns, following the directions of the satellite, before he pulled up outside an especially beat up four-story brownstone with water stains and dead, brown ivy vines still clinging to the walls.

Ibrahim handed the GPS back to her through the security window with the sticky-note attached to its screen and accepted her money.

"Will you wait?" she asked nervously.

"What kind of man would I be?" he asked sternly. "Of course I'll wait. You be careful!"

She nodded, swallowed and got out. She wondered why Ibrahim didn't ask her what her business was in such a place. It crossed her mind that he probably thought she was here to make a drug deal. It would have made her laugh if her knees weren't shaking so badly.

At the top of the stoop she paused, then knocked. There was no answer, so she tried the doorbell. After a pause there was the buzz of an electronic door lock and she pulled the door open and entered a landing at the foot of a set of stairs. To the left and right were empty rooms and straight up the hallway she could see an unlighted kitchen.

For lack of anywhere else to explore she started up the stairs. Even before she reached the top, a voice called out:

"Queen to king's knight four." The voice was measured, stiff and mechanical, clearly electronically generated. "I think I have you, Jet. Check mate. Ha. Ha. Ha. Ha. Ha."

Patricia hesitated at the first landing, then followed the sound of the voice through a pair of French doors into a spacious room that smelled of cleanser and disinfectant. To her left was what appeared to be a nurse's station, with monitoring equipment, sink, cabinets and such.

The voice came again from deeper in. "Don't sulk." It sounded oddly unemotional and cold. "You almost had me on the ropes that time."

She walked further in. Around the corner to the right the room opened up into a sort of sitting room. In contrast to the rest of the house, this room was furnished with an intimate grouping of couch, loveseat and chair around a braided rug, the windows were hung with tasteful drapes, there was a reading lamp, bookshelves overflowing with books, some stacked on the floor. In the center of the far wall was a large hospital bed. All around this bed were arranged the oddest assortment of equipment she had ever seen.

Some of it had medical applications, she could tell, such as the respirator and the IV stand. The rest was an assortment of flat-screen monitors and keyboards all on articulated mechanical arms and platforms. It set off a flickering sort of glow over the face of the man in the bed.

The man. His head seemed too big for his skeletal, atrophied frame. Even under the covers she could tell that the body underneath was of little if any use to him at all. But the head was large, chin clean-shaven with closely-cropped red-brown hair on top and the sharpest, liveliest, bluest eyes she had ever seen. He had a series of tubes propped up in front of his lips and he turned his head slightly to take each in his mouth and blow or suck.

Upon seeing her, his eyes opened wide. He shifted to one of the tubes and as he opened his lips to pull it in she saw bright metal where teeth should have been. He blew rhythmically in to the tube and the voice sounded again.

"Stay where you are," it said. "I won't tell you again. I am not without defenses."

Patricia was nonplused and stayed where she was only because she wasn't sure how else to react. Of all the things she had expected, this wasn't only the last, it hadn't even been on her radar.

"Who are you?" she asked, attempting a friendly smile.

His eyes registered puzzlement. He blew again, "Who are you? What do you want?"

She blinked. What did she want? Why had she come? Funny but ever since she had decided last night to come she had never once stopped to consider what she would do, what she would say, to whomever she found. Finally, she just shrugged.

"Can I sit down?" she asked.

"No," he said. "Answer my questions."

"I'm Patricia Duffy," she said helplessly.

His eyes widened, then narrowed again. He knew her, or knew who she was. He confirmed this when he said, "Your dog tracked me here over the hacked connection last night. Must have. He's good. There can't be ten people in the world who can beat me at that."

She didn't know what to say to that, so she stayed silent and shifted to her other foot. She really did want to sit down. "What's...wrong with you?"

"Quadriplegia," he said. "Subway accident ten years ago. Well, Patricia Duffy, now that you're here, what do you plan to do? Call the cops?"

She looked around her, saw a stool on rollers and went to get it.

"Stop!" he said. "I said stay where you are!"

She placed the stool where she had been standing about six feet from the bed, sat on it and placed her purse on her lap. Her head was now level with his. "There, now we can talk civilized. Why are you poking around in Dr. Gannery's personal files and databases?"

He regarded her with a measured gaze. It amazed her how much emotion he conveyed with his eyes alone, clearly barely able to even move his face. He was really quite young, late-twenties, not more than two or three years older than she. A handsome man, she supposed, but for the deadness of his blank expression. He couldn't help that. The stainless steel teeth were a distraction, but they didn't fill his mouth like braces, pushing his lips and teeth out like he had a mouthful of marbles. They seemed to fit his mouth just like real teeth would.

"Why should I answer that?" he asked.

She shrugged. "It would be polite. Let's put it this way, if I was interested in putting you in jail I would have sent the police here instead of coming myself."

"I'm not afraid of the cops," he said. "What are they going to do? Put me in jail? Like this? Could you see the press on that?"

She smiled in spite of herself. After the initial shock of hearing the electronically-generated voice she realized it was quite good. Not human by any stretch, but it still added inflection somewhat approaching human. She could almost forget it wasn't his own voice.

"I'm not going to call the cops," she said. "But you're going to some trouble to find out about my boss. I'm understandably curious why."

"You're pretty," he said. "I didn't expect you to be pretty."

She felt herself blushing. "You're a liar," she said.

44

She didn't need a mirror to know she was thin, covered in freckles, hardly any breasts to speak of, mousy brown hair, and an overbite that caught her lower lip behind it more often than she'd like. She'd grown used to her own looks and no longer thought of herself as ugly like she did in High School, but she was honest enough to admit she was decidedly on the plain side. "So who are you playing chess with? Who's Jet?"

"I'm not a liar, but I can tell by your body language that you don't know just how hot you are. Why do you work for a prick like Gannery?" he asked.

"What do you care?"

"Do you sleep with him?"

She felt an angry chill and gave the man in the bed a cold glare. "We aren't going to get anywhere asking a bunch of question neither one of us are willing to answer."

"I thought you'd never get here," he said.

At first this non-sequitur confused her, then Patricia gasped, launched out of her chair and spun around. The first thing she saw was the gun, large and black and deadly. It was a sawed-off shotgun leveled at her midsection. She'd seen enough movies to know that at this range such a weapon would cut her slight frame in half. Then she focused on the man holding it. He was tall, narrow of hip, long and straight of leg, wearing a beat-up leather hat and a dirty canvas duster. His face reminded her of old western movies, of the Marlboro man.

And he was clearly incredibly stealthy.

She thought she may have seen him somewhere before. But where?

"Take it easy, Ms. Duffy," his raspy voice came at her, soft but carrying the promise of hard consequences.

"Why don't you sit back down."

"Now who the fuck are you?" she asked, trying to sound tough but hearing the quaver in her own voice.

He motioned with the gun to the stool and she slowly sat back down again.

"Wait," she said, remembering. "You must be Jet. He thought I was you at first. Queen to king's knight four. Check mate. Right?"

He cocked his head and seemed as if about to smile, but didn't. "You're Beatrice Patricia Duffy, born 1980 in New Haven, Connecticut to Bob and Patricia Duffy. Graduated 2012, MBA with a 3.8 average. Snatched right out of school to work as personal assistant to Dr. Gerald Gannery. You hate your first name, you love your little pug who you named Monster who lives back home with your parents, and you drink your coffee regular – one cream, two sugars."

Patricia dawned to the realization during his monolog that she was in over her head. "Fine," she said. "It isn't just my boss you're spying on. I still want to know why."

"That's none of your business," Jet said, lowering the gun so that it pointed at a spot on the floor roughly half way between them. "What are you doing here, Patricia?"

The mechanical voice came from over her shoulder, "Her IT guy tracked me last night."

"I thought you said no one could do that," Jet said without taking his cruel grey-blue eyes off her.

"It was a fluke."

"Can't afford flukes, Gregory."

"I know, Bro. Sorry."

"Where's Margie?"

"She stepped out to pick up some more supplies."

"Look, I have a cab waiting," Patricia said. "You two clearly have some things to talk about. Why don't I just..."

"No," Jet said. "Stay where you are. Who knows you're here?"

"No one," she said, then stammered to correct herself, "Well, Derick, of course, our computer consultant. He's the one who gave me the coordinates." This was true enough, though he didn't know she was here just now.

Jet regarded her. "How did you get in?"

"Like she said," Gregory put in, "I thought she was you."

"What do you want, Patricia?"

Patricia glanced at the gun and swallowed loudly. "I want to know why you guys are poking around in Doctors' computer files."

"Why?"

Here it was. Why did she want to know? She'd always had a vague idea of why she came here in person, but before she knew how to say what she was going to say, it just came out, "Because maybe I can help?"

"Why would you want to help me?"

Me, not us, Patricia noted. "Does it matter?"

"Don't be flip with me, young lady!" Jet snapped.

Patricia jumped and her heart skipped a beat. He was deadly serious. She had underestimated his self-possession and overestimated her own charms. It shook her and she tried to reassess her predicament. She began trembling.

"Hey, Bro," the man in the bed whom Jet had called Gregory said in his canned voice. "Lighten up a little, huh? I think she's okay."

She expected Jet to shout at Gregory, too, but instead the bedridden man's words seemed to calm the gunman. "You said you thought it was me at the door," Jet addressed Gregory. "You didn't look at the security monitor before you let her in, did you? How many times do I have to tell you? That's what it's there for."

Gregory didn't answer.

"Why do you want to help me?" Jet asked Patricia again.

There was the distant sound of the front door opening, the rattle of keys and heavy footsteps on the stairs. Jet looked around him rapidly and the shotgun somehow vanished beneath the folds of his duster. He gave Patricia a glare of warning and turned as an impressive mass of womanhood waddled into the room carrying three plastic grocery bags.

"Jet," she said. "How are you?"

"Margie," Jet said.

Margie was tall and overweight, but she moved her impressive bulk as spryly as a rhinoceros as she began to remove things from the bags and put them away. Rather than groceries, what she was putting away were things like syringes, bottles of alcohol, soaps and sponges, gauze, etc.

"Hey, Superman!" she called out in a cheery voice.

"Hello, Margie," Gregory said.

"Margie," Jet said firmly.

Margie turned and saw Patricia for the first time. "Who do we have here? A visitor? I'm Margery Potter, but the boys here call me Margie. And you are...?"

"Margie," Jet snapped.

Margie finally turned and looked at him. "Yes, Jet?"

"Margie," Jet said levelly, "wait outside while we conclude our business."

"Jet," Gregory said.

Margie narrowed her eyes at the tall man and pulled her lips into a line.

"Please," Jet said stiffly. "If you wouldn't mind."

"Fine," she said tightly, then turned summarily and left the room, the sound of her footsteps receding down the stairs once again.

Jet turned to Patricia. "Go home."

Patricia hesitated. Did he remember that just minutes ago she'd offered to help him in whatever he planned against Gannery? She'd fully expected an enemy of Gannery's to jump at the chance to learn what she knew.

But it was Gregory who voiced her protest for her, "Jet..."

"God damn it, Greg," Jet hissed, low enough so that only the three of them could hear. "We aren't playing games here. She has no idea what she's asking to be part of. I can do this without her and I'm not going to risk exposure from amateurs."

"But..." Gregory had somehow lowered the volume on his mechanized voice to match Jet's caution against Margie overhearing them.

"No, Greg. This isn't a democracy." To Patricia he said, "Get out."

Patricia sat back in the stool and folded her arms in what she hoped was a show of stubbornness. But before she could finish settling herself into intractability Jet stomped over to her, took her arm roughly and marched her out of the room and down the stairs. Patricia tried to fight him but he was probably four times her mass, he was very strong, and he had a grip on her that could not be broken. Margie, who stood at the foot of the stairs, turned to watch in alarm, but said nothing. Jet dragged Patricia out the front door and all of the way across the street to the cab, opened the door and thrust her inside.

He leaned his head in and glared at her. "Go away. If you show up here again...you'll be sorry." He slammed the door. "What are you looking at?" she heard him address the driver.

Ibrahim ducked his head and peeled away from the curb.

Rubbing her bruised arm, Patricia turned and watched Jet out of the back window as he shrunk away in the distance. *I'll kill you*, that was what he had been about to say. *If you show up here again, I'll kill you.* She was sure of it.

She turned and looked forward again, still unable to control her trembling. Her eyes were opened to how stupid she'd been. She didn't doubt Jet's ability to kill, it soaked behind those dead blue eyes. Where Dr. Gannery had a sort of manic, almost lustful capacity for cruelty, Jet's came off as a quiet, unemotional one, cold and mechanical like a guillotine or a tree shredder. She was lucky to get away alive. This morning she thought she'd found a way to get out from under Gannery's thumb. Help these guys, whoever they are, make trouble for Gannery and maybe he wouldn't have time to care when she resigned.

That hope was dead now. She felt surrounded by cruelty and meanness, everywhere she turned. She longed for the simplicity of home, Saturdays fishing, Sundays watching football with her father and brothers. She should never have come to this city, it had only ever offered her nightmares, and she hated it.

CHAPTER 7

Gannery watched Vinnie Testarosa from his reclined chair and marveled at the man's economy of energy. Vinnie sat with his legs crossed, a newspaper held up in front of his face, reading casually as if he had all the time in the world. They'd grown up together, Gannery and Vinnie, in The Bronx, and though Gannery'd managed to parley his own single-minded greed into an academic scholarship, Vinnie had remained in the old neighborhood. It was widely known that what had once been the Mafia was now a mere shadow of itself, and Vinnie fancied himself the last remaining true *Cosa Nostra* gangster in New York. He ran a few girls, some gambling, smuggling and had an interest in a web of drug traffic, but most of it was local, neighborhood stuff.

As one female spa attendant gingerly massaged

Gannery's fingers in preparation for his manicure and another was wetting his hair for the trim, Gannery himself was watching his childhood chum with admiration. Vinnie was in his prime, narrow of hip and wide of shoulder, bulging muscles and thick, black hair. He had two dimples in his cheeks that drove the girls wild. He was sharp in a black Armani suit in spite of the heat of the day, with a black silk shirt and black tie. His shoes were shined to mirror perfection.

Vinnie wore five rings on his right hand, each with a letter boldly carved into the blocky gold: O-N-O-R-E. *Onore*. Honor. His big joke was that a man could read it in the mirror after Vinnie'd punched him in the face, which he only did to men without honor. The word "IRONY" would have fit on those rings equally as well.

Then Gannery looked past Vinnie to the rest of the day spa. There were other patrons at other stations receiving attention from other spa employees. Further on were racks and displays of high-end personal hygiene products. Then, standing in the middle of the center aisle about two paces inside the door with his hat on and his hands on his hips was the motorcyclist.

"Vinnie," Gannery said casually, eyes locked on the intruder.

Vinnie grunted but didn't lift his eyes from the paper.

The biker stood hip-shot and forked his fingers together one by one as if seating his gloves more firmly onto his hands. There seemed to be an indolent smirk on his face as he regarded Gannery just as casually as the doctor eyed him in return. People moved around the man as they came and went like a stream waking round a wedge of granite.

"Vinnie!" Gannery said more firmly.

Vinnie's head snapped up. His gazed followed Gannery's as he carefully folded the paper and set it on the floor next to his chair.

"That him?"

Gannery said nothing, but nodded.

Slowly, like a panther careful not to spook a deer, Vinnie stood. He extended his arm and pointed at the biker, then turned his hand over and crooked his finger in a beckoning motion, and completed the action by pointing firmly at a spot on the floor in front of him commandingly.

The biker flipped Vinnie off, turned and walked out.

"*Figlio di puttana!*" Vinnie spat. Then he added conversationally, "Did you know that flippin' the bird was originally a Italian gesture? I'll be right back."

Putting his hand inside the left breast of his jacket as if checking on something, Vinnie wended his way through the spa stations and product shelves and followed the biker out the door.

*

Paul fidgeted as he sat in the stark interrogation room of the police precinct. A lone cop sat on a chair by the door flipping through the pages of an issue of People magazine with Kim Kardashian featured prominently on the cover. The coffee in the cup in front of Paul had grown tepid after his first and only sip over an hour ago. Paul could see a perfect reversed replica of this room in the wall-mirror to one side. He thought he looked small and unimportant and hated himself for it.

Finally the door to the room opened and Detective Doreny came back in. He and the officer exchanged nods as the cop took his magazine and left, closing the door behind him. Doreny, a very fit-looking fiftyish man with gray in his hair and an anvil jaw, resumed his seat across from Paul and placed his file back on the table in front of him.

"Did it check out," Paul asked, unable to withstand the suspense.

"Nope," Doreny shook his head.

"Nope?" Paul asked incredulously. "What do you mean, nope?"

"I mean there is absolutely nothing to corroborate your story, Doctor," Doreny shrugged. "The number you gave us is out of service, and according to the company that owns the number it hasn't been in service in over a year. Bartender at Hunter's never met anyone like the man you described. Said you came in by yourself, tried to score some coke off one of the patrons, then left."

"He's lying."

"Did you get the plate number of the motorcycle?"

"Like I told you," Paul said irritably, "he came after me and left before I did."

"And you never asked his name," Doreny nodded.

"No," Paul snapped. "I asked his name. He didn't answer me."

Doreny sighed. "Doc, are you aware that if even half of your story is true that you are confessing to at least three, maybe four felonies that I can think of? Conspiracy to commit murder, fraud, money laundering – that one's Federal – and material accessory to murder if Dr. Gannery should, indeed, turn up dead?"

Paul sat back, exhausted. "Yes. I know."

Doreny studied Paul for a moment, then shrugged. "All right, we'll keep looking into it. Don't leave town, we may want to question you again."

Paul stood and shambled out. Officer Doreny chewed his lip, then stood, carried the file folder over to a corner where he dropped it into a large blue recycle bin. Turning to the phone on the table he dialed and waited.

"This is Doreny," he said to the voicemail recording. "Just had a Dr. Paul Jurgens here. I'm guessing you know the name. Stupid prick wants to confess, for fuck's sake. Got a martyr complex or something. Anyway, he has a pretty accurate description of you. You're lucky I was here to intercept him. I told you to be careful. Let me know if you need any more damage control on this one."

Doreny hung up, glanced once at the recycle bin, then left the room.

*

A manicure, trim, massage, mud-bath and steam-shower later, Gannery was ready to leave, but there was still no sign of Vinnie. As Gannery stepped out to the curb Palmer was leaning against the town car with a corded plug in his left ear. He pushed himself erect and opened the door for Gannery.

"Score?"

"Rangers up by one," Palmer said. "Office?"

"No," Gannery said, getting comfortable in the back seat. "Club. Have time to get nine holes in before I have to be back."

They pulled away from the curb and joined the stream of traffic as Gannery wondered what Vinnie was doing to the stranger. He didn't much care whether Vinnie went a little too far in scaring the guy off. Vinnie was a valuable asset when needed and Gannery would sorely hate to see him go to jail for murder, where he'd be of no use to anyone. But he wasn't Gannery's only asset.

"Boss," Palmer said.

"Mm-m," Gannery said distractedly.

Palmer was pointing out the windshield.

On the left sidewalk Vinnie hobbled along in the line of storefronts, other pedestrians giving him a wide berth. He hobbled because someone had cuffed his left wrist to his right ankle and his right wrist to his left ankle. He wore nothing but his white cotton briefs and his tie. His body was covered in coarse black hair, and his face was contorted in anger, red as the flames of Hell itself.

"Jeez," Gannery said in exasperation, pinching his squint with thumb and fingers so he didn't have to look at Vinnie. "Go get him, Palmer. Quickly, before a cop comes."

Palmer double-parked and hopped out, leaving his door open.

Gannery knew that Vinnie was smart, that he would have picked the right place and manner of intimidating Gannery's shadow and finding out what he wanted. Still, the biker had made Vinnie follow him easily, and had clearly gotten the upper hand on him. Gannery couldn't escape the feeling that he was moving according to the biker's plan, not his own.

In chess, the King's Gambit is a strategy by which you control your opponent's moves every step of the game, moving your own men in such a way that he only has one move available to him each turn, until you've forced him to sacrifice nearly every power piece he has, leaving his king so open he has no choice but to concede the game. Gannery liked that gambit because if well begun even a Grand Master is hard pressed to find a way to break out of the pattern.

He couldn't help but feel that he was already too late in spotting the pattern and was now locked into a King's Gambit of the biker's devising. The biker had seemed as if he had expected Vinnie to be with Gannery this afternoon.

That irked Gannery. His only hope to break out now was to somehow change the rules of the game.

CHAPTER 8

Paul saw the motorcycle parked at the curb as he pulled into his driveway. Casting about in all directions, he saw no sign of the fixer anywhere. With a lump of glowing coals burning in his chest Paul leapt from his car and rushed to the front door of his home, fumbling with his keys and bursting in like a cork popped from a bottle.

The house was quiet. He considered calling for his wife, his kids, then remembered. The kids would still be in school, and Gloria would still be at the battered woman's shelter where she worked as an attorney for the non-profit. Still, he paused and strained his ears for any sound.

"Come on in," came the familiar voice.

Paul stepped further into the foyer and leaned to peer into the living room to the left. The fixer sat on the settee – the one Gloria jokingly called her Princess Throne - with his boot heels crossed and propped on the table in front of him. Framed pictures of Paul's wife, his son and one of his daughters were ranked along the table facing Paul, reminding him disconcertingly of headstones.

The fixer turned the frame he was holding around to show Paul his remaining daughter's beaming countenance.

"Nice family," the stranger said.

"W-what do you want?" Paul asked, walking carefully into the room.

The fixer leaned forward and gingerly placed the frame he held on the table in a move that seemed at once careful and chilling, pausing to adjust it so that it, too, seemed arranged among the others like a cemetery. Then he sat back and folded his hands across his flat stomach and regarded Paul coldly.

"I want to know what the fuck you think you're doin', going' to the police."

"I..."

"You think goin' to some country club minimum security federal prison for tax fraud is so terrible you order a hit on the man sending you up," the fixer said intently, "and then you go and try to get yourself nabbed for a murder rap."

"I didn't go there lightly," Paul said. "But..."

"Shut up," the fixer snapped as he folded his legs under him and stood.

"Going to jail for something I didn't do is one thing," Paul went on, defiant. "But I'll have to live with Gerry's death on my conscience for the rest of my..."

It was alarming and terrifying how quick the lanky man in the long coat that billowed behind him like wings could move. One moment they were on opposite sides of a low coffee table, and the next second Paul found himself thrown against the archway of the room entrance with the stranger's steel fingers around his throat. He plucked ineffectually at the hand that choked him.

"You don't have the first fucking clue what's good for you," the fixer grated into Paul's ear. "You up for a tax rap, you'll be out in five years or less with good behavior. You up for murder and you never get out, maybe even get the chair."

"New York doesn't..." Paul tried to say and found his voice choked off by the grip on his throat. He pulled on the fixer's arms but they held like iron bars.

"Life in prison, you suckling shit! How do you think your family over there would deal with that? Hmm?"

Paul didn't try to answer this time. Of course he'd thought of that, he wasn't stupid. He eyes strained over and down to the pictures ranked along the edge of the table, happy smiling faces, faces he loved more than life itself, looking up at him in trust and adoration. Rage filled him but the man was just too strong to match muscles with.

"I told you to be sure," the fixer went on. "I told you I never go back on a gig. You hire me, that's it, no going back. You let well enough alone, you got no problems. You shut up and let me do my job, you'd be surprised how things work out for you."

Paul didn't understand what that meant.

"You meddle again..." the fixer said.

Suddenly Paul was let loose and he went to his knees, coughing and gagging and struggling to recover his breath. The fixer took one step toward the table and kicked it. As it flipped over, everything on it exploded into the air, including the framed photographs of Paul's family. Most of the pictures landed on the nearby couch, but the one of Gerry, his son, fell to the hardwood floor outside the rim of the rug on which the table had been sitting, the crystal shattering loudly.

Paul forced himself to his feet again and tried to roar in protest but his bruised throat would permit no sound. He glared hatred at the fixer.

"Get it?" the fixer demanded.

Paul wanted nothing more than to attack the man, knock him down. Instead he marched over to snatch up the broken picture and examine it to see if any of the glass shards had cut the photo inside. He heard the fixer's boot heels recede behind him, the front door open, then close, and finally the roar of the motorcycle outside as it sped away.

*

Patricia was startled by the window that simply popped up on her screen as she was typing a letter of thanks from Dr. Gannery to the producers of CNBC Evening News. It was a simple window with a blank area for text in the middle. And in the text-area was a single word.

Hi.

Patricia hesitated, then typed, not surprised to see her words appear one line below the first, a different font and color.

Is this who I think it is?

When the reply came, she was sure it was exactly who she thought it was.

Jet can be pretty intense some times. He's been through a lot, most of which even I don't know, and as a result he's wound pretty tight. Try to not take it too personally, he really is a good guy, in his own way.

Well he certainly has a way of making a lady feel welcome, Patricia typed.

I wanted to tell you, Gregory replied, *that you have nice legs. Were you a gymnast or a dancer in school? Figure skater, maybe? They have the best legs. Not like runners, who have gristly legs like a chicken, or cyclists who have legs more like their fathers than their mothers.*

Patricia was stifling her giggle behind her hand in case anyone walked by outside her office. It had been a long time since she'd heard a compliment. True or not, it felt nice.

Dancer. I wanted to be a ballerina once, but I started too late. They cultivate them pretty young these days.

I better go. Just wanted to apologize for Jet. He's really not such an asshole. Well, he is an asshole, but not in a bad way. Does that even make sense? Anyway, keep smiling, you have nice teeth, too.

Wait! She typed hurriedly.

There was no reply at first, then, *What?*

Patricia hesitated. It struck her that Gregory had complimented her on her legs and her teeth, two things that he, himself, must be quite self-conscious about. He was testing her.

She poised to type again, thought for a second, then wrote, *Why does he have you rummaging through Dr. Gannery's computer files?*

You don't give up, do you? He didn't type anything else for what seemed like an eternity, then: *I can't tell you that. It doesn't matter anymore anyway. He has moved me to another place and he won't let me help him anymore.*

Patricia typed, *Moved you? Just because I was there?*

Said he couldn't take any chances. Said he should never have endangered me to begin with by letting me help. Said he won't make that mistake again. Sometimes he can be such a pain in the ass. He pays for all my care and equipment and medicines and everything, why can't he see that I need to do something in return? A man can't just keep accepting the generosity of others forever. Sooner or later he has to repay it, or he begins to become less than a man.

Patricia put her hand to her mouth. *I like you, Gregory. You seem like an honorable man. Is there no way we can be friends in spite of Jet's objections?*

His answer was long in coming, in fact she began to suspect he wasn't going to respond when he typed, *I like you, too, Patricia. You're smart and you stood up to Jet when a lot of people just crumble. He's not an easy guy to stare down, but you did a pretty good job.*

Patricia felt herself blushing. All she really remembered of the encounter was being as frightened as she'd ever been in her life.

We'll chat again tomorrow, he typed.

Then the window vanished.

With the chat window gone a profound loneliness settled on Patricia. She hadn't realized before now how much she missed civilized conversation.

CHAPTER 9

Dr. Gerald Gannery looked at the faces around him. Hard faces, cold faces, faces of men on grim business and determined to prosecute that business with efficiency and dispatch. They looked like a phalanx of judges passing down a verdict of death. Judges with scarred faces and prominent knuckles and jewelry. Palmer drove, as usual, this time the limo, because Vinnie had insisted on bringing so many with them, five men besides Vinnie himself.

"Overwhelming force," he called it. "What 'shock and awe' should have been, that's what we're going to do to this guy. By the time we're done with him, he won't know what hit 'im. He'll be sucking his thumb and calling for his mother."

Gannery didn't care, just so long as Vinnie and his

65

men kept this fixer, as Paul'd called him, busy. Gannery was exhilarated in a way he hadn't been in a long, long time. Right on the verge of the national celebrity he'd sought for so long and then comes a hit man, one tough and resourceful enough to get the better of Vinnie. Would he kill Gannery in some spectacularly dramatic way, or would Vinnie and his men get to the fixer first? Would Gannery achieve his long-sought fortune and fame, or would the flame of his life be snuffed out right on the cusp of that dream?

Gannery fingered the matchbook that he'd taken with him out of Paul's office. He couldn't wait to see what would happen next.

"What's that?" Vinnie asked him.

"His number."

"Who's number?"

"The fixer. The one Paul hired to kill me."

Vinnie eyed the innocuous collection of cardboard matches as if he could burn into them every bit of hatred and virulence he felt after the humiliation he'd experienced at the hands of the hit man just earlier today.

"Trace it?" he asked.

"Haven't tried," Gannery said, amused. "But I doubt if it's traceable. I've a feeling this is a guy covers his tracks." He tossed the packet to Vinnie. "Welcome to try, though."

Vinnie put the matchbook in his breast pocket as the limo slowed, stopped, and Palmer got out. Moments later Gannery's door opened and he stepped out onto the curb of The Plaza Hotel. Vinnie and his men opened their own doors and climbed out.

"Dr. Gannery," the uniformed footman said as he approached, making a point of not noticing the thugs that gathered around them. "Good to see you again, sir."

Gannery nodded to the man and passed him the obligatory fifty-dollar bill, which ensured discretion. He listened vaguely to Vinnie while they walked as Vinnie deployed two men at the lobby elevators and two men at the eighth-floor elevators. Vinnie himself and another man escorted Gannery right up to the hotel room itself and stationed themselves outside.

Gannery used his own key card to let himself in, and was immediately greeted with the sense-blunting fumes of feminine-scented humidity. He didn't bother to call for her, he could hear the shower running. He walked into the suite and placed the flowers and chocolates he carried on the bureau.

The room was definitely lived-in. There were clothes scattered about, the bed unmade, an impressive array of toiletries cluttered and piled on the vanity, and the giant Teddy Bear he'd gotten her for her birthday sat in a chair in the corner with a pair of pantyhose draped over his nose. Ginny had made herself at home over the last six weeks.

He heard the shower die.

"Don't be startled," he called out. "It's only me."

"Who else would it be?" Ginny asked teasingly as she walked out of the bathroom utterly nude, dripping wet, and fastening a towel around her head. She jumped into his arms, straddling his hips, and gave him a mouthful of her lively, champagne-flavored tongue.

*

After the sex they luxuriated in bed together. Gannery didn't smoke, but somehow always craved one when he saw Ginny puffing on hers right after their killer athletic sessions of intercourse. As he often did, he took it gingerly from her fingers and drew a couple of shallow puffs and let the smoke out without inhaling it.

"Don't," she said sleepily, taking the butt back. "You waste it when you do that."

She took a deep lungful, then let it out as she asked, "So when does the show start?"

"Don't know yet," he said.

"What do you mean?"

"I mean the HBO people haven't set a date yet."

"But it's going to happen right?" she said, suddenly wide awake, pushing herself to a sitting position. "I mean, it's going to happen, right?"

"Yes, Ginny," he said soothingly. "It's going to happen. Meanwhile you get to live here, rent free. Not such a bad deal, really, right?"

"I told you I would pay you back," she said. "As soon as you get your show and you cast me, I'll pay you back. I won't be kept. I'm not a kept woman. I pay my way. You said the show had a green light and that you wanted me for the hostess, otherwise I would never have agreed to this arrangement."

"I know, baby," he tried to soothe her again. "Like I said, it's all but a done deal. Just be patient."

"All but?" she said, pulling the duvet with her to cover herself with as she climbed out of the bed to face him. She waved her cigarette for emphasis, "What's this 'all but done deal' bullshit? You said 'green light.' Those were your words, 'green', followed immediately by 'light.' You said it. I heard you say it."

"It is a green light," he said, exasperated. "There are just a few more wrinkles to iron out and we're all set."

"But it's going to happen, right?"

"I said it was going to happen, didn't I," he said,

beginning to get angry.

"Because there are other things I could be doing right now," she raged at him. "I had a shampoo commercial. I could be doing shampoo commercials right now, 'stead of lying here fucking you."

"What do you want me to say, Ginny? It'll happen when it happens. These are very delicate negotiations. You can't rush them."

Her eyes narrowed. "I'm starting to not believe you, Gerry. If you're lying to me, so help me, God, I'll..."

He was on her in a flash, left arm around her waist, right fist twisted in her hair, pulling her head back so sharply the bones in her neck crackled. She cried out and he waited for her to stop. When she did, he said, "You'll what? Don't threaten me, cupcake. And don't ever, *ever* call me a liar. I keep my word, unlike most men. When I say it will happen, you count on it. Because I will stop at nothing until it does happen, one way or the other. I have more determination than any ten men you'll ever meet. Do we understand each other?"

The pain, when it came, on the left side of his neck was excruciating. Unlike a common animal, however, Gannery didn't react immediately by pulling away. No, he was an evolved man. He looked first to see where the threat came from, before deciding how to deal with it.

Ginny had brought her cigarette up and was pressing the ember into the flesh about an inch below his left ear. Taking the arm from around her waist, he took her right wrist in his left hand and slowly pulled it away from his neck. The smell of tobacco and burnt flesh was sickening. He broke the cigarette off between her fingers and threw the burning half down, crushing it under his heel.

"Once more, with feeling," he said. "Do we understand each other?"

She struggled for only a moment longer, then nodded.

He let her go and she went to her knees, sobbing.

Standing over her, he felt the wound in his neck, hissed and left it alone. He didn't resent her for doing it. Every animal had a right to defend itself. He had made his point, and she would respect him more now for having asserted his alpha-position over her.

As he got dressed she eventually got up and went into the bathroom, shutting the door but not slamming it, he noted with satisfaction. When he was suited and ready to leave, he went to the bathroom door and tapped on it gently. "Leaving now, sweet pea. I'll be here at eight o'clock tomorrow night to pick you up for the awards banquet, all right?"

She murmured something unintelligible.

"Love you, too," he said, turned and walked to the hall door.

On the floor, just inside as if slid under the door, was a simple white envelope. Gannery bent and picked it up. Opening it he found a small, colorful card like the miniature Valentines children passed out in grade school. It was of a smiling cartoon bunny and a grinning cartoon turtle hugging each other, and the caption in the red heart above their heads read, "Yours By A Hare!" He turned it over and, as he expected, someone had written there in anonymous blue ink.

It read, *Do the right thing.*

He slipped the card in his pocket and cautiously opened the door. Carefully, ready to pull his head back in at the slightest sign of threat, he leaned out and looked both ways. He was not surprised to find Vinnie and the other guard gone, and relieved to find the hallway deserted of any others as well. Closing the door behind him, he walked along the passageway. Coming to another corner, he peered around carefully again, seeing nothing, not even the guards that Vinnie had stationed at the elevators.

Gannery went to the vestibule and pressed the elevator call button. When the elevator arrived he nearly lashed out when the doors opened on an elderly couple, peering out at him in alarm and fear.

"I'm sorry, folks," he said. "Just a little jumpy."

He got in as they came out and rode the elevator down, ready for it to stop on almost any floor and open on the grinning, deadly countenance of the fixer. He made it to the lobby without any such incident, again not surprised to find the guards stationed here gone as well.

Out on the curb he waited while the footman called Palmer in the chauffeur's room just off the garage. At any moment he expected to see a little red spot on his tie or the stylish handkerchief sticking out of his lapel-pocket over his heart, or to just hear the crack of a silenced weapon and a sudden, searing pain in his skull, but no such attack came.

Palmer pulled up and unfolded his length from the driver's seat, giving Gannery a rueful look.

"What is it?" Gannery asked, but Palmer just opened the back door for him and closed it behind him.

In the car were the six body guards, Vinnie and his men, and they were in bad shape. Many cradled their heads in pain, one held a wrist limp and broken and Vinnie held a handkerchief, white stained generously with crimson-red blossoms of color, to his nose and squinted out of his only remaining un-blackened eye.

CHAPTER 10

Patricia was nonplused to see Dr. Paul Jurgens standing in line at her favorite morning coffee joint.

She was reluctant to leave her desk on the various errands that Gannery sent her on, for fear that Gregory would try to contact her again and she would miss it. But she was never in any great hurry to get to the office these days, either. There was a serious rift ongoing between Dr. Jurgens and Gannery, she knew, and the partners didn't speak these days. No one on staff had a clue what it was, only that it was somehow related to the ongoing IRS audit, but as a result the staff of the practice had split as well, those loyal to Gannery and those loyal to Jurgens, causing a lot of tension there lately.

This place was like her staging area, a place to shore up her defenses before heading in to the office. To see Jurgens here was not only a surprise, but an enigma of protocol. They weren't at the office, and he'd always been sweet to her. Did she say hello, or pretend she didn't see him and let him make the first move?

As she watched him, considering this dilemma, it was resolved for her. He turned, as if feeling her eyes on the back of his head, did a double take and smiled wanly, almost ruefully at her.

"Good morning, Doctor," she said.

"G'mornin'," he murmured and turned back to place his order.

She felt oddly disloyal even talking to him, and this bothered her. She had always liked Paul, and lately he had seemed haggard, haunted, locking himself in his office between patients and leaving in the evening as quietly as a mouse.

They exchanged smiles again as he returned back up the line holding his hot cup gingerly, and as she stepped outside with her own cup she saw him sitting alone at one of the sidewalk tables thumbing through a medical journal. Making a snap decision, she marched up to his table.

"Dr. Jurgens."

He peered up at her, blinking at the morning glare.

"Um, can we talk?" she asked.

He frowned, and that frown seemed stiff with suspicion and distrust.

She took the other chair and busied herself with adding her cream and sugars while he closed his journal, set it aside and sampled his own coffee.

Finally, she sighed and asked point-blank, "What's going on? I mean, at the office, the audit, you and Dr.

Gannery. Something's going on, it's tearing the office staff apart and it's making you miserable, I can tell. Audits don't usually bring this level of tension unless there really is something wrong with the books. What's happening?"

Jurgens seemed taken aback by her bluntness and cast about him as if looking for escape. She reached across the table and grabbed his hands, pressed them together between hers and leaned earnestly toward him. "Look, I work for Dr. Gannery, but I'm not exactly his biggest fan. If it's something he's done, you can tell me. I know he isn't a boy scout. I won't be shocked."

Jurgens pulled away. Patricia was startled to see a certain sadness, a vulnerability cross his eyes, brushed away so quickly by his hand she couldn't be sure it was there at all. He stopped looking for escape and turned his eyes to the sky as if seeking strength. Finally he dropped his head, studied a spot on the table between them and started speaking. Stilted at first, then it all came out in a rush.

"More than ten years ago, he graduated two semesters before I did, so he got the practice started, up and running until I could get my license and buy in as partner. Those were giddy days; we were like two little boys with our first lemonade stand. We loved helping these people. Plastic surgery was still a sort of shadow industry then, not like it is now, with people openly, even proudly admitting they've had work done. Back then we did probably 50-50 vanity work – boobs, facelifts, rhinoplasty – versus burn victims, cleft palates, deformities, injuries, etc. These people were given hope by what we did, and it was gratifying, it truly was.

"Gerry...Dr. Gannery, had a better head for business than I did, so I left the business end of things to him. I lived for the work. I didn't even care if I was getting my share of the profits, strictly speaking. I mean, I trusted Gerald and I was having fun, and signing things he asked me to sign was the nuisance between the fun, I barely read them. I was so stupid.

"But time marched on and I got older. The patients became less and less deserving and more and more demanding. The new breed of plastic surgery consumer is a vain, hedonistic monster and I don't care for her very much anymore. The fun was fast going out of the work, and there was more work than ever. Plus, Gerry, who'd never been the top of our class to begin with, eventually stopped doing surgeries altogether. I don't think he's held a scalpel for three or four years."

Patricia knew this to be true. She'd never questioned it before, she'd always thought Gannery was the senior partner and had simply hung up his spurs in favor of his protégé, Dr. Jurgens. She'd never guess it was the other way around.

"Almost three months ago," Jurgen's continued, "we had an argument about that, me asking just what he brought to the partnership anymore. He made some veiled threat about me not rocking the boat, not upsetting the apple cart, not pulling aside the wizard's curtain or I might not like what I found behind it. That was when I began paying more attention to what Gerry was doing.

"I began to take more of an interest and he seemed to resent that. I soon found out why. The practice is heavily invested, actually owns other businesses, things not even related to plastic surgery. Do you know we own a chain of do-it-yourself car washes in Dallas, Texas? Why? Don't ask me, I don't know. But we're invested to the gills. There isn't a nickel of liquid asset to be had anywhere."

"That's kind of dangerous, from a business standpoint," Patricia said. She'd majored in business with a minor in economics, so she knew that what she was saying was, at best, an understatement.

Dr. Jurgens nodded. "When I confronted him about it Gerry became livid. He blew up at me, told me I couldn't leave the business affairs to him and then come in and start second guessing the decisions he'd made. He was right, I suppose, and I backed down. But I asked an independent accountant to come in and look at the books at night, after Gerry had left. What he found evidence of so much fraud he said he couldn't even begin to untangle it all in a month. Gerry wasn't just robbing Peter to pay Paul – no pun intended - the checks he was writing to Paul were based on imaginary assets that were yet to be realized. He had, in effect, mortgaged money several times over."

"What do you mean?" Patricia asked.

Paul squinted, "I don't have the head for business that Gerry has, but in short he has somehow managed to marginalize almost all of our assets. He's used assets twice, three times, sometimes even four times to secure investments and loans, assets that in some cases never existed, something my accountant calls 'assets yet to be realized.'"

"That's illegal," Patricia said. Mortgaging money, essentially taking out loans secured by future liquid assets, interest and proceeds from sales, etc. and then using cash from those loans as assets to invest deeper in other ventures, basically putting double, triple and quadruple loads on funds not even yet realized.

"Illegal," Paul nodded. "To say the least. But what

was worse, he had done it all in my name. All those documents I signed and didn't read. It was not just done with my apparent knowledge and approval but, it appeared, entirely without the participation or knowledge of the partnership."

"You're on the hook, he's in the clear."

"He's not just in the clear, Patricia. On paper, he's actually the victim of my fraud. Do you follow what I'm saying?"

"Oh no," Patricia put a hand to her mouth. "The insurance?"

"Exactly," Paul said. "I go to jail, the practice goes under, and to top it all off, he gets reimbursed by the insurance company, millions of dollars. It's brilliant when you think about it."

"It's evil," Patricia said. "That's the word for it. So that's why you called the IRS, isn't it?"

"I didn't know what to do, but before I could do anything, he called them. I don't know, he must've found out about my after-hours accountant, must've figured the jig was up, so he called the IRS. First I heard of it is when the accountant called me to tell me they'd shown up and seized all of our records."

Patricia shook her head. "I had no idea."

"It gets worse," he said. "I did something really, really stupid. I was drunk. I'm not used to drinking. I'd been drinking since I found out about the fraud, and the seizure of our records just pushed me over the edge."

"What do you mean?" Patricia asked.

"No, I can't use the drinking as an excuse."

"What, Paul," Patricia said, using his name for the first time. "What did you do?"

CHAPTER 11

Harold Bloom, Esq., stood with his toes right on the strip of red duct tape on the carpet, without going over, and took careful aim before chucking the dart at the target. Ten, on a double band that came to twenty, added to his prior score brought him to 305.

Darts was more a game of strategy, he reflected, than many people realized. In the standard game as played in international tournaments, you had 501 points to get rid of. Your closing throw had to score a double, with three darts to each throw. If you went over, your entire throw thus far, all three darts, was lost and you reverted back to the score at the end of your last throw.

It was supposedly possible to reach 501 in nine darts, but in the ages-long recorded history of darts, only John Lowe ever managed to do so on October 13, 1984 at the MFI World Match Play. Compared to that, after three throws, Harry didn't figure he was doing too badly.

"Harry," Dora's sing-song voice came over the desk speaker.

"Yes, Dora," Harry said irritably.

"HBO on line two."

Harry sighed. He went to the dart board, pulled the darts that protruded from the target and placed them all in their places on the rack before closing the cabinet. At his desk once more, he cleared his throat, pulled his neck up out of his tie, then picked up the handset.

"Daniel," he said. "How nice of you to call."

"This isn't Daniel," the unfamiliar voice said. "This is Steven, I'm one of Daniel's interns."

"Well why the hell are you calling me?"

"Daniel asked me to."

Not good. If you fell out of favor with a producer he would often relegate communication with you to an assistant. That Daniel Rontell of HBO had an intern calling meant Harry was out of favor and falling like a rock.

"You tell Daniel I don't talk to flunkies..." Harry started bravely.

"If I tell him that he's liable to stop taking your calls entirely," Steven the Intern said. "As it is, you and Dr. Gannery are lucky you're still in his email address book."

"Listen, I told him it has nothing to do with me," Harry said angrily. "Dr. Gerald Gannery assures me that his current obligation is all but dispatched. Just some loose ends to tie up. I told him what you guys wanted me to tell him. I'm not the obstacle here. I'm trying to facilitate this."

"Okay," Steven said in a conspiratorial tone. "Between you and me, I sympathize. It's not fair for Daniel to notch you down like this because of your client's excuses. I get that. I can put in a word for you."

Harry sighed. He wasn't stupid. "In exchange for..."

"Daniel told you what we want Gannery for, of course..."

"Yes."

"But he hasn't told me yet. He keeps ideas under development close to his vest. But if you could tell me what the idea is, and if I could see some behind-the-scenes role in it for myself that I can parlay into a permanent position here, well, I would kind of owe you one, wouldn't you say?"

"And what word is the *good* word of a mere intern?" Harry asked sarcastically.

"Right now better than you're getting from any other source," Steven said. "Especially if I am able to parlay this information into a real slot on the staff."

"You're a devious young man," Harry said. "I like you. I don't trust you, but I like you. Okay, you work for Daniel, I don't suppose I'm betraying any confidences. At any rate, no one told me specifically not to tell you. The show is an unscripted plastic surgery show – reality shows are all the rage these days. Dr. Gannery would perform surgeries on people and there would be a whole makeover segment and everything. The hook is, these people will only tell their family or friends that they are going on an all expenses paid vacation for several weeks, not that they're having any work done. Then the cameras follow them home and see if anyone recognizes them, get candid reactions, etc. Thing is, Gannery would also be co-producer, putting up much of his own money for the project in exchange for a cut. And that's why Daniel was so keen on the idea to begin with, because it would be only half the investment for HBO, which means half the risk."

"Interesting," Steven the Intern said. "I see a lot of possibilities to make myself indispensable to this enterprise."

"So I get my good word?" Harry Bloom asked.

"Yes, most definitely. I'm going to let you go now. Goodbye, Mr. Bloom."

"Goodbye," Harry said, hanging up. As soon as he did so his internal alarms started going off. Show business was a cut-throat business full of underlings ambitious enough to take any advantage, and Harry had a sinking feeling he'd just fallen victim to one.

"Dora," he said into the intercom. "Get Daniel Rontell on the phone like now!"

Dora was nothing if not efficient.

"Harry?" Daniel's voice greeted him. "What's up? I was just on my way to breakfast."

No hint of disfavor colored the man's voice.

"It's lunch time here," Harry said, trying to sound casual, conversational.

"Three hours makes all the difference. What's up?"

"Do you have an intern working for you named Steven?"

"Steven what?" Daniel asked.

Harry never got the upstart's last name. "I don't know."

"Well, hell, Harry, I don't either," Daniel said, laughing. "I got more interns up my ass than I have hairs on my dick."

"That's a lot?"

"Don't get personal," Daniel laughed again. "Hold on a second. Trista keeps those records. I'll check."

He put Harry on hold for about a minute, which seemed an eternity.

"Harry? Nope, we have a Stefan, but no Steven. Why?"

"Never mind," Harry said.

"You sure?"

"Yeah."

"How's Dr. Gannery making out?" Daniel asked.

"Any day now."

"Let us know. Later, Harry."

"Bye, Daniel," Harry said, then, "Dora? Can you trace the call that came in a few minutes ago?"

"No," Dora answered through the intercom. "Came through as unidentified. Is there a problem? Should I not have put them through?"

Harry didn't answer. Someone had just snookered him into spilling the beans about Dr. Gannery's show, something Harry thought he was too street-smart to fall for. And before they'd struck any official deal. Not good. Not good at all. He'd been distracted by the darts, yes, that was it.

Best to keep his mouth shut about this. His reputation depended on it.

Harry sat back and chewed his knuckles. After a few minutes he got back up and returned to his practice dart game.

CHAPTER 12

Dr. Gannery was only communicating with Patricia via email and voice mail right now, punishment, she knew, for her lapse the other day. Instructions came sporadically throughout the day and he expected her to drop whatever she was doing, no matter what, and jump to, prove herself worthy as his assistant. She hated herself for doing just that, for not quitting and walking away. It wasn't just that Gannery would not be likely to give her a positive reference, or even that he might blackball her entirely. Jobs were hard to come by these days, especially those that paid this well, especially with no reference from her former employer, all true. She wasn't even afraid of him insisting that she pay him back everything he'd paid on her student loans thus far in full.

Gannery was not someone who took rejection

well, from whom you could walk away with impunity. She would not leave him unscathed. Beating her to a pulp, leaving her to identify him as her attacker, was not his style. He'd plan her disappearance meticulously, then take great pleasure in executing his plan.

She was surprised at how eagerly she looked forward to hearing from Gregory. It was a single candle burning in the dusk that had become her life of late, and she yearned for that candle's tiny flame as a woman in the desert craved water. So when she returned from picking up Gannery's tuxedo from the dry cleaner's for tomorrow night's banquet, hung it on the hook inside his office door, and returned to her desk she was thrilled to see the chat-window appear on her screen as soon as she entered her password.

It said, *Hi*, again, as simply as before.

Hi, she typed back.

Where you been?

Out meeting fabulous people in fabulous places. You?

The same. Dancing the foxtrot and singing show tunes.

Don't make fun of yourself, she wrote. *Self-pity doesn't become you.*

You're right. I tell myself I do it to be funny, but it's not true. Okay. No more self-pity.

She frowned, hesitated, then, *Gregory, we need to talk.*

Uh-oh, sounds serious.

It is. Our friendship may hang in the balance. She hated sounding so melodramatic, but it was true. If he couldn't answer certain questions to her satisfaction she couldn't continue their association, new as it was.

Please, tell me you didn't know.

Perhaps you better come by.

You said Jet moved you and Margie...
I'll send a car to pick you up.

*

Margie waited at the curb as the taxi pulled up.

"Hello again, Patricia," she said warmly as Patricia extricated herself from the back seat. "I'll pay the driver. You go on up. He's waiting for you. Don't worry, Jet's not expected for a few hours yet."

This house was on the lower east side of Manhattan, yet another marginal neighborhood, with not so many dark and boarded up buildings, but some very old bricks and brownstones crowded against each other, a distinct sense of claustrophobia. As before, the facade of this one was deceptively decrepit. The inside was clean and smelled of disinfectant. There was another bank of stairs, this one bending up and to the right. At the top she saw light coming from one of the rooms and followed it into a large parlor. As before, Margie's station was set up to the left, with Gregory's equipment in the far right quadrant of the largish room.

"Hello, Beautiful," the mechanical voice greeted her.

Gregory sat in a wheel chair in the center of the room. He was dressed in khaki slacks and a NYU sweatshirt. A headrest that encircled the back of his head held it upright, the tubes were there again, within reach of his lips, and there was a flat-screen monitor mounted on a bar in front of him. Tubes and cords trailed behind him, umbilical connecting him to his life support softly hissing and humming in the far corner.

"Well if it isn't Fred Astaire," she said, failing to make it sound as cheerful a greeting as she had intended.

He blew into one of the tubes and the wheelchair

did a rather graceful pirouette, once to the left, twisting his cords around the wheels, then once the other direction, unwinding them again. This did make her smile and she gave a little delighted clap.

"What's the trouble, Bubble," he said. "I can see you're upset. Sit down. Talk about it."

She went to the stool she'd used before, at the other house, and pulled it up close to him.

"Do you know why Jet is spying on Dr. Gannery?"

"He never tells me details, even back when he was letting me help him. He only told me what he needed. But don't worry, Patricia, my brother's a private investigator, not a terrorist."

Patricia grated her teeth. "He's a hit man, is what he is."

"What?"

"He's poking around Dr. Gannery's business because he was hired to kill him."

"Calm down, Patricia. Where did you get this nonsense?"

They heard Margie return, so Patricia leaned in even closer and whispered almost directly into Gregory's ear. It struck her how perfectly formed this one little organ was, compared to the rest of his injured frame. She told him everything Dr. Paul Jurgens had told her, but when she got to the part about a man known only as the fixer, Gregory rolled his chair back abruptly.

"It's a lie," he said, blowing violently into his tubes to make the computerized voice that flatly refused to express his outrage.

"I don't think so," Patricia said. "Dr. Jurgens described the fixer. Gregory, it's Jet. What would Dr.

Jurgens have to gain by lying to me about this? If anything he exposed himself to arrest if I decided to go to the police."

"Why didn't you?" Gregory blew angrily, foam and spittle appearing on his lips.

"Is everything all right over there?" Margie called.

"Can we get a little privacy, Margie?" Gregory called, huffing in his distress. "I'm sorry, but please?"

"Sure, Sugar," Margie said. "I'm about due for a break anyway."

Margie slipped out.

"Why didn't you call the police?" Gregory asked again.

"Because I wanted to talk to you, first," Patricia said, hurt and showing it. "Because I wanted to see your face when I told you. I had to know that you didn't know anything about this."

"There's nothing to know about," Gregory said. His chair wheeled away from her, crossed the room, then wheeled back angrily. "It's all lies. The doctor friend of yours is delusional. I suggest you do call the police. He needs help."

"But what if it's true, Gregory?"

"It isn't."

"But what if it is?"

"It isn't, I tell you." Then, "Get out."

"Gregory..."

"Get out of here," he said. "You aren't welcome here anymore."

"No," Patricia said, folding her arms, much like she had when confronting Jet two days ago. "We have to decide what to do about this."

"I'll call Jet," Gregory said. "He can tell you."

"And what if it's true, Gregory? What do you expect him to say? What do you think he'll do to me? People in his line of work call people like me *loose ends*, Gregory. Do you know what they do to loose ends in his business? Do you?"

"Quit saying that," Gregory said. "I told you, it's all lies. I know Jet. He's not like that. He couldn't...couldn't..."

"Why would Dr. Jurgens lie?"

"Why tell you at all? He'd be in as much trouble as Jet."

"I asked him that. He said he told Dr. Gannery, thinking he would go to the police. When he didn't, Paul went to the police himself. They didn't believe him. He said he feels guilty and is willing to go to jail if it prevents any of this from happening. He told me because he needed someone, anyone, to believe him."

"Bull shit," Gregory said. "Come on, Patricia! It doesn't make any sense. Why wouldn't Gannery go to the police?"

Patricia felt the improbability of this next part, but she didn't back down. "Apparently he thinks it's funny."

"See," Gregory said. "Even he doesn't believe such a stupid story."

"Oh Dr. Gannery believed Paul. He thinks it's some sort of game. Like a test of wits or something. He thinks he can out-think Jet and turn the tables, or something."

"Jeeze, Patricia. Isn't it more likely that Dr. Jurgens is as guilty as your boss? That they both plundered the practice like their own personal piggy bank, and that Gannery was just smarter that Dr. Jurgens, enough to put it all on him?"

"It doesn't matter," Patricia said. "All that matters is Jet took the contract and is refusing to back off of it."

"I'm telling you Jet's no hit man."

"Is there nothing in your past that suggests he might be capable of killing someone, Gregory?" Patricia pressed. "Can you honestly say beyond a shadow of a doubt that you know him that well? You said he'd been through some things, not even you know half of it. I'm guessing some of it took place in a war. Maybe he was a soldier."

"Navy," Gregory said. Even his artificial voice sounded deflated. "Seals. He was a prisoner in China for four years. Disavowed. He made it back all alone. They still won't acknowledge his existence."

Patricia caught her breath, waited.

"They tortured him. Horrible things. He has nightmares."

"Gregory," Patricia said gently, "we have no evidence that he has ever carried out any assassination for hire before this one. If we can stop him, get him some help, there won't be any reason to tell the police, will there?"

"You met him," Gregory said. "Nobody tells him to do something, or to not do something. In fact that's the surest way to make sure that he does the opposite."

"So all we do," Patricia said, "we take away his reason for carrying out the contract."

"How?"

"He was hired to kill Dr. Gannery because of what he did to Dr. Jurgens. You downloaded the entire contents of Dr. Gannery's computer, right? What if we find evidence in there, proof of what Dr. Gannery has done? Then he'd go to jail, not Dr. Jurgens, and there'd be no reason for Jet to kill Dr. Gannery, right?"

"Sounds logical," Gregory said. "But what if he doesn't see it that way?"

"Doesn't matter," Patricia said. "Because Dr. Gannery will be safely behind bars, so Jet couldn't get to him even if he wanted to."

"I'm not saying I believe you," Gregory said. "I want that understood. But, well, if nothing else it would clear Dr. Jurgens' name and put Dr. Gannery behind bars. That's worth something, anyway."

"Fine," Patricia said. "But we need to get started now. There's no telling when Jet will decide to...um...do his thing. If you can print some of Dr. Gannery's papers out, I can help."

Gregory turned his chair and headed back to the steadily glowing bank of monitors and equipment and Patricia rose to follow him.

CHAPTER 13

Ginny was completely packed, even dressed for the road. She had never tolerated the kind of treatment from a man that she just got from Gannery, and she was determined to leave. And yet she sat on the edge of the bed, paralyzed. The fact was, she had nowhere else to go. She'd left all of her friends and family behind in Scottsbluff, Nebraska, and had no one in the city to turn to. She hated the idea of sleeping in alleys and in parks, or finding a shelter somewhere, especially in face of the luxury here at The Plaza.

When the knock came her guts clenched up and she fervently wished she'd made good her escape when she'd had the chance.

"Go away," she screamed.

"Okay," came the strange voice, "but I really

think you want to hear what I have to say."

"Who are you," Ginny called. "Who sent you? Tell Gerry I said to fuck off!"

"I'm no friend of Dr. Gerald Gannery's," the voice called. "That I can tell you for a fact."

"Who are you?"

"Open the door and we'll introduce ourselves properly."

"Nothing doing. I'm calling security."

"Aren't you even a little bit curious about what I have to offer you?"

"You have nothing I want, Mister."

"I have a plan to get Dr. Gannery's goat, make him squirm a little. Isn't that worth five minutes of your time?"

Ginny stared at the door. "Five minutes?"

"Less, if you aren't interested. More if y'are."

She cast about her. The champagne she'd ordered from room service for breakfast still sat in the ice bucket, long ago warm. She picked it up and dumped its stale contents into the bucket with the melted ice. Hefting the long-necked bottle like a club, she nodded and went to the door.

"I'm armed," she said, turning the deadbolt and backing away. "No funny business."

He opened the door slowly and peered in.

He looked like Dirty Harry. No, more like The Rifleman. He even wore a pair of worn cowboy boots and a rodeo belt buckle. His long canvas coat bore stains in spots and someone had beaten the hat he wore nearly shapeless. His face was weathered and tanned, and she had never seen a deader shade of blue eyes.

"Sit down," she said, motioning to the vanity.

"Move slowly."

"You have every reason to be suspicious," he said, his voice neutral. He took the indicated seat, perched on it like a crow on the wobbly head of one of the giant sunflowers that grew near her family's farm. "I heard your fight. With Gannery. Through the door there."

"You were eavesdropping?"

He nodded. "I would have helped, but I knew he wouldn't hurt you badly. Gannery isn't sadistic, not really. His thing is controlling people, making them do what he wants. He never asks politely if he can manipulate or force you instead."

"How do you know Dr. Gannery?" she asked, sitting on one of the chairs near the table where the hours-old remains of her breakfast languished, but keeping the bottle up between them.

"That isn't any of your business," he said without malice. He smelled of leather and sweat, a manly odor and not an entirely unpleasant one. "But if you help me with something, I think I might be able to make it worth your while."

"Money?"

"No," he shook his head slowly. "Something better. A chance to get what you want. I'm not going to lie to you like he does and tell you it's guaranteed. You'll have to work for it. But I can get you the chance to earn it."

"I never wanted any handouts," she said defensively. "All I ever asked for is a chance. I can do the rest."

"I don't doubt it," he said. "Have I earned more of your time?"

She regarded him soberly. She lowered the bottle,

placed it right-side up between her feet and folded her arms.

"I'm listening."

"Good," he said, all business. "Now, first thing we do is get the lock on this room changed. Step two, do you have an evening gown? Real sexy number? Something to turn heads?"

"Dr. Gannery had one delivered here today. I'm supposed to wear it to his goddamn awards banquet tomorrow night. It's actually quite beautiful, damn him. Why?"

The stranger grinned at her.

*

When Patricia walked past the open door to his office she saw Dr. Paul Jurgens staring at a bottle in front of him, a fifth of vodka. After confessing to Patricia this morning he disappeared into the operating rooms and she hadn't caught sight of him until now. She stopped and looked in. She'd always liked Dr. Jurgens, he'd always been the more gregarious of the two partners, the friendliest, most likely to join in the conversation in the break room, always ready with a pat of the back for work well done.

Now he looked like his own corpse, Patricia thought. It was clear he hadn't been sleeping. There were dark circles under his eyes and his jowls seemed to hang like funereal drapes. His clothes were still well pressed and brushed by his wife, but he wore them loose and hanging now, like shrouds.

He hadn't yet broken the seal on the bottle to take that first drink. He sat with his chin on his chest staring at it with a look of utter misery on his face. He was bereft of hope, she could tell from her morning's conversation with him. It struck her that she'd been entirely selfish in her fear and hatred of Dr. Gannery, in her desperation to help Gregory and Jet put things right for her own benefit. Here was a man, a good man, with much more to lose than she had.

She felt ashamed of herself and intense pity for Dr. Jurgens.

Her knock on his doorjamb galvanized him. He sat up suddenly and ran his hands down his face, first the left, then the right, as if wiping away ennui and gamely trying to replace it with a more professional countenance. He reached for the bottle, but she got to it first, swept it from the table, regarded the label, and clucked her tongue.

"This isn't the answer, Dr. Jurgens," she said, dropping the bottle into the trash bin near the door with a bang that made him jump.

"Thought I'd self-anesthetize while I waited for the cops to show up. You called the cops, didn't you, Patricia?"

"No," she said.

He ran a hand over his damp face and sighed. "What does a felon have to do these days to get arrested?"

"This may be fixable without the wrong people going to jail," Patricia said.

"I can't look at myself in the mirror anymore," he told her. "I've done something terrible, and I can't undo it. I feel like a rat with its tail on fire. I want to run, but I don't know where to run to."

"Things aren't as hopeless as they seem," she said. "Take my word for it."

"What do you mean?"

She perched on the far edge of his desk and looked down at him with a smile. "I mean what if there was a way to make sure the right man goes to jail. There won't be any reason for this fixer to kill him anymore. Even if he wanted to, he wouldn't be able to. Not in jail."

Dr. Jurgens shook his head. "You don't know this man, Patricia. You haven't seen him, looked into those vacant eyes of his, heard his dead voice. He won't stop. Not ever."

"I have met him. I mean, I've met men like him. He'll stop. He may not give your money back, but he'll stop when he sees he can't get to Gannery anymore. And he won't have any reason to, because you'll be cleared of all charges."

Patricia saw Dr. Jurgens's face blanch and his eyes twitch. He stood and placed himself directly in front of her, brow furrowed, face red, and glared into her eyes. "Listen to me, Patricia, don't get involved. That isn't why I told you everything. This guy is deadly. He's crazy. I tried to go to the cops and he found out, somehow. He threatened my family, Patricia. He's evil. He's insane. And he'll kill you, too, if you get in his way."

Patricia's mood darkened as he spoke. Now she pulled away. "He threatened to hurt Gloria and the kids?"

"Not in so many words, but yes, he did. He said if I did anything to get in his way, they'd be the ones to suffer for it. Do you see now, Patricia? I made a stupid mistake in a moment of anger and weakness, and I've only made things worse. I've placed everyone I know and love in this guy's sights. I couldn't take it if anything happened to them, or to you, because of me."

"I'm sorry, Dr. Jurgens," Patricia said, "but Dr. Gannery can't be allowed to get away with this. Not without at least a fight. I'm doing this for my own reasons, too, and we aren't going to get ourselves killed."

"I'm not worried about me," he said. "If that's what it takes for him to leave my family alone then I'd welcome it."

"What I meant was," Patricia said, "I have a friend. A friend who knows a thing or two about this fixer of yours. A pretty smart guy, and between us I think we can put a stop to this."

"How could you?" Dr. Jurgens said, "I only just told you about him this morning."

"Never mind," she said, "suffice to say I'd already run into him before you told me you were the one who set him on Dr. Gannery's scent. Until this morning I thought they were just a couple of hackers after bank accounts and credit card numbers."

"No, Patricia. Promise me you'll stay out of this. Promise me you'll stay away from this hit man. Promise me."

"If we play our cards right, this friend and I," she said, "then none of us will ever have to see this fixer again."

"You're in over your head," Dr. Jurgens said. "Hell, I'm in over my head."

"Maybe," Patricia told him, "but we're in it now, no choice but to swim. I'm not just doing this for you. Dr. Gannery has to be stopped. He's hurting people, and he's getting away with it. It isn't right. No, Dr. Jurgens, I won't promise you anything of the sort. There's a way, somehow, to have Dr. Gannery put away for a very long time, to put wrong things right, and to keep one very wrong thing from happening. I'm going to see it through. I'm sorry if that isn't what you want to hear."

"I'll tell him," Dr. Jurgens said. "Gerry. I'll tell him what you're up to. I will. I'll get you fired if I have to. For your own good."

"Do what you have to," Patricia said. "But if I were you I'd go home. Your family needs you and you need them right now. The booze is only giving Dr. Gannery what he wants."

Dr. Jurgens looked at the bottle in the trash can. "I don't think I was ever going to get around to drinking it. I bought it because I thought I might, but a hangover isn't going to make me feel any better." He dropped miserably into his chair and covered his face with his hands. "Ah, Patricia, what can I say to keep you out of this?"

"Nothing," she said, then turned and left the room before he had a chance to start in on his protestations again.

CHAPTER 14

Dr. Gerald Gannery was late to the banquet. He'd been lunched and wined and dined all day by members of the Municipal Women's Auxiliary, wives of politicians, commissioners, high ranking police and fire officers and wealthy philanthropists. With no spare moment to pick up Ginny, he sent Palmer for her after dropping him here.

The ballroom was a vast hall bedecked with gold brocade and filigreed mirrors, chandeliers and free-standing fountains of crystal, sculptures and a dizzying array of bouquets anywhere one looked. Nearly all of New York City's elite and influential were here or expected. It was the swankiest of the swanky, the corridors of power to which Gannery had aspired all his life, all here to honor him.

Gannery was in his element.

He winced as the collar of his tux pressed the bandage at the side of his neck and the hole in his skin beneath it left by Ginny's cigarette. When asked about it tonight he had offered several humorous quips from having cut himself shaving to having a run-in with a vampire. The true culprit galled him, and he decided she was not done paying for it yet.

A hopelessly forgettable rush of faces passed before him as person after person stopped in their circulation of the room to shake his hand and congratulate him. He wished Patricia was here to help him keep them all straight. The poor girl had been ostracized enough, Gannery suddenly decided magnanimously, basking in the glow of this night. In the morning, he'd greet her at the office personally, praise her for her loyalty and conscientious service over the last three days, and give her the day off. With pay. She'd earned it.

Vinnie and his men, twelve of them now, each wearing high-end fashionable suits concealing more weapons collectively than an entire platoon of marines, stood stationed all around the room. He caught Vinnie's eye and returned the other's nod surreptitiously. Vinnie's nose was still badly swollen, but nothing that a minor corrective procedure couldn't set right.

"Gerald." Harry Bloom appeared in front of him, taking his hand. "Congratulations on the award."

"Is Rontell going to be here?" Gannery asked.

"Daniel?" Bloom asked. For the first time since they met, Harry seemed unable to meet Gannery's gaze. "You're kidding me, right? From California? And no deal signed yet? You're lucky you're still in his email address

101

book."

"Fuck you, Harry," Gannery whispered, smiling warmly for the benefit of onlookers. "What if I just took my business to another firm?"

"I wish you would," Bloom spat, smiling as well. "You're doing my reputation no good, stalling like this. Do that, or get your other business taken care of and sign this deal. Either one would suit me just fine. And fuck you right back, Gerry." Then Bloom added in a louder tone, "No one more deserving. Really, Gerry. Congratulations."

As Bloom moved on it was all Gannery could manage not to glare after him.

He spotted Palmer standing discreetly by the top of the entry staircase, signaling him unobtrusively. There was no sign of Ginny. Gannery excused and extricated himself from the press of well-wishers currently within his orbit and made his way quickly to his driver.

"Don't tell me she's sulking in the car," Gannery murmured to Palmer.

"No sir, she wouldn't come at all. The key-card you gave me didn't work no more, and she sicced security on me. But she said to tell you she'd be here, come on her own when she's good and goddamn ready. Her words, boss."

Just as he'd thought, reflected Gannery, sulking.

Determined not to let Ginny sour his mood, Gannery patted Palmer on the shoulder, sending him back down to wait in the bar, and turned back to receive his public.

Ginny still hadn't shown her face by the time Mrs. Howard Lillary took to the podium and urged everyone via a whistling microphone to take the seats assigned to them by silver-embossed placards at the head of each place setting. Gannery mounted the dais himself and took his own place between the mayor and the podium.

Dinner was served, and still no sign of Ginny, the place he'd reserved for her at the very front table as vacant as the gap in a hillbilly's smile. Dessert came and still she'd not put in an appearance. Speakers were announced, each taking his turn to sing Gannery's praises, a spectacle he particularly wanted the stubborn little wench to witness, and still no Ginny.

At last it was his turn to accept the plaque and present his acceptance speech. Grating angrily inside, Gannery stood and shook a gaggle of congratulatory hands and found himself at the microphone, the plaque he hadn't even gotten a good look at yet balanced on display in front of his plate for the audience to admire.

"Ladies and gentlemen," he began. "Governor, Mr. Mayor, prestigious members of the board, distinguished guests. I..."

Completely non sequitur to the building momentum of his address, Gannery caught sight of Ginny. He stammered because the sight of her took his breath away. She was nothing short of radiant in her deep, royal-blue off-the-shoulder gown with elegantly draped lace patterning. Her lips, though earth-toned, glistened enticingly and her flawless face glowed around a pair of impossibly large and arresting meadow-green eyes. The tiara she wore was small and understated. He was momentarily hypnotized as she made her way carefully but gracefully among those seated toward her assigned place at the front table.

"Ladies and...and...I..."

There was a flaw in this scene of unequalled

glamour, however, and it took his mind several heartbeats to register it, to tear his eyes from her enough to make note of the escort who, with hand chivalrously on the small of her back, both guided and protected her as she worked her way forward. By now others in the audience were turning to see what had drawn his attention and as they saw Ginny there were murmurs, some in agreement with his apparent distraction, and some were salacious.

"I wanted to say, that is I need to thank..."

He tried gamely to recover, but now her companion was drawing his attention. Gannery knew him. Tall, lanky, face like a storm. Stylish in a tuxedo, he still wore that ratty old hat and scuffed boots. The biker. Paul's hit man.

The fixer.

Gannery had to swallow several times to stifle the rage churning beneath his skin like the lava of an imminent volcano. The two smiled benignly - no, smugly up at him as they reached Ginny's seat. The fixer held it for her as she sat, then borrowed a vacant chair from a nearby table and ensconced himself directly behind her. Very, very closely behind her. He placed a hand on her shoulder from behind. Ginny reached up and took it with one of hers, held it.

"Um...I...the...this award is..."

Movement on the verges of his vision made him focus further out toward the skirts of the crowd. Vinnie and his men had spotted the fixer. They were moving now, working their way up, closing in.

"No," Gannery shouted, and the crowd startled almost as one. "I mean, um, I'm sorry. An old friend...in the crowd...haven't seen in a while. We should get together later. But soon. Not now, though. Not now.

Because we have all these wonderful witnesses, this audience, who want to honor me with this...this wonderful plaque. We'll talk later, okay?"

He was relieved to see that Vinnie seemed to have taken the hint. He was signaling. His men were retreating to the fringes of the room once more. Gannery sighed in relief and wiped at a brow suddenly gone very damp. He reached for his glass with a trembling hand, spilled droplets on his tie as he took too big a gulp of wine and struggled to swallow it.

He barely heard his own speech, wasn't even entirely sure that he delivered it correctly. His gaze kept dropping to Ginny and the fixer, as if gravity itself conspired to pull his gaze downward. They often whispered to each other, smiling and even laughing quietly at some shared humor. His own pulse roared in his ears. When he was done his fingers cramped as he unclamped them from the edges of the podium and took his seat amidst enthusiastic if somewhat perplexed applause.

Firmly in his chair again, Gannery looked up, but Ginny and the biker were gone. Ignoring the closing speaker next to him, Gannery stood and scanned the crowd desperately. He spotted them, making their way through the crowd once again, toward the back of the room, the stairs and escape. Gannery's gaze sought and found Vinnie's. To the question he saw there Gannery nodded once.

Vinnie and his men converged on the hapless couple once more.

Gannery excused himself to the mayor and hurried off the dais, dropping down to floor level and rushing along the border of the banquet hall toward the stairs. He needed to get to Ginny, intercept her while Vinnie and his men dispatched the fixer once and for all. This affront could not go unanswered. His pride, his dignity demanded redress.

Many outriders in the audience stood to intercept him with offers of praise and well wishes. He accepted them distractedly, hurriedly at first, then as his sense of urgency took hold he simply brushed past these people in annoyance and rushed on.

He reached the stairs, with no sign of Ginny, the fixer, or Vinnie and his men. Taking the steps two at a time he threw himself down to the lobby and out through the front vestibule, breathless with rage and suspense. At the curb, the fixer was closing the door of a taxi. Ginny's beautiful face peered out at him in genuine fear and concern. Vinnie's men were arranged in a half circle on the sidewalk. One stepped forward and gripped the handle of the cab, but the fixer stopped him.

Gannery never saw a man move so fast. The fixer's foot was a blur as it came up under the man's wrist, dislodging it from the door handle, then came down and out, crashing into the man's hip with an audible snap, sending him sprawling.

"GO!" the fixer bellowed.

The taxi peeled out and joined the stream of traffic with alacrity.

The fixer turned and faced the remaining eleven men with a feral look in his eyes. Gannery fancied himself a notch above the average horde, an evolved man with the will, the strength and the intellect to rise above his inferiors. Here was his antithesis, a man more animal than human. A barbarian. A beast in the city.

"What are you waiting for?" he cried angrily to

Vinnie.

At a signal from Vinnie the men all drew weapons and leveled them at the fixer. Tires in the street squealed, pedestrians screamed and scattered, and quite suddenly the night was filled with panic and terror. The fixer made no move to draw a weapon of his own and for a brief halt of breath nothing moved on the city block.

Then two things seemed to happen simultaneously. The fixer spun with that same cobra-speed, fanning his tuxedo coat behind him like wings, and fled. Vinnie's men opened fire and filled the night with the spatter-roar of violent death. Whether they hit him or not, Gannery couldn't tell. The fixer vanished behind a row of cars and Vinnie's men gave chase.

Lagging back, nevertheless Gannery followed, salivating to see this interloper's bullet-riddled body before the night was over. He watched as the fixer's head popped up from the seemingly endless row of cars parked at the far curb, further along the street each time as he ran like the coward he was. Vinnie's men fanned out and followed, scattering pedestrians and halting cars before them like gods of paralyzing fear.

Reduced to taking pot shots each time the fixer showed his head, they pursued him along the street and down a side road, away from the bright lights of the main thoroughfare and onto darkened side streets, as if the night could hide his escape. As they lost sight of him Vinnie ordered his men to fan out and check every nook and cranny.

Vinnie was further up the road and entirely missed the next appearance of the fixer, but Gannery witnessed it from almost too close. From a dim recess between darkened storefronts, a blacker shadow amid the blackness of night, the scarecrow silhouette of the fixer emerged long enough to throw something that flashed like lightning as it flew, crossing some errant beam of moonlight. The man nearest Gannery, only two car lengths ahead of him, dropped his gun, grabbed something protruding from his throat and gurgled in an attempt to cry out.

The fixer was gone before it struck.

Gannery crept up on the man, staying low. He yanked the haft of the throwing knife, the double-edged blade sliding from the man's throat like hot wire through butter, but it was too late. The man died clinging to Gannery's sleeves as if he could climb up out of the yawning maw of hell into which he fell.

Shaking himself free, Gannery kept the blade and crept forward some more. He witnessed two more deaths by much the same means, collected those blades, too, holding them together in his right hand.

"Vinnie," Gannery called.

"Yeah, Ger," came the answer in a stage whisper from somewhere up ahead.

"Heads up. He's throwing knives."

"Shit," someone else spat. "It's too damn dark out here."

"Quit your bitchin' and shut up," Vinnie ordered. "Listen for him. Watch for him. He's not running. He thinks he's got a shot against twelve of us."

Gannery didn't see the need to correct his friend's math at that moment.

Gannery witnessed another death, a movement in shadow, the flash of steel, a man choking on the blood flowing from his carotid artery into his throat and lungs.

The killer moved so goddamn fast.

As Gannery reached this body the man was already dead. A circular, star-shaped blade protruded from his throat. Gannery collected this, too, careful not to cut himself on any of the razor sharp edges of these implements of death.

His blood was pumping, his head was clear, his breath coming in short, excited puffs. He felt alive, exhilarated, more in tune with his own mortality than ever before. He relished this moment and prayed the fixer would prolong it. The fear and the proximity to the deaths of other young, strong, strapping men were intoxicating.

Five down so far: one with a broken hip back at the banquet hall who would probably live, and four dead here on this darkened boulevard. That left seven more, counting Vinnie and not himself. Six, Gannery amended, as he saw another rush of shadow, another flash of bright silver and another man fall, clutching his neck.

In true sniper fashion the fixer had doubled back and was now working his way up the ranks from the rear. Either he had missed Gannery back here so far, or he was leaving him for last. Gannery knew lesser men would run, let Vinnie and his thugs deal with the killer, but Gannery was an evolved superior to the common herd. All of these men were here because of him, he was the catalyst that brought this scene into existence. It was he whom the fixer hunted, and it was for him that these men died. It validated Gannery's conviction in his own gravitas, that he should be the eye around which the hurricane of such events raged.

No, he would face his fate head on, not slink from it in the night. And if by chance Vinnie and his men did get the better of this predator, and dispatch him,

Gannery wanted to be there to share in the glory of the moment.

This time, when the fixer appeared to deal his silver death, someone spotted him and opened fire as the fixer's target went down, dead. Vinnie and his men converged on the spot where the fixer had appeared, firing an almost steady barrage into the dark alleyway. A cat yowled and was silenced.

"Goddamnit, Vinnie," Gannery yelled forward to them. "He's picking you guys off like flies. Do something."

"Just stay back, Ger," Vinnie answered. "We'll get him, I'm tellin' ya."

Gannery had collected three throwing knives and three throwing stars, each spotted with a different man's blood. They were growing sticky in his grasp, but the spoils of war were not to be shunned. These would make adequate trophies when this menace who called himself the fixer was finally six-feet under.

The arms that encompassed him suddenly from behind pinned his own arms at his sides like a band of iron he could not break, struggle though he did.

"You have some things that belong to me," the fixer whispered wetly, intimately into his ear from behind.

"Vinnie," Gannery bellowed, despising the childlike screech he heard edging his voice.

They came running, Vinnie and his men. As they tried to flank him, the fixer scuttled backwards, dragging Gannery with him, hurting his arms. Gannery cried out with the pain and eventually the men stopped trying to run alongside, and arranged themselves in front like a firing squad.

Not like this, Gannery said to himself. Not like

some stuck pig. "Don't shoot," he told them.

They held their fire. Sirens grew in the distance. Finally, someone in the neighborhood had thought to call the cops.

"We're at a stand-off," Gannery gloated. "You best let me go. You aren't going anywhere, and no one here wants to be jailed by the local constabulary."

Gannery felt the fixer's uncertainty at his back. Finally, his captor dragged Gannery back again, making him scuttle as fast as his feet could shuffle, back until they came to a narrow gap between two buildings that hardly qualified as an alleyway. The fixer backed himself into this and placed Gannery at the entrance like the cork in a bottle.

One arm freed him, and Gannery was dismayed and ashamed to find that the one was still more than adequate to keep him utterly, helplessly immobile.

"I'll have those back," the fixer said behind him, tugging the blades Gannery had collected from his grasp. When he was released, to the sound of footsteps receding quickly into the dark gap, Gannery cried out for the men not to shoot, lest they hit him instead.

But the fixer was gone.

CHAPTER 15

For the first weekday in she didn't know how long, Patricia wore sweat pants and tennis shoes. Her sweatshirt was inside out because she didn't like the feel of the terry-side against her skin, and her jaw-length dusty-brown hair was in a pair of short pigtails. Gannery had called her this morning and given her the day off, with uncharacteristic praise for her work over the last few days since their falling out.

She sat cross-legged at the foot of Gregory's bed with six stacks of papers arrayed in front of her across the landscape the blanket made over his atrophied legs, trying to decide which stack to put the next paper in. She was as reluctant to start yet another stack for another category of fraud as she was afraid she might just have to.

She looked up at Gregory and sighed.

"What?" he asked.

She was growing accustomed to his computer-generated voice, had learned to add inflection to it in her mind based on the expression in those alarmingly expressive blue eyes. But today it was different.

"Did you change the tone?" she asked.

He smiled. "Yes. Last night I broke down the dynamics of a certain movie star's voice and integrated it with the algorithm that generates my voice. What do you think?"

She tilted her head, listening. "George Clooney?"

"Wow," he said. "Never thought you'd guess."

"Well I hope you didn't do that for my benefit," she said. "I liked your voice the way it was."

"Maybe if I gave myself a British accent..."

She laughed. "You're silly. I think you should give yourself Darth Vader's voice. *Luke, I am yo-ah fah-thah.*"

She laughed again, and though he didn't have the lung capacity to laugh, his smile spread into a wide grin, showing off his bright platinum teeth. Just as quickly he stopped smiling and his too-pale face colored, and she knew it was her fault — she must've shown some of the shock she still felt on seeing those metal choppers.

"I'm sorry," she said. "I'm ashamed of myself."

"They aren't an affectation," he said.

"Oh, I didn't think..."

"I'm barely able to swallow," he said. "Even though Margie brushes my teeth well, my own saliva tends to eventually corrode any material they make implants out of — acrylic, porcelain...mahogany, pine. These are the jokes, folks...insert laugh track here."

Patricia smiled but was too embarrassed to laugh out loud.

113

"So," he went on, "I elected to have implants made of surgical steel. I don't really need them for chewing, I'm not permitted solid food, weak esophageal muscles would only lodge something halfway down and choke me. At best Margie sometimes gives me hard candy to put under my tongue and suck on. For meals I'm spoon-fed puree, a lot like baby food."

Normally, Patricia would feel such an overwhelming pity for a life lived in such a way that she would almost find it impossible to be around Gregory. But in the past few days she'd seen a Gregory bed-ridden and yet more full of life and humor and intellect and wit than any other man she had ever met. She actually felt inspired and energized being around him, and these were new feelings for her. It was all she could do to leave in the evening to return to her stark apartment in SoHo.

Returning to the papers, her smile faded and she sighed again. "I actually expected to have to really dig to find evidence of fraud. I didn't expect to find so much that we'd have to sift through it like this. It's staggering how many laws Dr. Gannery has bent or broken. Surely we have enough to put him away for the rest of his life."

"Unfortunately," Gregory said, "we don't really have anything. Even if we could explain how we got it, all of this is circumstantial. Even if we were to direct them to his computer and they were to find it for themselves, none of it proves anything without something physical connecting it to him."

"Being on his computer isn't enough."

"No. He could claim that someone else put the documents in there, or that he collected them during his own internal investigation. We need something to prove *he* committed the fraud, a signature, or at the very least some proof that these funds ended up in a bank account in his name. All we currently have is proof that Dr. Jurgens signed off on these things."

She lifted one entire pile to show Gregory. "We have about five off-shore back accounts, from Buenos Aires to Switzerland."

"Yes, but nothing showing any of these funds went to any of those accounts. He knows what he's doing Patricia. Anything really, truly incriminating is being kept somewhere else. Does he have a safe deposit box? Or a safe in his office?"

"I never saw one. Doesn't mean it isn't there. I sure wouldn't have a key or know what the combination was, even if he did have one."

She perused the piles again, sighed and started another one in spite of her reluctance. She placed several more documents on their appropriate piles before looking up at Gregory again.

"What?" She had gotten so good at reading his eyes in such a short time that she could tell when he was struggling with something.

"Don't take this the wrong way."

"What?" she said again.

"Are you sure you have it right? Are you sure that Dr. Jurgens didn't actually commit all this fraud and is now trying to squirm out of it by pointing to Dr. Gannery."

Patricia considered this. "No, I believe Dr. Jurgens, and I'll tell you why. For as long as I have worked for him, Dr. Gannery has never performed any but the most minor surgeries."

"Really?"

She nodded. "Dr. Jurgens did most of the work.

He loved the work, you could tell. Even though according to his story by the time I was hired he was already getting burned out, I could still tell he loved it. From the moment I started working there I could see what he didn't see, that while he did all of the work, Dr. Gannery was taking all the credit. Hardly anyone knows Dr. Jurgens' name, but ask anyone in the industry who Dr. Gannery is and they can tell you. Dr. Gannery spent his days schmoozing with celebrities and politicians and corporate mucky-mucks. He golfed with them, went to their benefits, dined in their homes, attended their kids' bar mitzvahs. With all of the social engagements I was booking for him he didn't have time to do any real work, even if he was inclined to."

"And no one saw it but you?"

"No one paid the kind of attention that I did. You see, I'm convinced that Dr. Jurgens is the single best plastic surgeon in the city, probably the country. It was that quality of work that Dr. Gannery was getting the credit for. He did do a lot of the consultations and preliminary work-ups, but then he just passed on the actual surgery to Paul. Since the patients were all sedated for surgery, they never saw who actually worked on them."

"Didn't Dr. Jurgens notice?"

"Either he didn't notice, or he noticed and didn't care. Like I said, he loved the work and would have done it in some deep dark cave somewhere. He didn't care about the publicity, or so it seemed."

"Honorable," Gregory said. "Humongously naïve, but honorable."

"That's Paul Jurgens," Patricia shrugged. "You could tell he didn't much care for the business end of things. And what he says about signing whatever Dr. Gannery put in front of him? I saw it happen several times. Of course I didn't know then what I know now, so I minded my own business."

"And, of course," Gregory added for her, "we look at who benefits the most from all this. Everything points too neatly to Dr. Jurgens while not a single shred of it points to Dr. Gannery. If it was Jurgens, he made no attempt whatsoever to hide his tracks. You'd have to be more than an idiot to leave a trail that clear, you'd have to be monumentally stupid, and you couldn't be stupid to manage some of these bookkeeping stunts."

Patricia nodded. "Dr. Jurgens says he thinks the IRS knows that Gannery is the real criminal, but since they can't pin anything on him they are going for the bird they can cage. I agree."

"So who called the IRS to begin with?" Gregory asked.

"Paul says he doesn't know. He said maybe Dr. Gannery found out about Paul's secret accountant and blew the whistle himself. You know, as sort of a preemptive strike."

"Why would he do that," Gregory asked. "Doesn't sound to me like he had anything to fear even if Dr. Jurgens did find out what was going on. It wasn't likely Dr. Jurgens would call in the feds, knowing everything pointed to him. No, we're missing a piece of the puzzle."

"Doesn't matter." Patricia shook her head. "What matters is what we do about it now."

"Give them something, anything, to shift the focus back to Gannery, where it belongs," Gregory said.

"Exactly." Patricia nodded. "And we need to do it

fast, before Jet kills him."

"I'm still not convinced about that part of it, Patricia," Gregory said.

She shrugged. "Like we agreed, either way, we are helping him clear Paul's name. If we do that, then what Jet was actually hired to do is moot."

"Good morning?" came a small voice from the far side of the room.

Margie, who sat in a chair well out of earshot across the room watching soap operas on a small portable color television, was closest to the door and stood to greet the newcomer as if she knew her.

"There you are, Sweetheart!"

The young woman in the doorway wore an oversized man's shirt like a nightgown. Her hair was mussed and she rubbed her eyes with a childlike fist hidden by a copious sleeve as if she'd just awakened.

"But it's nearly lunch time," Margie said, leading her into the room. "You've slept a long time."

The girl shuffled in just her socks. Girl? To Patricia she could have been 15 or 25, it was hard to tell.

"Who is this?" Gregory asked.

Spotting him, the stranger stopped in her tracks and stared.

"This," Margie said formally, "is Virginia Miller."

"Ginny," the girl said mechanically, looking at all of the equipment surrounding Gregory.

"She's a friend of your brother's," Margie explained. "She got in last night. She'll be staying with us for a little while."

"Jet?" Patricia asked, unable to keep the shock out of her voice. Even without make-up and bleary from sleep she thought Ginny looked like a movie star.

"S'that his name?" Ginny asked, focusing on Patricia. "Hey, I know you. You're Gerald's secretary."

"Personal Assistant," Patricia corrected her. "Where do you know Dr. Gannery from?"

Ginny blushed and looked away.

"Where do you know my brother from?" Gregory asked.

Ginny looked at him again and seemed stymied by the sheer number of questions jumbling around in her own head. Finally she stammered, "I'm not sure I..."

"Now, now," Margie scolded Gregory. "You two have your secrets, and I'm sure Jet has his. Let's not make everyone uncomfortable with a lot of questions. It's time Gregory had some lunch. You girls will need to excuse us."

CHAPTER 16

"The guy isn't real," Vinnie said as Gannery watched him take a bite of cacciatore and grind it to a pulp between his teeth. To Gannery's disgust, Vinnie held his fork in his fist like a shovel and he had sauce on his chin and his knuckles. "I mean who moves that fast? And he throws knives better'n Paulie does. Y'know, Tony's brother?"

Six men dead, Gannery reflected, one crippled. Even if he heals completely, that one, he'll get a twinge every time it rains for the rest of his life. And the cops weren't stupid, they knew most of the dead men they found last night and, today were as thick as flies on a corpse questioning everyone in Vinnie's gang. Vinnie was right. The fixer was not your average street thug. He was something more.

They sat in Mrs. Testarosa's sweltering kitchen,

which smelled cloyingly of garlic and butter and heavy with spice. Gannery had to be quite forceful in refusing a plate of food from Vinnie's impressively intransigent mother, such that after fixing her son's lunch she gave Gannery a glare to make a lesser man flinch and slink away in shame.

"Comin' at him head-on," Vinnie said, slurping, "that ain't gonna work."

An evolved killer, Gannery thought. An evolved predator for an evolved man. The poetry appealed to Gannery.

"Gonna have-t find some other way," Vinnie mumbled through his food. "Find some way he don't expect."

Gannery still smarted at the appearance of Ginny on the fixer's arm. He knew the man had followed him to her hotel room because he had dispatched five of Vinnie's men so efficiently there. But he hadn't expected the man to have the gall to approach Ginny, and he would never have guessed the girl had the gall to show her face at the banquet with him.

"Overwhelming force," Vinnie sniffed, mocking himself. "We got to stop lettin' him pick the battlefield."

This was a foe like none Gannery had ever faced. Most of his opponents had been acquaintances, men Gannery knew, men with a personal stake in the outcome. Men whose weakness could be found and exploited.

"It's clear to me now," Vinnie was saying, "it was a mistake to try to get this guy out in the open and come at him all at once. He only has so many hands, so many weapons he can throw at once. I expected maybe one or two would go down, but I thought if we swarmed him, there's no way he can get us all."

Problem was, as Gannery saw it, he didn't know this fixer, had no handle on him, and no way to get one. Not on what little information he currently had.

"No," Vinnie amended, "that ain't right. As a group we are only as fast as our slowest guy, only as strong as our weakest, only as invisible as our least stealthy guy. He's already taken too many of my men. I gotta find some way to get him, he don't see it comin'. Some way he can't do nothin' about."

Paul Jurgens didn't know the fixer, that was clear to Gannery. He was just some hired gun. Paul wouldn't have the first clue about the hit man's weaknesses, his exposures. No, Gannery needed some means to get leverage here. Some way to make the fixer think twice before he came at Gannery again. He had to de-claw the guy somehow. Someone he knew, someone he wouldn't want hurt. Did guys like him have loved ones? How to find out?

"Make him think he's winning." Vinnie's mind was visibly churning now, so much so that he put his fork down and wiped his hands absently on a paper napkin. "Make him think we're giving in. Get his guard down. Then hit him. Hit him hard and fast from some blind side he don't expect."

Gannery remembered how the fixer put Ginny in a cab last night. When Vinnie's man had tried to open it the fixer put him down and hard. Gannery recalled, could even hear it now, the edge of panic, subtle but there, in the fixer's voice as he screamed at the taxi driver to "GO!"

Vinnie had the matchbook with the fixer's number on it in his hand again. He seemed to play with it a lot lately. He looked deep in thought, which amused Gannery. Thinking was not Vinnie's strong suit.

The fixer didn't want Ginny caught in the middle of the fight. He may have used her to goad Gannery, but he clearly cared enough not to want her to get hurt.

"I have to go," Gannery said. "I have a call to make."

"Oh?" Vinnie's head snapped up from the matchbook and he blinked at Gannery as if waking from a dream. "Sure. Listen, I'll send the other guys with you. I got something I gotta take care of."

"Fine," Gannery agreed, standing and pushing his chair in. "My best to your mom."

"Sure," Vinnie said.

Gannery saw himself out of the house. Seeing him, Palmer pushed away from the town car where he'd been leaning, stashed the cellphone on which he'd been tapping deep in his chauffeur's coat pocket, and opened the back door for Gannery.

"Where to, Boss?" he asked.

"The Plaza," Gannery told him.

*

"That Gerry Gannery is sarcastic and rude," Mrs. Testarosa snapped as she came back into the kitchen and snatched up Vinnie's napkin from the collar of his shirt where it'd been stuffed for a bib. "His mother indulged him too much, I always said it." She took Vinnie's face roughly in one hand and wiped the sauce from his chin with the cloth. "I don't think you should invite him over anymore."

"Ma, that's Gerry," Vinnie said. "He's my best friend."

"I don't care who he is," she said in a hurt tone.

"He's not welcome back in my house."

"Ma, I gotta go," Vinnie said, standing and pulling away from her.

"You tell him," she called after her son. "Tell him."

"I will, Ma," Vinnie said petulantly. "Ma, I gotta go."

He kissed her on the cheek and left the kitchen. Up the hall, he turned into his father's den, *his* den since his father's death five years ago. Locking the door behind him, he sat in the plush, leather bucket office chair and picked up the phone. Placing the matchbook on the desktop, he dialed quickly, then just as quickly put his finger on the hook and thought for a moment. His lips moved as he rehearsed what he was going to say, then he lifted his finger and dialed again.

After one ring the connection was made, but there was only dead air.

"Yo, you there?" Vinnie asked.

"What do you want, Vinnie?"

"This the fixer?"

"The what?"

"The fixer. You're after Dr. Gannery, right?"

"fixer? Never been called that before. Yeah, Vinnie, I know who Dr. Gannery is and I know who you are. You got the right number. Question is what you think I want to talk to you about."

"Well you don't yet 'cause you don't know what I want to talk to you for. Maybe is you'll want to talk to me after I tell you what I want to talk to you about. Maybe is we got some business to talk about, you'n me."

"Get to it, Vinnie, I'm a busy man."

"I know. You killed six of my guys last night."

124

"Self-defense," the fixer said.

"Could say that," Vinnie said. "Could say you want to kill a friend of mine. Could say we was just defendin' him against you."

"S'that all, Vinnie?"

"No, that's not all," Vinnie said angrily. "What's your hurry? What else better you got to do than to listen to me offer you a truce."

"A what?"

"A truce," Vinnie said. "We stop tryin' to kill you and you stop tryin' to kill Gerry."

"Thing is, Vinnie, I've already been paid, you see? I get paid, I do the job. I don't see myself giving refunds."

"I figured you'd say that," Vinnie nodded, as if the other could see him through the phone. "That's why we gonna pay you to back off. How much did Dr. Jurgens pay you?"

"None of your business."

"I just wanna know so's we can match it," Vinnie said. "We pay you, same amount as he did, and you go peddle it somewheres else."

"He paid me half a million," the fixer said.

"Fuck you!" Vinnie shouted reflexively.

"Thanks, but no."

"You're shittin' me!" Vinnie said.

"I wouldn't shit you, Vinnie. You're my favorite turd."

Vinnie sat for a moment speechless, mouth opening and closing soundlessly like a sphincter. Finally, he managed, "Okay. We pay you half a mil, you're no longer Dr. Gannery's problem. Deal?"

"You don't have it," the fixer said flatly.

"No, but Dr. Gannery does," Vinnie said. "He'll

pay it."

"Let me see the money first," the fixer said. "If it's all there, and if it's all real, then we have a deal. The Hotel Excelsior in Queens. Rent room number 29. Call me, tell me when the money's there. I show up, anyone else is there, or anyone takes a pot shot, or the money isn't all there, then I take care of Gannery and you become my new special project. You got me, Vinnie?"

Vinnie had to grit his teeth for a moment to get his outrage under control, then he said, "Jeez, such a paranoid guy. I got it."

The fixer hung up.

*

"No, we aren't sleeping together," Ginny said pointedly. "I didn't even know his name was Jet until I heard it here, today."

"That's not what he was asking," Patricia said in an apologetic tone.

"Yes it is," Gregory said immediately.

"No," Patricia said, shaking a finger at him, "it wasn't. What he meant was, will you be staying here long?"

Patricia sat in her customary place, tailor-style on the foot of the bed. Ginny sat on the stool nearby. Margie had returned to her daytime television shows across the room.

Ginny shrugged and chomped her gum loudly. Her breath smelled of cigarettes and mint. "Don't know how long, he didn't say. I was ready to walk away and go see if those shampoo commercials were still available, but...Jet?...he asked me to stick around for a little bit, rent free. I had nowhere else to go, so I said okay. Sure, I was suspicious at first, but have you seen him? Wouldn't be the worst thing in the world if he wanted a little quid pro quo."

Ginny giggled, a not entirely unpleasant sound, Patricia confessed to herself. Patricia found she liked Ginny. The girl – young woman – wasn't very well educated, wasn't the deepest, intellectually, but she wasn't stupid either. Just, well, young.

"Why did he bring you here?" Gregory asked.

"Gregory," Patricia scolded.

"That's okay," Ginny said. "I understand, he's your brother." Patricia noticed Ginny was still having difficulty looking Gregory directly in the face. She looked at his chest, the wall, his monitors, her own hands, the ceiling, Patricia herself, anything to avoid meeting Gregory's eyes.

"I suppose he sent me here as a sort of protection," she shrugged.

"*Sent* you here?" Patricia asked.

"Yeah. He stayed behind to fight with Gerald's body guards."

"What?" Patricia found herself closely echoed by Gregory's manufactured voice.

"They were very rude," Ginny said. "They chased us out of the banquet and they would have taken me out of the cab if Jet hadn't stopped them."

"What did Gannery want with you?" Gregory asked.

Ginny blushed, then shrugged. "We *were* sleeping together. Thing is, he was going to get me a job, too, hosting his show on HBO."

"Show?" Patricia asked.

"What show?" Gregory put in.

Ginny told them all about the HBO show

Gannery was trying to close the deal on.

"Patricia, did you know anything about this?" Gregory asked.

"Me?" Patricia said. "Of course not."

"If he made that deal while his partnership with Dr. Jurgen's was still in force..." Gregory started.

"Then Paul would get half of everything Dr. Gannery got out of the show," Patricia finished for him.

"So Dr. Gannery had to find a way to have the partnership dissolved," Gregory said.

"He called the IRS."

"The accountant had nothing to do with it," Gregory concluded, the look in his eyes triumphant.

"What are you guys talking about?" Ginny asked.

"We still need proof," Gregory said.

"Well it isn't here," Patricia said, picking up one of the stacks now neatly arranged on a nearby easel that Gregory usually used to prop books he was reading, then slapping the stack back down again in disgust. "Like you said, nothing we have here connects him physically to it all."

"What are you guys talking about?" Ginny asked again politely.

"It's got to be somewhere," Gregory said.

"It has to be back at his office," Patricia said. "Somewhere."

"In his safe, maybe?" Ginny asked.

They looked at her.

Ginny ducked her head self-consciously. "I only know he has one because he said he kept my tiara in it after he bought it for me, before he had it sent over with my evening gown yesterday."

"Tiara?" Patricia asked incredulously.

"Do you know where the safe is?" Gregory asked.

Ginny shook her head.

"Or the combination?" Patricia asked.

"Huh-uh," Ginny said, shaking her head again.

"Knowing it's there is half the game," Gregory said. "We have to get into that safe, somehow."

"It has to be me," Patricia said.

"Patricia," Gregory started to protest.

"I'm the only one who has free access to the suite and his office in particular," she said firmly. "I know his schedule...hell, I make his schedule. I can do it, Gregory. The thing is, even if I find it, we still don't know the combination."

*

Gannery stepped off the elevator, followed closely by Vinnie's four remaining mechanics, and walked up the hall toward Ginny's room. When he turned the corner he saw the maid's cart outside and the room door was wide open. Gannery passed the cart, making sure not to brush against it as he did, and entered Ginny's room while the men stationed themselves outside. He could tell almost immediately that it was vacant. Ginny wasn't a messy girl, but she didn't clean the place up this well the entire time she'd been here.

The maid, a tall, stocky blond, was making the bed. "Can help you, Sir?" she paused to ask in a Russian accent thicker than borscht.

Gannery turned and marched out again. As he pressed the button and waited for the elevator he reflected that once more the fixer was one step ahead of him. He was caught in the King's Gambit and couldn't seem to find a way to break the pattern. But break it he must.

Break it he would.

When the elevator arrived Gannery stepped in, waited for the four others to join him, then slugged the ground-floor button with his fist.

CHAPTER 17

"It's odd," Patricia observed out loud, but *sotto vocé*, "hearing your voice in my ear, but you're not here. It's like you're sitting on my shoulder."

"Ma'am?" The taxi driver looked at her in the rear-view mirror, but Patricia waved him off.

"Careful," Gregory's voice came to her out of the miniature transceiver in her ear, much as if it came from within her own head. "You don't want people to think you're crazy, talking to yourself." It was funny how she'd come to accept this computer-synthesized vocalization as Gregory's voice, when indeed she'd never actually heard his real voice.

"Let me try." Patricia heard Ginny's excited voice in the background.

"Just talk," Gregory said. "She can hear you."

"Can you hear me, Patricia?"

"Uh-*yes*," Patricia coughed into her hand. The driver looked at her in the mirror again. "Excuse me," she smiled at him.

"This is freaky," Ginny's disembodied voice giggled.

"Okay, that's enough," Gregory said, "or we're going to blow it before she even gets there."

It was infuriating to Patricia how much Gannery had managed to keep from her. As his personal assistant, she thought she was privy to every intimate detail of his life, but she didn't know about Ginny. She didn't know about the safe, about any tiara or an evening gown, and the TV show came out of left field, as far as Patricia was concerned. All of it explained why she was only given limited access to Gannery's computer, why she wasn't allowed in his office when he wasn't there, and why she had access to his office voicemail but not his cellular voicemail.

It infuriated her because it revealed how little he really trusted her. She'd known he didn't trust anyone else, but she thought she'd put up with his shit enough to earn his trust. Of course, here she was betraying that trust, but she wouldn't even be doing this if he hadn't abused his position as her boss and treated her like crap. She'd felt justified in what she was doing after coffee with Paul, when she found out what Gannery was doing to his own partner. Now, learning how much he kept from her, Patricia felt like she was on a crusade to rid everyone of a disease that had sickened their lives for much too long.

The taxi pulled up to the curb outside the building that housed the offices of Gannery & Jurgens, MDs. She paid the driver – Gregory had wanted to give her money for the ride, but she assured him that she was well paid for the abuse Gannery piled on her – and she walked inside to the elevator.

"At the elevator now," Patricia murmured, with no one in sight.

"Are you sure he's not going to be there?" Gregory asked.

"If Dr. Gannery keeps to his schedule," Patricia said, "he's got a meeting with his editor all afternoon, polishing up his latest book. Everything he learned from Dr. Jurgens, with no intention to share the credit."

"And you're sure you can get in without anyone noticing you?" Gregory worried. "It is important that everyone think you took the day off the doctor gave you, that you weren't anywhere near the office today."

"Yes, Mother," Patricia said, stepping onto the elevator and picking her floor. "And I washed behind my ears, too."

"Ha ha," Gregory said, and Patricia reflected that they needed to find more natural laughter for him to include in his artificial-verbal repertoire. "It's just that this is pretty risky," he went on, "and if I could have I would have stopped you from doing it. But since you insisted, the least you can allow me is a little worry."

"Okay," Patricia said. "I'll be fine. Don't worry. You'll see."

The elevator opened and she peered into the hallway to be sure no one from the outer office was in the vestibule before she stepped off and went the opposite direction from the main entrance to the suite. Gannery & Jurgens occupied three-quarters of the entire floor, sharing the rest with a dentist and a jewelry designer whose clientele was so exclusive that the entrance was locked and had an intercom next to the door and security camera overhead.

Patricia slinked past these two neighbors and came to one of the locked doors that gave access to the back hall of the practice that Dr. Gannery and Dr. Jurgens had built together and were now squabbling over. Using her master key, she slipped in. The rooms off this hall included storage and empty examination rooms that were only used during peak seasons, which was primarily the early spring, just before the prime beach-lounging months, and the fall when most of the power elite prepared to head south with the gulls to warmer weather. The rest of the year was pretty steady, but these were the money-raking times, when Dr. Jurgens would seem his most tired and yet happiest.

It was really rather simple to get to her office from here and the door adjoining Gannery's corner office, the trick was she had to walk past the pharmacy and Paul Jurgens' office. The pharmacy was basically locked storage lined with cabinets both refrigerated and dry, but the nurses came and went quite often to fetch fresh lines of prepared blood-collection tubes, samples of Viagra and Zoloft, or to gossip about others in the office. If Dr. Jurgens was in his office, he would likely have his door shut, and he had never bothered to hire an Executive Assistant like herself. But if he wasn't in his office, he could appear in the hall at any time, returning from wherever he was.

As she peered around the corner, she saw Nurse MacDenna step into the pharmacy, and a few moments later heard her step out again and squeak up the hall and into an examination room. Patricia took a breath, then rushed up the hall. As she came up even with the glass door of the pharmacy she saw Nurse Crone – her name was Cohen, but she was such a crank that she'd earned the nickname – in the pharmacy unloading a carton of bottles and placing them on the counter. Patricia froze, almost ran on, then nearly ran back, thought to just run forward again and finally ducked back out of sight just as the older, gray-haired woman turned toward the door.

Breathing hard, Patricia felt trapped. Crone would be in there for a while now: after inventory of the shipment there was labeling – adding the personal contact information of Gannery and Jurgen's, MDs. to each bottle – then numbering, indexing and finally placing them in the cabinet where they belonged. Patricia had to move fast, either brave on or retreat, before someone came into the hall again.

Deciding she hadn't come this far to punk out, Patricia peered around to be sure Crone had her back to the door once more, then rushed on in a deep crouch. She came to another turn and ducked around as she heard the pharmacy door open. "Nurse MacDenna, is that you?" came Crone's irritable croak. "Hello? Whose there, goddamnit!"

*

Gannery found it difficult to listen to what Kimberly Pine, Editor for Beacon House Publishing, was saying to him. She was a sweet girl, but she had too much of the stink of purity about her for Gannery's tastes. He liked them sweet but with an underlying sluttiness. Like a porn star.

Like Ginny.

How she could cast her lot with the fixer, Gannery couldn't fathom. What could some ragamuffin hit-man offer the girl that could compete with the role of

Hostess of HBO's latest hit reality show? It might be sex, he reflected. The fixer's age was hard to pin down, given his sharp, rugged features and the overall weathered look to his complexion, but he was undoubtedly younger than Gannery's fifty years. Still, *they* say that fifty is the new thirty, and Gannery was in as good shape as he'd been then, with only the very beginnings of sag to the flesh of his arms, his chest and his scrotum.

"Is that okay?" Kimberly asked.

She was clearly off her stride. She didn't like all the men sitting in the lobby, men who looked as if they'd stepped right off the screen at the latest revival of De Niro flicks: *Goodfellas*, *Casino*, *Heat*, etc. Gannery could tell it made her look at him differently, too.

"Dr. Gannery?"

"I'm sorry, what?" he said, coming to himself again.

"I said with only a few changes we can move the collage of you at the Children's Burn Unit back eight pages. That would balance out the inserts better and puts your anecdote about Cher and Joan Collins crossing paths in the hallway of your office more toward the end. That gives us a much stronger final chapter, don't you think?"

"Sure," he said. "Whatever you say."

"And are you sure you want to refer to them by name?" she asked. "We can leave enough hints in description and dialog that readers can guess who they are without having to give their names. Isn't naming them some violation of doctor-patient privilege or something?"

"Fine," he said again. "Whatever you think's best."

"Dr. Gannery," she said, but it was the irritation in her voice more than her use of his name that snapped his attention to her. "You seem to have a lot on your mind today. We've only been at this for thirty minutes and you just can't concentrate. Would you like to reschedule this for another day?"

Suddenly the thought of returning to the office appealed to him. He really didn't care how they edited his book. With the tell-all nature of his book, and he the premier plastic surgeon in the country, it was guaranteed to make the bestseller lists. Meanwhile, sitting here was getting him no closer to breaking free at last from the partnership with Paul, or to finding a solution to this whole fixer problem.

"You know what?" he said, standing and donning his coat with a flourish. "You edit the book any damn way you please, okay? Don't call me again until it's time to promote. Deal?"

"Deal," Kimberly said, standing. She looked surprised but sounded relieved. He had sensed before that she didn't relish working with him, but did so only because she could see the book's blockbuster potential perhaps even better than he could.

"Thanks," he said, shaking her hand and ducking out.

He needed to get back to the office. He needed to light a fire under these damn IRS guys and he needed to find a way out of the King's Gambit the fixer had him trapped in.

*

"I know there's someone out here," Nurse Crone called out into the hall. "Very funny."

Patricia held her breath and pressed her back against the wall, willing herself to be silent and invisible.

Finally, the woman huffed indignantly and

137

Patricia heard the pharmacy door close once again.

Patricia took a moment to breathe. The hall into which she had ducked dead-ended at a window overlooking the neighboring building. There was a couch, a table burdened with out-of-date magazines, a small flat-screen TV, a small refrigerator stocked with sodas, and a coffee machine. This was the patient's lounge where those who did not wish to be seen in the main waiting room, celebrities or those frequently seen on New York's society pages, awaited their appointment. To Patricia's relief it was deserted.

"I can hear you breathing hard," came Gregory's voice in her ear. "Are you all right? Who was it that called out?"

"Nurse Cro...Cohen," Patricia whispered breathlessly. "She nearly spotted me, but I'm fine."

"Remember what we agreed," he said. "If anyone sees you, abort the mission. Tell them you're there to pick up some theater tickets you left in your office or something and get the hell out of there."

"I remember," she scolded him in a whisper. "Hush now, just a little further to go."

The hall out of which she'd ducked continued on past Dr. Jurgens' office and then to hers, with its adjoining door to Dr. Gannery's office. She was nearly there. Peering out into the hall again, she saw that it was deserted. She slipped out again and crept quickly onward.

As she neared Dr. Jurgen's office she saw that the door was open. Since he had taken to locking himself away when not with a patient, she felt safe in assuming that an open door meant he was not there at the moment. Prepared to tiptoe past it, she heard a noise from inside and quickly pressed herself up against the wall outside.

She strained her ears but the sound, a sort of dry sliding sound, didn't come again.

She leaned out and looked in. Paul Jurgens was there. On his desk was a collection of moving boxes, and much of his shelves had been cleared. He stood now with his back mostly to her. He was looking forlornly down at a framed photograph he held. She couldn't see it, but from the check stuffed in front she knew it was the photo of him and Gerald Gannery, arms around each other's shoulder, smiling outside the door to their fledgling practice, the freshly painted frosted glass of the door bearing their names.

The check was the first one they'd gotten. It was for $575 for a single eyelid lift, a bilateral ear-pinning and skin-grafting to hide a scar. Today one would be lucky to get a consultation with either Dr. Jurgens or the eminent Dr. Gannery at that price. It was the actual check, not a photocopy, they'd never cashed it.

Patricia paused, caught up in the melancholy that clearly caused the man's shoulders to droop, his head to bow. Then he sniffed, tossed the photograph into the box and reached for another stack of books. Patricia wanted to talk to him, to tell him not to give up yet, that if she and Gregory succeeded it would be Gannery going to jail and not him.

She heard the rustle of clothes behind her and turned to see Nurse MacDenna enter the hall, looking down at the clipboard in her hand. The nurse turned away, heading toward the pharmacy again. Patricia stood frozen, exposed, with nowhere to retreat or hide. She held her breath and waited for the inevitable.

CHAPTER 18

MacDenna stopped by the pharmacy door, rapped on it without taking her eyes from the clipboard, then entered when Crone's wrinkled, liver-spotted old arm opened it from the inside. Never once did she look up in Patricia's direction. Patricia almost sighed, but she remembered Dr. Jurgens in his office and didn't.

Peering again, she saw that he still had his back to the doorway. Moving quietly – toe-heel, toe-heel – she slipped past the door, took nine steps to her own office and, holding her keys tightly in her fist to keep them from jingling, let herself in. She closed the door behind her with a final sigh of relief that sounded deafening to her own ears.

"I'm in my office," she whispered.

"No one saw you?" Gregory asked.

"No," she said.

"I still don't understand," she heard Ginny put in. "She works there. What does it matter if someone sees her or not, even if it is her day off?"

"Because," Gregory said, and Patricia knew she couldn't actually hear the exasperation she imagined she heard in his artificial voice. "If she finds what we need, she'll be taking it with her. Copies won't do, we need original signatures. That means sooner or later Gannery is going to notice them missing. He might not notice it for several days, weeks, months...he may never notice. But we know how meticulous and careful he is, so it is entirely likely that he'll notice them missing right away. Patricia's unexplained presence on her day off, the same day these documents or whatever go missing, will be too great a coincidence for him to ignore. As it is, he is liable to suspect her right away. But, for today at least, she has an alibi."

While he explained this to Ginny, Patricia had crossed the room to the door adjoining Gannery's office and let herself in. Once more the cloying richness of the room's décor made her feel stifled, as if the over-opulent atmosphere of the room itself made it difficult to breathe.

"I'm in his office," she said.

"Good," Gregory said. "Check the obvious places, like we discussed: behind pictures, the backs of cabinets, in the floor under his chair, etc."

Patricia was doing so with alacrity even as he spoke. As they expected, there was nothing to be found in such obvious hiding places. For the safe to remain hidden from her for the nearly three years that she'd worked for Dr. Gannery, even though she was rarely in here when he was not, it would have to be well-hidden indeed.

She opened every drawer in the desk, then the filing cabinet, and then the sideboard along the far wall, all of which she had been provided keys for, in case of emergency. She moved every piece of furniture that wasn't too heavy, careful to return the feet of each back to their own impressions in the carpet. She ran her hands along every inch of wall, seeking a seam, recess, unevenness or bulge.

"Nothing," she said, perching on the edge of the desk.

"I was afraid of that," Gregory said.

"What do you mean?" Patricia asked.

"Well, the only other explanation for how he was able to keep the safe secret from you for so long is that there isn't one. Not there, anyway. It could be at his house. Or maybe there isn't a safe at all. Maybe he has the papers stashed in a deposit box somewhere."

Patricia nodded, even though Gregory couldn't see her. She was disappointed. She'd hoped finding what they needed would be just this easy. She knew now that had been an unrealistic expectation. Gannery was a smart man. Smart and paranoid as such men are. He would have taken a lot more precautions in hiding such incriminating evidence than just stuffing it in a hastily concealed office safe.

"But he mentioned a safe to me," she heard Ginny protest.

"You must have been mistaken," Gregory said.

"If there is a deposit box," Patricia said, "there has to be a key, right?"

"Yes. So?" Gregory said.

"So a key can be hidden in many more places

much smaller than a safe," Patricia said, standing and looking around her more critically.

"No," Gregory said, "he wouldn't hide a key, he'd have it on him. I mean, most likely. Doesn't matter. If it's in a deposit box you can't get to it unless you're authorized, anyway."

"Maybe I am authorized," Patricia said, pulling books down off of shelves and shaking them to see if anything fell out. "I am his Executive Assistant after all. Just because he never told me about any deposit box doesn't mean he didn't put me on the account. Just in case."

"You're reaching, Patricia," Gregory said.

"It's better than just giving up," she snapped, feeling under each of the drawers for duct tape.

"I'm not giving up," Gregory said. "I'm just trying to be logical about this. Go ahead and look, but don't be too long. You want to be gone long before Gannery gets there. Don't even cut it close."

"He's supposed to be with his editor all afternoon," Patricia said, checking under the desk blotter and inside the desk-lamp diffuser. "We have hours yet. You worry too much."

*

Palmer pulled the limousine up to the curb outside the Wall St. building that housed the offices Gannery shared with Paul. Vinnie's men insisted on pouring out of the limo first, then Gannery climbed out. From a nearby cab, Vinnie came trotting up to them.

"Told ya I'd catch up," he said. "Any sign of him?"

Gannery gave him a wry look. "Did you get your business taken care of?" he asked distractedly, not really caring.

"I have a feelin'," Vinnie said triumphantly, "that by this time tomorrow, this whole fixer thing will be pretty much over and done wit'."

"What makes you say that?" Gannery asked with only slightly more interest.

Vinnie shrugged. "Oh, just a hunch."

"You'll forgive me if I reserve judgment," Gannery said, turned and headed for the entrance.

Vinnie rushed to open the door for him. "You'll see. You'll see."

*

Patricia found something.

Or she thought she had. When rechecking the inside and outside walls of all the drawers in the filing cabinet for a taped key, she noticed that the bottom drawer was just as wide and just as deep, but wasn't as long as any of the others. At the moment she was struggling to unhook it from its tracks so she could remove it.

"Look on the sides," Gregory offered over the tiny hearing-aid-sized transceiver in her ear. "Is there some sort of catch or lever?"

"No," she said, frustrated. She tried tilting it up and tilting it down as far as its proximity to the floor would allow, but the drawer would only come out so far and no further. In frustration she tugged at it, and noticed that the drawer hit its outward limit, not solidly, but with a softer thunk. Pushing it almost completely closed again, she braced herself, then pulled it out as hard and as fast as she could.

The drawer came free so suddenly that Patricia fell over onto her rump, pulling the drawer with her and spilling the entire contents of the hanging file folders therein on top of herself. Papers scattered everywhere and covered her like giant flakes of snow.

"What happened?" came Gregory's voice in her ear.

Desperately, Patricia scrambled to rearrange the folders in the drawer and to return their contents to them. As she was thus bent over, she glanced over to the one foot square black hole left behind at the bottom of the cabinet by the vacated drawer. The light reached in, and though not deep enough to penetrate the entire gloom, there was enough diffracted light for her to see that there was, indeed, something at the back of the cabinet.

"Patricia," Gregory demanded.

Leaving the chore of cleaning up for later, she crept forward on her knees and bent to peer even further in. There, at the back of the cabinet where the shorter drawer had been, was another, smaller drawer on the same tracks. She lay on her belly, reached in, grabbed the handle and pulled it out. It didn't want to come easily and squealed on the tracks as if infrequently used, but it came and rested at the edge as its predecessor had done.

"Patricia," Gregory said again. Having only known him a short while, still she could sense him trying to infuse his mechanical voice with more urgency than the slightly inflected drone it always possessed.

"Calm down," Patricia said. "I found something. It might be the safe we were looking for."

The drawer had a hinged lid over it and a latch like a common strong box. In the loop of the latch was a simple padlock and on the bottom was nothing less mundane than a simple set of six tiny thumb-wheels in which to enter the combination.

145

"It's numeric," she said. "The combination is numeric. Six digits. We don't have to worry about letters."

"Good," Gregory said.

Patricia reached into the hip pocket of her sweats and pulled out a sheaf of papers that she unfolded and placed on the floor in front of her. On the sheets were two-column lists that she and Gregory had assembled after painstaking review of every personal name, date, address, or etc. that they could find that might even remotely serve as the combination to a lock. Gannery's mother's birthdate, his childhood address, the registration number on his medical license, anything. It had been an arduous process, given that they hadn't known how many characters the combination would be, whether it would be strictly alphabetical, numerical, or some combination of the two, or even that there would be a combination as opposed to a key.

Patricia carefully but hurriedly sifted through the pages, discarding everything with too many digits or letter. Isolating only the six digit guesses, she set to trying each one. She jumped up just briefly to fetch a pen from Gannery's desk to cross off everything that didn't open the lock. She could feel herself hyperventilating with exhilaration and couldn't help it. This was one of the most frightening, dangerous and exciting things she'd ever done in her life.

"Well?" Ginny's voice came over the earpiece.

"Shhh!" Patricia hissed impatiently.

"Quiet, Ginny," Gregory said. "Let her work."

The list was alarmingly, depressingly short after she had eliminated everything alphabetical or with too few or too many digits. As she neared the end of it all too soon she huffed, then grunted in frustration with every failed attempt. When she reached the end of the list she hit the lock with her fist in anger, then sucked the heel of her hand where the lock had hurt her in return.

"No luck?" Gregory asked.

"I'm going to start at the beginning," she said, rearranging the sheets in front of her. "Maybe I missed some or didn't do them all just right."

"No," Gregory said. "Waste of time. Think. Let's try to be smart about this. What would it likely be?"

"We tried his mother's birthday," Patricia said, "his ex-wife's birthday, his daughter's birthday, *his* birthday, even Dr. Jurgens'. We tried his address, the address of the office here, his mom, etc. What if it isn't anything? I mean anything specific. What if it's just a random set of numbers?"

"There's one last chance," Gregory said. "Clear the combination."

Patricia did as she was told, spinning the thumb-wheels freely. "Okay."

"Pull on the lock," he said. "There should be a little play in the latch. Pull on it and keep that tension. This should engage the tumblers even though they aren't aligned. Starting with the last wheel and moving to the left, turn each wheel until it stops by itself. If we are lucky, each tumbler, once it finds its place, will resist moving beyond it. But don't do the first one. Wait on that one."

Patricia did as she was told. The last number stopped at 7, the next to the last at 9, the next at 9, then 2, and then 0. Only one wheel remained, the first. "Okay," Patricia said.

"Okay, release the tension," Gregory said, and Patricia let the lock drop. "Now, try each number one at a time on the first wheel. It might open on one of them."

The first wheel was currently on nine and the lock had not opened. Patricia turned it to 8 and pulled.

Nothing.

Sighing, she thumbed the wheel to 7 and pulled.

CHAPTER 19

Gannery stepped off the elevator behind half of his entourage and the remaining men trailed behind him. It was beginning to be distracting, having all of these men around him. He hadn't complained yet, because as ineffective as they had proven against the fixer, they were still his only protection, however incompetent.

He walked at a no-nonsense pace to the private entrance of the practice, used his key to let himself and his men in, and marched up the hall toward his office. As he passed Paul's office he stopped when he noticed the room nearly entirely cleared out. Paul stood in the center looking lost.

Gannery stepped into the room.

"What the fuck is going on here?"

Paul turned to him and his face grew red with

useless fury. "I'm getting my affairs in order," he said from behind clenched teeth. "I suggest you do the same. It won't be much longer before you're in the ground and I'm in jail, and you know what? I just don't give a shit anymore."

He was advancing on Gannery as he spoke, working his hands against each other so hard that the knuckles were white.

"You win, Gerry," he grated. "You reduced me to something I never thought myself capable of. You brought me down to your level, and now there's no way out. Not for either of us."

"Bullshit," Gannery said. He kept his usual rakish air about him, trying not to show how Paul's words echoed his own growing fears. If he didn't find a way to outmaneuver the fixer, he would, indeed, be six feet under. He turned and started back up the hall but Paul launched himself forward and latched his arms around Gannery's neck.

The two staggered and struggled for a moment until Vinnie and his men were able to peel Paul off Gannery. He saw raised fists, some laced with iron, and he called out to stop them.

"Knock it off," he snapped. The men stopped to look at him, then withdrew, letting Paul go, thug's tools disappearing as miraculously as they'd appeared.

Paul stood poised against the hallway wall as if ready to throw himself into attack-mode again.

"Dr. Gannery?"

Gannery turned to see Nurses Cohen and MacDenna outside the pharmacy. It had been Cohen who'd called out. "Is everything all right?" she asked in a voice she tried to make strong but that quavered with trepidation anyway. She was looking at all of the men choking the passageway with a combination of angry indignation and fear.

"Everything's fine, Wilma," Gannery called back. "At any rate, it isn't any of your business. Go back to what you were doing."

"I don't want any of the recovering patients disturbed," she said, stepping forward, emboldened, while Nurse MacDenna plucked at her sleeve in warning. "The recovery room is just up that hall."

"Go back to what you were doing," Gannery said again, putting a chill of warning into his voice. "Now."

She seemed to try to hold her ground a little longer, finally wilted and retreated to the pharmacy with her colleague, closing the door behind them.

"Get him into his office," Gannery said and Vinnie and his men grabbed Paul none-too-gently and nearly carried him, struggling, back into the office. Gannery followed them and closed the door behind them.

*

"What's the matter?" Gregory asked.

Patricia hadn't realized she'd stopped breathing. She'd let the lock drop and was on her feet, heart pounding and unable to swallow, her mouth gone desert dry. There was no doubt in her mind that that'd been Dr. Gannery's voice in the hall, calling out to Wilma, Nurse Crone.

"He's here," she said, breathlessly.

"Who?" Gregory asked. "Gannery?"

"Yes."

"Get out," Gregory said.

"Oh god," Patricia heard Ginny cry behind him.

151

Patricia looked at the papers scattered all around her and seemed unable to move. At any moment she expected the sound of his key in the door, and the terror that gripped her now would not unfreeze her joints and let her at least attempt a clean escape. Part of her wanted to just run, but the more reasoning part of her, petrified but still functioning, if sluggishly behind her fear, told her to make at least some attempt to clean up until the very last possible moment, then bolt.

"Patricia," Gregory said. "Don't bother to return the drawer. Just get out. Now."

"Jesus," Ginny said urgently.

Finally Patricia dropped to her knees and reached for every sheet of scattered paper she could find. There was no time to place them in the files that they belonged in, so she just stuffed them into folders at random. Her heart quailed in her chest as she imagined the scrape of the key in the lock, waiting horribly for the actual sound itself.

By the time she had returned the drawer to at least some semblance of order, the door hadn't opened. She was about to shove the drawer back into place, pushing both it and the hidden drawer in, when she looked over her shoulder. The door should have opened by now. Gannery should be standing there now looking at her in rage.

But he hadn't come.

There was no question that she'd heard his voice moments before. She knew it too well, had feared it for too long to mistake it. But clearly he had been distracted by something.

"My birthday," Ginny said, quietly.

"What?" Gregory said.

"October twenty-ninth, nineteen ninety-seven," Ginny said triumphantly. "The combination is my birthday. The first number is one, Patricia!"

"It's too late," Gregory said. "We can try it another time. Get out, Patricia. Now."

Patricia knew Gannery's delay was the proverbial gift horse in whose mouth one should never look, and that she should flee. Instead, she put the drawer down and turned back to the lock, turning the first wheel to the digit 1.

*

"Don't make a scene, Paul," Gannery snapped at him. "Christ, you're so melodramatic."

Vinnie's men had ensconced Paul on the couch under the window and sat around him like a mob of gargoyles ready to pounce. For his part, Paul sat with his hands on his knees. There were dark rings around his eyes and he glared at Gannery as if he truly didn't care what happened to him.

"I have some advice for you, old friend," Gannery went on. "If you know what's best for you, you'll take it."

"You're the second man this week to tell me what's best for me," Paul said from between clenched teeth.

"That's because you're an idiot, Paul," Gannery said. "People see the need to talk sense into you. What I've done isn't fair. I don't claim that it is. You were in the way of something I want very, very badly and I couldn't have that. But it isn't as if your life is over. You'll go to jail for a few years. You're the goody-goody type, you'll get out on good behavior. Your life will go on."

"Fuck you. I'll never be able to practice again," Paul said.

"Well boo-fucking-hoo," Gannery shouted. "You'll do something else. But you'll be older. You'll be smarter. You won't be such a schlub anymore. And you'll be a free man. But you go making waves about this whole hit man thing and you could go to jail for the rest of your life."

"That's just what he said."

"Who?"

"*Him*," Paul said, looking at Gannery pointedly.

"Oh, him. Well he's right. You don't see me going to the police."

"I don't get that," Paul said, his face releasing its clenched crimson rage, if only a little. "Why not? If you want me in jail that would be one sure way to do it."

"Because I don't need the legal entanglements either," Gannery said. "My project is hanging by a thread as it is. Even the hint of a scandal and they'll pull the rug for sure."

"What project?" Paul asked, a little too casually.

Gannery stood and patted Paul on the cheek bracingly a few times. "Don't you worry yourself about that. Just ride this out. It'll be over soon, and you'll see. Older and wiser, like I said. You might even see as how I've done you a favor here. I doubt it. Few people appreciate true altruism. But you might. Just behave. I don't want to have to make things harder on you than they already are. Right, Vinnie?"

"Right," Vinnie said, reaching out and twisting Paul's ear cruelly.

Paul cried out, ducked his head and pulled away. He swung a fist back at Vinnie, who deflected it easily, laughing with his men.

"Come on," Gannery said. "This place stinks."

He opened the door and headed up the hall, followed by his bodyguards. Reaching his office, finally, he slipped the key in the lock and opened the door.

*

With no time to sift and discriminate, Patricia took everything she found in the little lockbox-slash-hidden-drawer, files and papers and manila envelopes, the lot. She placed them on Gannery's desk, closed the lid of the hidden drawer, and replaced the lock, even taking the time to spin the thumb-wheels randomly.

She slid the drawer back as far as she could reach, then turned and lifted the original drawer and placed it over the hole. It didn't fit. How could it not fit? It had come out of this self-same cabinet.

She looked to be sure the tracks were lined up and they were, but every time she pushed the drawer to slide it into place it lifted up off the tracks. She whimpered, half out of frustration and half out of desperation.

"What's the matter now?" Gregory asked.

Taking a moment to calm her shaking hands, Patricia took the drawer and tried placing it carefully, precisely in the tracks. This time, when she pushed it, the drawer slipped up again and jammed in the hole.

"Fuck," she hissed.

"What?"

"The drawer won't fit," she spat irritably.

"Leave it," Gregory urged. "Patricia, for God's sake, get the hell out of there."

One last time.

She jammed the drawer down onto its tracks, pushed, and it slammed against the drawer above it once more. Intending to flip the entire thing into the air out of

155

frustration, Patricia lifted the front of the drawer high...and with a *kathunk* it not only slipped into its tracks, but slammed closed so loudly she nearly cried out.

Jumping to her feet, she shoved the key in the cabinet lock, pushed in the button and turned the key. Taking the stack of pilfered treasure from Gannery's desk and holding it to her chest, she rushed to the door adjoining her office.

A key ground into the lock of Gannery's office door. She looked down and saw shadows moving under the door. She hit the light switch and slipped through into her office. She turned to close her own door when the one to Gannery's office slammed open, impacted the door to her office and drove it shut with a forceful bang.

She heard angry voices in the other offices as she turned to flee. She nearly cried out as she drove her hip directly into the sharp corner of her desk. The folders, papers and envelopes in her arms scattered everywhere as she fell to one knee and bit her lip, whimpering, tears stinging her eyes.

"Patricia?" came Gregory's voice in her ear.

Impatiently, Patricia yanked the earpiece from her ear and stuffed it into her bra. Biting her lips, Patricia forced herself to move, to gather up all the papers and order them again. Once more pressing them to her chest, Patricia opened the hall door, made certain the coast was clear, then slipped out into the hall.

Dr. Jurgens' door was closed when she went by this time, and Nurses Crone and MacDenna were too preoccupied with the new shipment in the pharmacy to see her slip past the glass door. She found herself in the elevator vestibule with considerably less effort than it had taken to get into the office. She danced impatiently, glancing at the doors to the practice lobby, until the elevator arrived and let her in.

As she rode down she put the papers on the floor long enough to pull down one side of her sweats and look at the giant, ugly bruise developing on her hip and thigh. As she did so she heard a tiny sound coming from somewhere below her.

"Oh," she said, taking the transceiver back out of her bra and inserting it into her ear once more.

"...don't answer now I'm calling the police," Gregory was saying.

"Relax," Patricia said. "Hey. Gregory. I said relax. I have the papers. I'm in the elevator. I'm fine."

CHAPTER 20

A man named Jet, known to recent chosen adversaries as the fixer, anonymous in jeans and white undershirt, fully capable of passing inconspicuously when it suited him, as it did now, stood across the street from The Hotel Excelsior, leaning against a light pole outside a drug store. It took surprisingly little effort to alter one's appearance sufficiently to pass unrecognized, and in fact subtlety was the key. Jet chose to stand slightly hunched as if defeated by time and fate, having grayed his hair with simple everyday talcum powder. He wore a pair of half-lens reading glasses.

He watched Vinnie arrive in a cab with another man. Vinnie carried a suitcase of only moderate weight, given how he handled it. The other man, an Irish-looking fellow with thin face and sandy hair, carried a chest-like satchel of considerably more weight, judging by how it made him lean away from the hand that held it.

Vinnie looked around them, always cautious. His eyes scanned right past Jet without stopping, and the two men turned and entered the rundown hotel. The watch on Jet's wrist said 8:42 AM. Aside from shifting weight occasionally from one foot to the next, he didn't move.

The Hotel Excelsior had been built in the sixties during a time when other parts of the country seemed enamored with the Southwestern-inspired art-deco movement, and so had a sweeping, rounded façade with circles of various sizes cut into it in patterns. It had since fallen into disrepair and a similar disrepute, with flaking paint, an off-kilter revolving door that hadn't turned in a decade, and windows covered with drooping, faded, coarse-weave tweed drapes.

Loitering without appearing to be up to no good and drawing the attention of cops was an art. It didn't do to act drunk, or to look passers-by or drivers in the face, as if looking to make a connection. You watched traffic and pedestrians in a distracted sort of way, as if waiting for a person or vehicle in particular, with no real interest in anyone else.

Time passed and Vinnie and his companion reappeared, Vinnie without his suitcase, the Irishman with his but without the distinctive list to one side – *his* case was much lighter now. They hailed a cab and rode away, less attentive as to any possible observers – their business was done and they were, presumably, home free.

Jet's watch read 10:32. Nearly two hours before the scheduled pick-up.

Much more cautious than Vinnie, Jet scanned sidewalks, windows, and rooftops with a professionally trained eye for spies. Seeing none, he pushed away from the pole and took his time crossing the street, pausing for passing traffic as if he had all the time in the world. Reaching the other side, he scanned the storefronts casually, as if with no real interest, then walked into the Hotel Excelsior.

The lobby was shallow, with matching worn couches and end-tables to each side of a tiled runway leading to the front desk. A wrinkled, thin old man dozed loudly on one of the couches. To the left of the front desk were stairs going up into darkness, to the right an elevator with a circular window in the door. The clerk in his bullet-proof glass enclosure lifted drooping eyes from a small portable TV and scratched a stubbly chin. When Jet ignored him and veered toward the stairs the clerk went back to his flickering program without comment.

On the second floor Jet turned right, toward the odd numbered rooms. To his left were ranks of doors with numbers on them, and to his right a bare wall with faded, stained and peeling wallpaper. The hall smelled of cigarettes, urine, and something else, bitter and unidentifiable.

At room 29 he paused. Bringing his nose within inches of the jamb, he carefully scanned the entire circumference of the door's seam. He then placed his hand on it, feeling every inch of its surface. Finally, drawing a Berretta from a holster at his calf, he knocked authoritatively.

The door to room 27, one door to his left, opened and an emaciated man with splotchy hair and black raccoon circles around his eyes looked out. Seeing Jet and, more importantly, the gun trained on him, he ducked back in and slammed his door. Jet waited a beat

160

longer, but if there was anyone waiting for him inside room 29, they were not going to open the door.

Looking both ways, Jet took a key from his pocket from which depended an oblong plastic fob with the word Excelsior embossed on it above the large number 29. Fitting this into the lock, he squared himself, then opened the door rapidly and squatted, gun raised in his right hand braced with his left, key still dangling from the lock.

The room was long and narrow, with a bed to one side, a table bearing a lamp on the other and a curtained window opposite the door. No TV, no phone. In the far corner by the window was a booth fashioned from plasterboard and fitted with a folding closet door. Inside this room he could see a toilet and a sink with dripping faucet, a makeshift privy added to this room as an afterthought.

The room was vacant.

Jet quickly stepped inside and closed the door behind him, keeping the key. Re-holstering the berretta, he looked at the suitcase on the foot of the bed, the self-same one left behind by Vinnie minutes before. This, presumably, held half of a million dollars. Jet got down on his hands and knees and peered under the bed. It was filthy under there, but he ignored the grime on the floor and examined the bed frame. Carefully he reached up and felt the underside of the frame and the box-springs. Waddling on his knees, he examined the entire perimeter of the bed.

Finding nothing, he stood and wiped dust-coated fingers on the seat of his pants. Leaning over, he examined the exterior of the suitcase with as much scrutiny as he had the bed, trying especially to see anything underneath. Again, with nothing obvious revealing itself to him, he stood and removed a small pen knife from his pocket.

Touching the top of the case with only two fingers of his left hand to steady it, he used the knife to worry at the tops of the hinges of the latches holding the case closed. He worked them expertly, bending weak brass pintles the size of sewing needles and sliding them free of their tubular seatings. Hinges now disassembled, the case could now be opened without use of the two latch-release buttons.

Jet pulled two pillows out from under the ratty olive-green duvet. He lay on the floor hard against the bed and arranged the pillows over him length-wise. Reaching up with the pocket knife in his left hand, he worked the blade into the seam presented between the lid and the case itself. It was a simple matter to carefully lift the lid and turn it back until wide open.

Satisfied, Jet cast the pillows off and stood. Inside the case were rows and rows of banded $100 bills, five across and five deep. If each stack held a hundred bills then there would be exactly $250,000 in the case. Two layers would total the agreed upon sum. But the case was deep and these stacks of bills came up nearly to the rim.

There was definitely something underneath.

Jet examined the part of the case's interior every bit as minutely as he had the door and the bed, again rewarded with no outward sign that anything was amiss. Using his knife, he carefully placed the point on the top bill of one of the stacks in the middle, pushed a feather's weight, then turned back the smallest corner of the bill impaled by the blade.

As suspected, a slip of gray construction paper cut

to the exact dimensions of the United States Treasury's finest works of art was underneath the genuine article. With every reason to believe the remainder of this stack, of all of the stacks, was similarly fraudulent, Jet let the bill go.

Leaning down and placing his face level with the rim of the case, he carefully slipped the blade under one of the bands bundling each of the stacks and tried to lift it without tearing it or cutting it. There was nothing under the first band, and nothing under the second. Under the third was a wire as thin as a cat's whisker, and under the fourth and fifth as well.

At this level, he could smell the dusty chemical smell of C-4 plastique, a smell as distinct and familiar to him as his own musk. There was no doubt, the case was wired with enough explosive to incinerate the room and leave nothing but ash of its entire contents.

He stood and smiled, closing the knife and returning it to his pocket. Jet was certain that Vinnie had acted on his own, planting this bomb. From all he'd observed, it just wasn't Gannery's style. That man would prefer to outmaneuver Jet, not blow him up in some anonymously impersonal way. A man like Gannery would be disgusted by such brutish and inelegant tactics.

Using his hands, Jet closed the lid carefully and replaced the hinge-pins, his knife making another appearance to bend them back into place. The tension on the tiny inner springs that would have caused the latches to spring up when the latch-release buttons were pressed had been spoiled, but that couldn't be helped. Whoever next opened the case would have to lift them manually.

Turning away, Jet left the room and returned to the lobby. Approaching the desk, he waited for the sleepy clerk to look up. When he didn't, Jet said, "Hey."

The clerk strained his eyes away from the TV without turning his head, looked Jet up and down, then went back to watching his TV. "Uh-huh." His voice was as soggy sounding as he smelled.

"What's the rate by the week?"

This drew a longer look from those dim eyes. "A hunnert."

Jet drew out a money clip and began counting out bills. The clerk lifted his head and began to watch with more attentiveness. Jet counted out four fifties and slid them under the slot at the bottom of the glass partition.

"Two weeks, room 29."

"That room is booked," the clerk said, eyeing the bills. "But room 30 on the other side is free. 29 will be free tomorrow."

"I'm taking it now," Jet said. "Guy who was just here? Friend of mine. Change of plans, is all."

The clerk shrugged and pocketed the bills. "Whatever you say."

"The book," Jet said.

"Huh?"

"Mark it in the book."

Sighing, the clerk drew a bent spiral notebook from under the desk. On the cover were obscene sketches. He opened it and made a note inside, then returned it to its place.

"Satisfied?"

"Listen up," Jet said, placing a fifty on the desk and sliding it under but keeping his hand on it. The clerk looked at the bill and licked his lips with a pale, worm-like tongue.

"No one goes in that room without a key," Jet

said. "I mean no one. I find out someone's been nosing around in there, you or one of your buddies, I'm going to come down and put a bullet into your skull. We understand each other?"

"Yeah." The clerk laughed sarcastically, rapping the bullet-proof glass with his knuckles. "Right."

Jet reached around and hit the wall of the booth to one side of the window with his closed fist, hard enough that they could both hear plaster knock loose and rattle free inside the hollow wall.

"Yeah, right," Jet said.

The clerk looked at his side of that wall and swallowed.

"Okay," he said and reached for the bill.

Jet held on a moment more. "No one," he said pointedly.

"I got it," the clerk said rather petulantly.

Jet let him take the bribe.

"Is there a back way out of here?" he asked.

CHAPTER 21

"Wow," Gregory's canned voice said.

Patricia only swallowed.

"We have him," Gregory said.

Patricia folded her arms as she sat opposite him at the low table in the overly warm room and shivered. She wasn't afraid, exactly, but she was in awe of her own audacity. Gregory sat opposite her in his wheelchair. Between them, arranged in stacks, were the original documents pilfered from Gannery's computer, topped off with more physical evidence than their best dreams could have hoped for. These were the documents among the stuff Patricia had stolen from Gannery's little hidey-hole.

Ginny had gone shopping and wouldn't be back for hours. Margie sat in her easy chair by her TV across the room snoring softly.

Patricia looked at Gregory and tried to swallow, only to find her throat parched. For his part, his eyes were wide and bright with excitement.

"What is it?" he asked. "You're white as a sheet."

She tapped one of the stacks.

Among all of the folders and envelopes she had brought with her back from the office they had finally found signed deposit slips for the off-shore accounts that they'd been able to cross-reference almost directly one-for-one with every instance of investment fraud and embezzlement from the firm. They'd found hundreds of demonstrated acts of tax fraud in Gannery's own hand.

But the stack she tapped was the most damning.

Cases settled out of court, over twenty of them. Malpractice cases, each depicting horrendous cases of botched surgeries, demonstrably egregious cases of negligence resulting in the disfigurement and maiming of patients. Two resulting in actual wrongful deaths. Each case settled out of court, some for staggering amounts, and each with the absolute stipulation that nothing would ever be revealed to the media.

All of them had occurred in the two years before Dr. Jurgens had graduated, passed the board and joined the practice. It was nearly every surgery that Dr. Gannery had performed prior to the forming of the partnership. The man had been more than a hack, he'd been a butcher.

"Give him credit," Gregory said. "He stopped practicing as soon as Dr. Jurgens came on board."

"Yeah, and then started taking all the credit for Paul's brilliant work," Patricia spat bitterly. "And what about these?"

She lifted a stack of check stubs next to this stack.

Each was made out to someone named Salomé Johnson, each in the amount of $5,000, one a month for the last twenty-five years and change. Patricia had been able to identify Johnson as her own predecessor – Johnson had been Gannery's executive assistant until three years ago. And yet the checks continued, even after she left.

"Hush money," Gregory said. "I'd bet my life on it."

"Nearly a million and a half over 25 years," Patricia said.

"At least she isn't dead. It also explains why he was much more careful not to let you in on any of his secrets."

Patricia slapped the stubs back down on the table. "Quit that putting-the-best-face-on-things bullshit," she snapped. "He's a beast. An absolute beast." She felt close to tears. To think she'd trusted this man, even in a way admired him, in spite of his abuse of her. He'd been irascible, unreasonable, demanding, but she'd never suspected that he was evil.

"I don't disagree," Gregory said.

"I almost think we should let Jet kill him," she ground from behind clenched teeth.

"You don't mean that," Gregory said. "That's not for us to decide, that's not for Jet to decide, that's not for Paul Jurgens to decide. It's for the law to decide."

"I know," she said ruefully.

"If everything Dr. Jurgens told you is true, and that's a big if, I don't want my brother to go to the gas chamber over a slime-ball like this," Gregory said, his eyes becoming intense. "Gannery isn't worth it."

"I know," Patricia said again. "I said 'almost.'"

They sat in silence for a few minutes, each lost in

their own thoughts.

"So we call the FBI," Gregory said. "Probably the IRS and the treasury department, as well. Give them the proof. Then it's over."

"Wait," Patricia said, "we can't do that. We acquired all of this stuff illegally. Worse, we can't offer any plausible story on how we got it without causing all sorts of questions. At the very least I could go to jail for breaking into Dr. Gannery's lockbox."

"That's unlikely," Gregory said, "given Dr. Gannery isn't going to want to admit the evidence is real to begin with, much less that he had it hidden away in a secret safe that you broke into."

"No, but such questions could lead to your brother. We didn't cover our tracks quite that well."

"So?"

Patricia sighed. "So it will come out that he was hired to kill Dr. Gannery. That could jam up both Jet and Dr. Jurgens"

"I still don't buy that," Gregory said.

"Again, why would Dr. Jurgens lie about something like that?"

"Okay, maybe Dr. Jurgens did say that to Jet," Gregory said, "but while I can believe maybe Jet intends to help him somehow, I don't believe he actually plans to commit murder."

"So what then?" Patricia asked impatiently. "If you tell me we got all this stuff, went through all this for nothing, Gregory, I swear I'll scream."

"No," he said. "But we need to get this into the hands of someone who could plausibly have gotten his hands on it through entirely legal means."

"Dr. Jurgens?"

"Exactly," he said.

"But first, we need to show it to Jet," she said.

"Okay," he said. "But why first? He'll be as pissed as hell that we got involved."

"Because," Patricia said, "on the outside chance I'm right and Jet does plan to kill Dr. Gannery, we need to show him that he no longer has any reason to. Because Gannery will be going to jail, and Dr. Jurgens will be off the hook. Killing Gannery would be pointless now."

"Fine," he said. "Then you'll see I was right."

"Somehow," Patricia said, thinking back to the one and only time she'd stood face to face with Jet, "I don't think it's going to be as cut and dried as you think. Just please be open to the possibility that what Paul told me about hiring your brother is true."

Gregory looked away.

"When he got in last night," he said, "Jet came in to check on me, like he always does."

They'd always been very careful not to allow Patricia's and Jet's paths to cross here at the house. Gregory's older brother would not be happy to see her. In fact, to use Gregory's own words, he'd "have kittens" if he knew they'd maintained contact, much less were working on their own to undermine Gannery.

"He seemed to be in a pretty good mood," Gregory went on. "I asked him if the Gannery thing was going well and he said yes. When I asked him what, exactly, he'd been hired to do, he avoided the subject. When I asked him, as if it was a joke, whether he'd been hired to kill Gannery, he looked right at me. Through me. I've seen that cold look he gets. You don't want it aimed at you, let me tell you."

"Actually, I have," Patricia said.

"Oh yeah," Gregory said, his eyes smiling at her. "I know he makes it a point of never lying to me. He may withhold things, but he has never, to my knowledge, lied to me. So anyway, he asked me what I knew. I told him nothing, I was just joking. He told me to mind my own fucking business and marched out. He didn't come to say good morning to me this morning."

"I'm sorry, Gregory," Patricia said. "You know I didn't want to be right. But you weren't there, Paul was compelling. I don't know him well, but I've never known him to lie, either. Not when it counted."

"I still don't think Jet's capable of such a thing," he said.

"You said he was a Navy Seal," Patricia said. "You had to know he killed people before."

"In the line of duty, maybe," he said. "But this isn't that. This isn't right."

"How long has he been...a private investigator," Patricia said.

"Not long," Gregory said. "A couple of years."

"Do you think he has...killed...before, and just not told you about it?"

Gregory looked away from her again. She thought he wasn't going to answer her when, after a time, he said, "I don't know."

"Does he even have an investigator's license?" she asked.

Gregory looked at her, his eyes registering surprise. "I've never seen one. I just assumed..."

Patricia looked back sympathetically.

"If he's been a hit man while all the time he was telling me he was a private investigator," Gregory said, "then I'm wrong about him, and he's not who I think he

171

is."

"You didn't know," she said. "In fact *we* don't know. We're just speculating."

Gregory looked away yet again, this time showing his anger. "I don't want you here," he said. "When I show him what we've found. I want you to go home. We have a lot to talk about, Jet and me. I don't want him distracted by the fact that you helped me."

"You mean you don't want him to blame me," she said. "To accuse me of leading you into a betrayal of him."

He just looked back at her.

Patricia stood up and picked her backpack up off the floor, placed the strap over her shoulder. "Just remember, Gregory. Whatever he's done to hide things from you, whatever lies he told, I'm sure he did it for you."

Gregory didn't answer.

Patricia turned and walked out. "Good night, Margie," she called, snapping the woman awake as she passed.

Out on the street Patricia turned her cell phone back on — Margie didn't want it on around all of Gregory's life support equipment for fear of magnetic field interference — and called herself a cab.

CHAPTER 22

Gerald Gannery looked up from his computer and rubbed his eyes. Vinnie and another man dozed over on the couch in Gannery's office. The others had been stationed as inconspicuously as possible around the greater offices of the practice, keeping an eye on entrances. Not inconspicuously enough, since Nurse Cohen had demanded to know what all these cologne-smelling Guineas were doing in *her* office. Gannery had to firmly tell her to mind her own business, but even then she huffed every time she passed one of them in the hall. One of them tried to cow her by looming over her and glaring, but she took a swipe at him with a dirty scalpel and now they all gave her a wide berth.

It struck Gannery he should have hired her as his body guard instead of Vinnie and his stooges.

With Paul gone, Gannery had been swamped with demands for surgeries scheduled that his partner was no longer available to perform. Gannery wasn't about to do these operations himself, it'd been twenty-five years or more since he'd even touched a scalpel, a fact few suspected, he was sure. Even then, his heart had never really been in it.

Since Patricia had yet to show her face today, he was forced to have the office staff cancel and reschedule as many of these as they could. Even then, many of the patients, self-important snobs every one of them, demanded to speak to him personally to demand an explanation. He was either on the phone all day or on the computer answering impatient emails.

Irritably, he snatched up the phone and hit the redial button for the umpteenth time today. It rang, as before, but then she picked up.

"Patricia," he snapped.

Vinnie woke with a snort and reached under his arm for his gun. Gannery waved him down and the man smacked his lips and closed his eyes once more.

"Where the hell have you been?" Gannery demanded.

"Running the errands you left for me," she said, then added, belatedly, "Doctor."

He should never have given her the day off yesterday. This was what you got when you coddled your employees. Laziness and insubordination. Well, he wouldn't make that mistake again.

"Dr. Jurgens is gone," he informed her. "Just packed up his office and walked out. The place is a madhouse. I need you here."

"Now? It's five o'clock."

Gannery glanced at his watch. "Well, no, not now. But in the morning I want you here, in the office. I want to see your face. We have a lot of damage control to do."

"Can't you do the surgeries yourself?" she asked him.

The goading he heard in her voice must have been his own imagination. Mousey little Patricia would never have the guts to taunt him. He rubbed his temple. He was tired and paranoid and not really enjoying this game with the fixer so much anymore.

"No," he said. "I don't have time. I have a million other business matters to attend to. You know that's always left in my lap. Paul was never good with numbers."

"Oh," was all she said.

"Tomorrow, Patricia," he said warningly. "In this office. Or else. Do we understand each other?"

"We do," she said.

Did she sound amused? No, he was tired. Just tired.

He hung up and turned back to the computer. Then he looked up and stared at the phone.

She hadn't asked why. She hadn't been particularly surprised that Paul had abandoned the firm and she hadn't asked why he did it. It seemed like a perfectly natural question, but she hadn't asked it. Why not?

Could it be she already knew? Could it be Paul talked to her, the squealer? Could he have turned her to his side? Gannery guessed it was possible. He was relatively certain that he had Patricia by her short hairs, with her student loans and his agreement to pay them for her in exchange for a six year commitment from her. But as miserably uninterested in enriching himself as he seemed to be, still Paul was not without resources of his own. He hired the fixer, didn't he? It wasn't beyond the realm of reason that he'd bought Patricia out.

Gannery shook his head again.

No, Paul just wasn't that smart, and he didn't have that much imagination. His despondency yesterday had been genuine, Gannery'd stake his life on it. And Patricia was too nice a girl to be so duplicitous. It was one of the reasons he'd hired her, a lesson he'd learned after dealing with the last anaconda that'd held her job, a mistake he was still paying for. Any agreement they had between them, Paul and Patricia, would be completely open and above board, the saps, so that she could feel justified in confronting Gannery himself and scolding him for how he was treating Paul.

"Vinnie," he snapped.

The man woke up and blinked at Gannery. The other, next to him, woke up, too, and stared around blearily.

"Get the men," Gannery said. "It's time to call it a day."

Gannery turned to his computer and began to shut down the various applications he had opened. Preparing to close the NTSE ticker that scrolled by at the top of his screen, he paused just long enough to see one of the symbols, a stock in which the firm was heavily invested, scroll by.

"What?" he said, smiling.

The stock had gone up an almost exponential amount. Gannery laughed and opened his stock calculator. He needed to know the exact amount invested. For that he turned to the filing cabinet and pulled open the bottom drawer, looking for the file that held the statements for that particular account. At first he couldn't find the folder. It was out of place. Then, finding it, he opened to a mess of meaningless shit.

These documents were in the wrong file, and the one he was looking for, the latest statement, wasn't there. In fact, he noticed on further examination, none of the files in this drawer were in order, and some of the pages were off kilter and dog-eared. So many of the papers he corrected turned out to be in wrong folders that he settled into going through every hanging file. None of them were in the right place.

"What the hell?" he snapped angrily.

Everything in this drawer was a mess, as if someone had spilled the contents and hurriedly replaced them.

"Shit!"

He pulled the drawer out to its limit, reached under and unlatched the tracks and set the drawer aside.

"What is it, Ger?" Vinnie asked.

"Shit-shit," was all Gannery said, now on his knees reaching to the back of the vacant hole left by the removed drawer and pulling forward the hidden one. He lifted the small lock and looked at the combination. It was wrong, but that didn't mean anything.

Quickly he thumbed the six digit-wheels into place, yanked the lock free and flipped open the lid.

"Fuuuck!" he bellowed in a voice that could be heard clear out to the elevator vestibule.

*

Vinnie fetched him a cone-shaped paper cup of cooler water, which Gannery downed and crushed in almost the same motion. He sat on the couch next to

Vinnie trying to slow his breathing, trying to stop hyperventilating. Names raced through his head like a stock ticker gone haywire.

The fixer. Dr. Paul Jurgens. Patricia Duffy. Ginny Miller. Salomé Johnson. The fixer, Dr. Paul Jurgens, Patricia Duffy, Ginny Miller, Salomé Johnson. The fixer Dr. Paul Jurgens Patricia Duffy Salomé Johnson Ginny Miller. The-fixer-Dr-Paul-Jurgens-Patricia-Duffy-Salomé-Johnson-Ginny-Miller.

They were all in it together. He was sure of it.

"Thefixerdrpauljurgenspatriciaduffysaloméjohnso nginnymiller," he said.

"Ger, you're talking gibberish," Vinnie said.

Was he?

He was.

They couldn't all be in on it.

He put greater effort into leveling his breathing and tried to think clearly, logically. Salomé could have gotten past the office staff, having been a familiar face around here for many, many years, but she had no reason to do this, she was set up for life, and those papers could only have spoiled that.

Patricia hadn't been in the office for two days.

Paul left the office abruptly yesterday, which was suspicious, but Gannery still couldn't accept that Paul's depression had all been an act, the man simply wasn't that good. Still, Gannery couldn't entirely discard the possibility that his partner had stolen the files.

Ginny couldn't have gotten into his office without someone stopping her.

"Ger?" Vinnie was pressing. "You okay now?"

The fixer was hired to kill Gannery. Why would he be messing around with papers, even if he had gotten past the office staff somehow? Hit men were technicians, not spies. They were blue collar, very good at what they did, but ultimately single-minded.

"You're color's coming back."

Paul had opportunity and motive but no imagination, Patricia had opportunity but no motive, Salomé the same. If Ginny had cast her lot with the fixer, as it seemed she had, she had motive, but still no opportunity.

"You wanna tell us what's going on," Vinnie pressed him.

Whoever it was would have had to pick the door-lock and somehow figure out the combination to the padlock on the secret drawer's lid. Ginny's birth date, though she had no way of knowing that. Ginny and the fixer, together, at the banquet. The fixer looking at the last number dialed on his cell phone at the diner.

The fixer had to be after more than just killing Gannery. He'd had ample opportunity on at least two occasions and hadn't taken advantage. He seemed to be goading Gannery, taunting him. Did he want Gannery to buy out the contract?

Gannery's heart resumed beating in excitement and relief.

That had to be it. Gannery was in no danger, yet. Never mind how he got in here or how he and Ginny guessed the combination to the padlock, the fixer wasn't going to take those papers to the police. He was going to blackmail Gannery with them. He and Ginny. It was the only thing that made sense. These were motives Gannery could understand, identify with. Yes, he'd have another leach on his ball-sack like Salomé, but he wouldn't be going to jail any time soon and the TV deal still had a chance of going through.

"We going or not, Ger?"

Gannery stood, shot his sleeves and straightened his tie. "Yes, Vinnie. I'm better now. Let's go."

He let himself be led out.

It was only a matter now of waiting for them to contact him with their threats and demands. Whatever the deal, Gannery would insist on getting those papers back. That would have to be part of the agreement. They could make copies, probably were doing so even now, but Gannery needed the originals back. That or no deal, on that he had to stand firm.

On the elevator, however, the relief that followed on the heels of terror now gave way to gall. Gannery balled his fists and grit his teeth. Once more he was being forced to dance to the fixer's tune. It pissed him off no end, and the more he thought about it the angrier he got. There had to be something he could do to turn the tables, get the upper hand once more.

"Put this fixer out of my misery once and for all," he hissed.

"Huh, Ger?" Vinnie asked.

"Never mind," Gannery said, his voice tight. Vinnie had proven himself clumsy and ineffective against the fixer. It was left to Gannery himself to end this game grown tiresome.

The gambit was an opening set of moves in chess that, when well begun, sets the tone for the entire game, then it is up to the master to maintain the advantage gained and capitalize on it. But just as wise is the player who recognizes when it is time to execute an endgame. Sometimes even more crucial than the gambit is the suite of moves intended to bring the game to its inevitable conclusion. Even when behind, a well-executed endgame can turn the entire match on its ear.

Gannery had been a step behind up until now. It was time to bring this game to an end. It was time to play the endgame.

As usual Vinnie and his men cased the exit before they let Gannery pass through. Palmer waited at the curb with the limo. He let the bodyguards open their own doors, but he held Gannery's for him. Gannery adjusted his butt in the seat, stared out the window and resumed planning.

Gannery felt that planting a bomb in the money the fixer was bound to demand as first payment was an amateur's cliché move that a professional like the fixer would surely be expecting. And it wasn't personal enough for Gannery. He needed to defeat the man on his own terms to satisfy his sense of indignation and humiliation.

Which meant he needed leverage on the fixer. Something, someone. This was not the first time the idea had occurred to him. That time, he'd gone after Ginny, but the fixer had already spirited her away somewhere. He was very protective of her. Gannery could understand why, she was a phenomenal fuck. It galled him to lose her.

She was the only connection Gannery had to the fixer, the only certain thing he knew the fixer cared about. The leverage had to be her. Which meant he had to find some way of getting to her. He was familiar with her routine. It was Thursday. What did she usually do on Thursday?

Gannery smiled.

"Palmer, turn around. We're not going home just yet. Head downtown. Take me to Bergdorf's."

CHAPTER 23

Patricia forced herself to stop chewing her thumbnail as she stood amid the crowd gathered on the sidewalk. She watched and waited for Jet's return to the house. The crowd was waiting to get into a house party blasting away from one of the apartments in the brownstone across the street from the place Jet had ensconced Gregory.

When Jet came she almost missed him, a proverbial shadow within shadows as he took the outside stoop three stairs at a time and slipped through the doors in nearly one motion. Patricia counted to ten slowly, picturing Jet climbing the interior stairs to Gregory's room. Then she made her way across the street and, moving slowly, tried to be as quiet as she could in letting herself into the house using the key Gregory had Margie make for her.

Gregory'd made it clear he didn't want her here when he confronted Jet with what they'd discovered in Dr. Gannery's records. He said he was concerned that if Jet knew she'd remained involved after he thought he'd scared her away and even went to the trouble of moving Gregory, that his rage would turn toward her. Gregory felt he could withstand Jet's anger storm more than she could, being Jet's brother.

As she made her way stealthily up the stairs toward Gregory's room she supposed he might be right, but she had her own convictions that felt just as valid to her. For too long she'd been passive, allowing herself to be domineered and controlled by fear. In the past week she'd been taking action, and in one very notable case quite bold action toward a very specific goal. It felt good, and with each success they'd met she'd been more and more awakened to life and her place in it.

So now it just didn't feel right leaving Gregory to weather that storm alone. Now that she started on the path of action, she was more sensitive to the apathy that tried to pull her back into complacency. Where it would have been comfortable to sit back and let others act once, now it chafed. She didn't want to go back anymore, never again.

As she neared the top of the stairs she stopped. Light inside the room and dark here in the hall she doubted if anyone in there, who might glance out, would see her here two or three steps below the top stair.

Gregory sat in his chair by the couch over in the little tea grouping at the opposite side of the big bay windows from his bed. The windows overlooked the playground at the back of the house and several neighborhood teenagers were enjoying the dusk with laughter and most likely the passing around of a few joints.

Jet stood in the center of the room facing him, his back to Patricia. "That's not your decision, Greg," Jet was saying, "she works for me..."

"She takes care of me," Gregory said, upping the volume on his voice synthesizer. This would show Jet that this was going to be a serious conversation.

"Where's Ginny," Jet asked.

"She's shopping downtown," Gregory said. "We need to talk, Jet. Sit down."

The lanky man walked over slowly and sat down on the couch. Patricia couldn't see Jet's eyes under the brim of that stupid hat of his, but from the angle of his head she thought it a good bet that as intended his attention was drawn by the stacks of papers arranged on the coffee table in front of them, but whether he sensed Gregory's mood or out of plain politeness he didn't touch them and he didn't ask who'd put them there.

"What, exactly, did Dr. Jurgens hire you to do," Gregory asked.

This time Patricia did catch two small glints as Jet eyed his brother. "I take it since you're asking, you already know," he said. "Who told you?"

"Never mind," Gregory said. "Is that what you've been planning to do?"

Jet regarded him, but didn't answer.

"What does Ginny have to do with it?"

"Nothing," Jet said quickly. "Not that part of it. She only helped me in drawing him out. I would never endanger her or anyone."

"Except Gannery himself," Gregory said.

"You don't have to know this," Jet told Gregory

with a warning note in his tone. "In fact, it's better if you don't. In case...in case...."

"In case you get caught," Gregory finished for him.

"I won't."

"So you *are* going to do it, aren't you?"

Jet refused to answer.

"What if you don't have to?" Gregory asked. "What if I told you I have found enough proof to put him in jail instead of Dr. Jurgens?"

"Not in the stuff you downloaded from his computer," Jet averred.

"I've found more than enough physical evidence to not only put him away for a lot of years, but to ruin him professionally for the rest of his life. Look."

Jet followed Gregory's eyes and began reviewing the documents on the table. Gregory, and Patricia from her place in the shadows, waited patiently for several long minutes while Jet picked through the stack, occasionally looking at Gregory with a steadily darkening brow. Beneath the brewing storm on Jet's brow she could detect wonder and even some outrage. But over it all was an anger reaching the pressure point.

After glancing at the last item Jet shot to his feet and marched away, across the room toward Margie's station and the doorway. If he kept on marching out the door Patricia wasn't sure she could find a hiding place fast enough to keep him from stepping right on her. At any rate hiding wasn't what she'd come here for. She got ready to stand and face him. But he stopped, looking straight ahead, and for a moment she thought he was staring right at her. Then he strode halfway back and took a wide-legged stance, facing Gregory again.

"God damn you, little brother," he said in a quiet, dangerous tone. "What did I tell you? What did I tell you! I wanted you out of it. I should never have involved you to begin with. It was too close a call, that IT guy tracking you down. It was my fault for getting you mixed up in this, for endangering you. What are you trying to do to me?"

By the end Jet sounded utterly miserable and distraught.

"What are you trying to do to me?" Gregory demanded back. "What would happen to me if you got yourself sent up for murder?"

"You'd be well taken care of," Jet waved his hand. "I've seen to it that you'll be well taken care of."

"That isn't what I mean," Gregory snapped. "How many, Jet? How many have you killed?"

Jet turned away, his hands working into fists and then releasing repeatedly, as if helpless. "Too many," he said. "More than I can count."

"I mean since you...got back...from...from that place."

Jet shook his head. "None."

For that Gregory must feel some relief, Patricia thought.

"What happened to you, Jet," Gregory asked. "When you showed up in Japan alive after we all were told you were dead, I was so excited. But then, when you came home, I saw that you *were* dead. You were still breathing, but those people in that place, they killed whatever it was that was Jet, deep down, inside. The only spark of life I saw in you at all was when you told me you decided to work as a private investigator. It wasn't much of a spark, but it was there, and I had reason to hope that it would grow.

"But it didn't. If anything, it receded again. You talk about setting the wrong things right, but when you talked about it back then, your eyes lit up and you seemed excited. Now when you talk about it, you seem to get angrier. Do you even have an investigator's license?"

"No," Jet said. "They wouldn't give me one. They said I had a history of mental instability."

"Because of what you went through," Gregory asked.

Patricia was ashamed to admit, if only to herself, that she didn't entirely disagree. From what Gregory had told her, since Jet's return he'd always seemed to Gregory to be walking a razor's edge between sanity and the proverbial deep end. The problem was, it wasn't anything he, Gregory, could put his finger on...just a feeling, he'd told her. Something only someone who knew Jet as well as he did would be able to detect.

"You have to stop this," Gregory said. "It isn't helping things. It's making them worse. You have to stop."

"No," Jet said, his back still turned to Gregory, his eyes once again shrouded from Patricia by the brim of his hat.

"Please, Jet."

"You don't understand," Jet said, lifting his head. The ice in his eyes now was in shards, with jagged edges and needle sharp tips. He turned once again. "I can't. If I stop, I'll die."

Gregory seemed about to protest again, but didn't. Patricia wondered if the implications of what Jet was saying chilled him as much as it did her, chilled him until he couldn't summon the breath to blow into the tube that generated his fake voice. If he had, she was certain she would be able to see steam rise from his mouth like on a cold day in winter. Instead, the brothers locked gazes and didn't speak for several heartbeats.

"Moving," Jet said in a cracked voice. "It keeps the...memories away. Moving. Acting. Setting the wrong things right. It's a sick world out there. The bad guys win more and more every day. To the point where even the good guys are starting to look like the bad guys. Time was when a man who returned a lost hundred dollar bill was admired, today he is called a fool. Where once a woman made a guy want to be a better man, now women have stooped down to wallow in the mud with him.

"Evil is man-made, little brother. Evil is selfishness, evil is a disregard for your fellow man, evil is soulless greed. Do you know what evil is, Gregory?"

Gregory shook his head slowly.

"Evil is men like Dr. Gerald Gannery. He's gotten by all his life, built his fortune and his fame on the back of Dr. Paul Jurgens. Then, when it is no longer convenient for him to do so, he betrays Jurgens and destroys him."

"Dr. Jurgens is the good man, then?" Gregory asked.

"Dr. Paul Jurgens isn't perfect," Jet said. "He's weak. I despise his kind of voluntary weakness. He's a coward. He's not very smart in spite of all his degrees. He could have prevented Gannery from making him a victim if he'd paid more attention. But those are his weaknesses, and it isn't up to me to judge him for that. What makes him a decent man is that he treats others with kindness, he's honest, he's hard working, he cares about excelling in his chosen profession. Dr. Jurgens takes no short cuts.

He pays his dues. He deserves what he gets because he's earned it. Problem is, because of people like Gannery, he doesn't always get what he deserves."

"If you can't judge Jurgens for his weaknesses," Gregory observed. "How can you judge Gannery for his...for lack of a better word, evil?"

"Because Gannery's evil hurts others. Gannery's greed isn't mine to judge, but when what he does to feed that greed hurts others, that I can judge. We are all obligated to judge that."

"And as judge, jury and executioner," Gregory said, "you have decided that he deserves to die. For that."

Jet didn't answer at first, then he strode over to the table and slammed a fist down on one of the stacks. "For that! And that!" Fisting another stack with a loud *wham*! "And that!" Yet another. "For all of it!" He swept the stacks off of the table so that they flew up, then drifted to the floor like dead moths. "For all of it," he said again, this time in a whisper, watching the papers settle around him.

Patricia rose at that moment ready to intervene, but after the papers had settled and Jet lowered himself wearily to the couch once more, Gregory asked, "And what about you, Jet? Who judges your actions? What happens when you go to jail? Who will set the wrong things right then? What happens when, God forbid, you kill the wrong man?"

Jet remained silent.

"Regardless of all this," Gregory said, "as you see, it's no longer necessary to kill Dr. Gannery. We have him dead to rights. Tomorrow we give this proof to Dr. Jurgens, coach him on what to say to the authorities, and he's home free while Dr. Gannery goes to jail. So you don't have to kill him now. Right Jet?"

Jet remained frozen in place.

"Right, Jet?" Gregory pressed.

"I wasn't hired to send him to jail," Jet said.

"What are you talking about?" Gregory demanded. "You know why Dr. Jurgen's hired you. Because of what Dr. Gannery was doing to him. Well, now we've undone that. So the reason for killing him doesn't exist anymore. There's no need to kill him, Jet. He's going to jail."

"It isn't enough," Jet said, then repeated, "it isn't enough."

"Goddamnit, Jet." Gregory sent the volume on his voice-emitter way up. "You don't have to kill him!"

Jet stood again and confronted Gregory square on. "Who helped you with this?" he asked.

"No one," Gregory said.

"I know you didn't do it alone," Jet demanded. "You just used the word 'we' several times. Who helped you? Was it Ginny?"

"It wasn't Ginny," Gregory said. "And I won't tell you who. It's none of your business. It has nothing to do with what we're talking about."

"We're talking about you not minding your own business," Jet said dangerously. "We're talking about you sticking your nose where it isn't needed, where it isn't welcome. We're talking about you doing things behind my back that could get you, me, or someone else killed. You're going to tell me who helped you, or I'm going to knock you out of that goddamned chair."

"Try it," Gregory said boldly.

Jet took a step toward him.

"I did," Patricia said, stepping out of the shadows

of the door across the room. "I helped him."

Jet spun on her.

"Jet," Gregory called, the fear in his artificial voice palpable, fear that his brother might unleash his mounting rage on Patricia. To her, Gregory said, "You should have listened to me and stayed at home."

"How did you get in here?" Jet demanded.

Patricia raised a bundle of keys on a ring, holding one between her thumb and forefinger.

"Where did you get that?"

"Had it made," she said, putting her key away and striding forward. "And if you lay a hand on Gregory you're going to have to go through me first."

She brushed past Jet and perched one hip on the arm of Gregory's wheelchair, putting her own arm across the back of it protectively.

"What are you doing here?" Jet demanded, angrily watching her.

"I'm visiting my good friend, Gregory," she said. "My best friend, these days."

Gregory said, "I told you to stay home. I can handle this."

"And let you take the credit for all of our brilliant detective work," she said, looking at the papers on the floor and frowning. "That someone just threw all over the floor. Not on your life."

"What business do you have with a key to my house," Jet demanded. "What are you doing here?"

"Margie trained me on how to take care of Gregory's basic needs," she said, "how to read the monitors, how to prepare his meals, etc. Anything goes wrong that I can't handle I have her emergency number, and failing that there's always 911..."

"I told you to stay the fuck away," he said. "I told you if you ever showed your face again I'd kill you."

"You said I'd be sorry." She smiled sweetly. She'd be damned if she was going to show him the fear he coursed in her chest. "But I knew what you meant. And to quote one of the greatest men I know, 'Try it.'"

"Patricia, don't," Gregory said.

She had no idea how close those dead blue eyes staring out from under the shadows beneath Jet's beaten leather hat were to erupting, but she could guess it was close indeed. She wasn't leaving Gregory alone with Jet in this state.

Gregory said, "Jet, I contacted her. It isn't her fault. I enlisted her help. And she performed brilliantly. Even you would have been impressed."

If anything Patricia made her sarcastic sweet smile broader and she stuck out her chest in pride. "I have a question of my own," she said. "If you were hired to kill Gannery, why not just do it? Why have Gregory hack into his computer files like that?"

Jet's eyes shifted, as if momentarily confused, then came back strong as ever. "I needed to know all about him. I needed to be sure that he deserved...that he was..."

"You wanted to make sure," Gregory interrupted, "that he deserved to die."

"Still," Patricia pressed, "after you found out, why not kill him? I know Ginny was Gannery's girlfriend, she told us that much, and about some banquet you took her to when she was supposed to be Gannery's date. What does she have to do with all this? What are you playing at?"

Jet straightened and walked away, then turned

around again to face them. "It seems you two have been busy behind my back, without my permission. Well amateur hour stops now. Do you hear me?"

"He was harrying him," Gregory said.

"What?" Patricia asked.

"He was toying with him," Gregory explained. "Whether he thought Gannery deserved to die or not, he still couldn't do it in cold blood. He was harrying Gannery, trying to get him to make the first move." He moved his chair forward, forcing Patricia to stand, and confronted his brother. "Then you could justify killing him by calling it self-defense. That's right, isn't it, Jet?"

Jet growled under his breath. "Gregory, if I have to I'll put you in a home, no matter what I promised before. I'll take away your computers. Do you get me?"

"No," Patricia said before Gregory could get his own protest out. She stood and advanced on Jet before she knew what she was doing. She suspected it was a bad move, but he needed to know she wasn't going to back down. Not from anyone, not any more. "No," she went on, "I don't get you. What the hell is your problem? Are your feelings hurt? Are you jealous because we were able to do what you couldn't? Or are you such a small man that you can't say, 'Hey, Greg, Patricia, gee, thanks for all your help. Thanks for saving me the trouble of having to kill that son of a bitch, Dr. Gannery. Thanks for saving me a trip to death row.'"

By the end she was leaning toward him and screeching. Jet had rocked back on his heels slightly during her tirade. But he still regarded her with that deadly dangerous storm over his brow.

"Jet," Gregory said, and Patricia stepped aside so the brothers could address each other again. "Even you have no right to tell me who my friends can be. Even you can't keep me locked in a tower where no one can get to me so I won't ever be hurt again for the rest of my life. I know you blame yourself for what happened to me."

Patricia had never heard the story of what happened to Gregory to paralyze him. When she looked at him now he answered the question he must've seen in her eyes. "It happened while Jet was in that prison in China. What could he have done to stop that bum from trying to cross the tracks with two shopping carts full of aluminum cans, or to keep the subway train from jumping the tracks when everything got tangled underneath? Even if he'd been here, what could he have done?"

Patricia turned to Jet, who continued to glare at the two of them as if he could burn them to cinders with his eyes.

"It wasn't bad enough that I was the sole survivor," Gregory went on as if talking to them both now, "that there is no logic, no rhyme or reason behind why I lived when so many others died senselessly. No, I had to come out of it utterly and completely helpless, forced to rely on others for food, mobility, to wipe goddamn shit from my ass for me."

Gregory rolled his chair past Patricia again and put himself directly in front of Jet. "It's a good thing you weren't here, because you would've coddled me, just like you're trying to do now. You wouldn't have given me the chance to rise above it all. To build what small miracles of independence I've managed to acquire. To find the many small ways in which I could regain my dignity.

"Jet, you have to let me live my life, Bro. Otherwise, neither of us is going to be happy." Then Gregory rolled his chair over to the side of the bed.

"Patricia?"

She came over and undid his restraints, cradling him in her arms like a child, lying his wonderfully warm head snugly against her throat. She placed him in his bed and turned to adjusting his equipment around him the way he'd shown her that he liked. While she did this she saw Gregory turn his eyes to Jet, as if daring him to watch her care for him.

When she was done she waited by the side of the bed. Jet watched them for a moment, his expression unreadable. Then he went over and knelt by the coffee table. Quietly, he gathered the papers together again and placed them back on the table. Gregory watched as Jet paused to study some pages. He took one, folded it, and placed it in his hip pocket. Then he stood up and turned to them with worry on his face.

"What time is it?"

"It's seven, seven-thirty," Patricia said. "Why?"

Jet turned and strode out of the room, saying over his shoulder as he went, "Ginny shouldn't be out this late. Not alone."

CHAPTER 24

The evening gown, Ginny kept. You didn't get much for second-hand clothes anymore, even a designer gown like this one, and it was such a nice dress anyway she hated to part with it. The tiara, on the other hand, she was able to hawk at a jewelry pawn for almost two thousand dollars. And that was worth a trip to Bergdorf-Goodman on 5th Avenue.

It was her favorite place to shop. Even when she didn't have any money she came here to daydream. It was easy when Gannery had her set up at The Plaza, just a block away. The ache in her heart at all the beautiful things offered for sale here got to be so poignant, however, that she had begun to limit herself to one day a week there. Thursdays. For her own sanity. Just until she made it big, she promised herself, only until then, and then she would shop here every single day.

She sat now in the shoe department with skyscrapers of stacked boxes forming a miniature city skyline around her. On her feet was a pair of little midnight blue pumps with transparent acrylic heels, so beautiful she wanted to cry. They would have gone so enchantingly with that velvet blue strapless dress she'd bought in the dress department only an hour before.

She regarded them, shapely legs extended out in front of her, and sighed while the salesman stood to the side, shifting his feet impatiently.

"Ginny? Is that you?"

Ginny's joy shriveled, her heart quailed as she looked in the direction of that too-familiar voice. Gerald Gannery stood in the aisle nearby. Behind him were two men she didn't recognize but could have been two of those from the night of the banquet.

"Gerald," she said, trying to sound cold. "What are you doing here?"

He held up a small bag with little rope handles on it. "Shopping for perfume. A gift. For you. A little apology for our tiff."

The nearby shoe salesman made a rude sound of impatience and marched off.

Intrigued in spite of herself, Ginny licked her lips as she looked at the bag. "It was more than a tiff," she said. "You pulled my hair."

His smile faltered, but came gamely back. "You burnt my neck with a cigarette," he said, craning his neck so that she could see the bandaid sticking up from underneath his collar. "But I deserved it," he said, pouting a little. "I was being just a real shit."

"Yes," Ginny said, "you were."

"But I want to make it up to you," he said. "Come with me to dinner now, so I can give this to you and apologize properly. No hard feelings. Okay?"

She craned around to see if there were any more of his thugs lurking around among the racks of shoes. "I don't think so,."

He sighed. "No more than I deserve, I guess. Still, I'd like to give you this. Will you come out of there so I can do that, at least?"

"I don't know," she said from behind her walls of shoeboxes, like a princess in a castle. She wished Patricia was here, but Patricia had declined to join her. Or better yet, Jet.

"C'mon," he said coaxingly. "What am I going to do to you, here, in public?"

Glancing around one more time, she stood and began to work her way out of the maze she'd assembled around herself.

"That's it," Gannery said encouragingly. "No one's going to hurt you."

One of the guys behind him was sneering, and that almost made her turn back. In the end, she thought, as he had said, that it would be impossible for him to hurt her or to take her away, here, in public, without someone interfering. And Gannery had earned a reputation for buying the most delicious presents for her. His taste was impeccable.

Finally free from the ramparts of shoeboxes, she stopped two paces away and looked at the bag he held out to her. She leaned way out and snatched it from him, and he laughed pleasantly like an indulgent uncle. Looking in the bag, she squealed in spite of herself.

"Desperation," she said. "Oh, it's my absolute

fave!" She dropped the bag and struggled to open the box.

"May I," Gannery asked, holding out a hand and taking a tentative step toward her.

Wary, still she nodded and took a step toward him, handing him the box. He extracted the adorable little dispenser and handed it to her and she wasted no time applying it to her neck, her wrists, and rubbing the latter together vigorously. She inhaled deeply and moaned.

"May I," he said again, pointing to her wrist.

Without hesitation she held it out to him. He took it gently in his hand and lifted it to his nostrils, inhaling, his breath tickling the tiny blond hairs there.

"Mmm," he moaned. "That's just wonderful on you."

Gently he pulled on her wrist and she came forward, tilting her head permissively as he brought his face down to her neck and inhaled once more. His arm went around her waist and held her warmly.

Something horribly sharp burnt into her buttock underneath his hand.

She struggled and pulled away and glared at him. He smiled at her as he recapped a small hypodermic needle and slipped it into his breast pocket. His face slid down and onto the front of his shirt as she tried to back away from him, and arms serpentine and wavy like tentacles reached out to steady her as the floor pitched beneath her feet.

"You asshole," she said, or tried to say as her tongue fluttered beyond her control and spilled drool down her chin. The edges of her vision closed in slowly. She tried to scream, but her whole body was going numb and she was forgetting what it was that was so frightening after all.

*

"She's diabetic," Gannery explained urgently to a security guard who intercepted them. "We have to get her to an emergency room fast." He carried Ginny in his arms like an infant, her head lolling back limply as she gurgled.

"I'll call 911," the guard said.

"I can get her there just as fast in my car," Gannery said. "It's just outside. I'm her doctor."

"Well, I don't..." the guard hesitated.

"Do you want me to show you my board card while she drifts off into a coma?" Gannery snapped. "Or do you think it's a good idea we get her there as fast as possible? You can come if you want to."

"No," the guard said. "I can't leave my post. I believe you. Go on ahead."

"You're making the right decision, pal," Vinnie said, clapping the guy on the back as Gannery rushed past him toward the parking garage.

Outside in the garage, the limo rested at the curb and Palmer leapt to open the door for them just as Gannery heard the loud rattling roar of a powerful motorcycle. Looking up, he saw the fixer as the man power-skidded to a stop at the top of the ramp and looked down at them.

"Hurry," Gannery screamed as he ducked into the car with Ginny's tiny frame clutched to his chest. The others climbed in as the motorcycle's engine roared and Palmer pulled away just as the fixer pulled alongside them. At first it seemed as if the fixer's eyes met his, even though Gannery knew the windows were too darkly tinted for the other to see in, and then they left the fixer behind briefly as they sped down the other ramp.

But in a flash the man was alongside them again, on the outside of the turn, glaring in as if he could shoot bullets from his eyes. Too close, Gannery realized, for his own comfort. He'd learned to fear this man.

"Ram him against the side," Gannery roared.

To his credit, Palmer tried, but as he veered into the far wall, the front and back end of the limo made a sickening crunch and grinding noise against the sharp curve of the wall. The vehicle was too long and the fixer rode in safety in the bridge between the two ends. Gannery roared in frustration.

The fixer could have blown the window out at any time, but he never drew a gun. Come to think of it, Gannery didn't recall ever seeing a gun in the man's hand, nor on his person anywhere, even that night chasing through the dark streets after the banquet. Could it be the man did his work unarmed except for those ridiculously accurate blades of his?

Gannery felt his spine compacted as Palmer hit street-level at speed and bottomed out, then raced on through the thinning midtown traffic. The fixer fell back again only briefly, then pulled up alongside once more.

"Will you ram this guy once and for all?" Gannery demanded.

Palmer swerved again, squeezing the biker up against the row of parked cars. The fixer snaked expertly between the bumpers of two cars parked at the curb and up onto the sidewalk as Palmer shattered the side of the limo up against the flanks of the parked vehicles. Gannery cried out, as it was on his side, and cursed while they all jostled around violently.

"Here," Vinnie said in the seat facing backward.

Drawing his gun, he reached across and pulled Ginny from Gannery's lap to his own. He pressed the button at his elbow and the window by his head dropped precipitously on its motivator. Holding Ginny up to the window, he held the gun to her head and looked out.

The fixer, still racing down the sidewalk as if it were a runway glanced over, then immediately fell back. Vinnie made a sound of satisfaction, when suddenly the fixer was back beside them. His right arm arced across his chest, silver flew and Gannery cried out a warning.

A throwing star sprung from the back of Vinnie's gun-hand. The man cried out and blood spurted. He dropped the gun, which rebounded off the window's rim and fell to the pavement outside, to be left behind by the racing vehicles. As Vinnie quickly wrapped his tie around his hand to stem the spurting life fluids, Gannery reached across and retrieved Ginny while one of Vinnie's men leaned across his boss and rolled the window up.

"Kill the fucking bitch," Vinnie roared in rage.

"No," Gannery snapped. "She's our leverage."

"Fuck leverage," Vinnie bellowed. "He near cut off my hand."

Gannery glared back until Vinnie looked away once more. The star still stuck out from under the wet silk tie binding the wound around it. Vinnie touched it, testing, hissed and left it alone.

"Boss," Palmer called back in a warning tone.

Gannery looked out again and saw that the fixer was pulling out ahead of them. "What's he up to now," he asked Palmer, who didn't answer.

He watched as, up ahead, the fixer power-skidded again, hopped off the bike and climbed up onto the roof of one of the parked cars.

"Look out," Gannery yelled, he's going to..."

As they passed, the fixer leapt onto the roof of the speeding limo and Gannery heard him briefly scrambling for a handhold. "...jump," Gannery finished belatedly. "Well what are you waiting for?" he shouted at the men around him.

They drew their weapons and began firing into the ceiling as fast as they could pull their triggers. Gannery raised his hands to his ears and even though he was shouting at the top of his lungs for them to stop they couldn't hear him until they began to run out of bullets and had to pause to reload.

"I meant go out after him," he screamed at them.

They looked around at each other sheepishly, then the two nearest the opposite windows from Gannery and Vinnie rolled them down and prepared to climb out and onto the roof. A hand appeared, once, twice, quick as lightning, silver flashed and two more men went down, one with a knife in his chest and the other with one embedded in his face.

Before the next two could react, a pair of boots swung in and slammed into the side of one man's head. Then the fixer was inside and, in spite of the close quarters, was making quick work of the two uninjured thugs.

"Stop," Gannery screamed and Palmer fishtailed to a halt.

Gannery kicked open the door on his side, leaping out and dragging Ginny with him. He limped, hauling her under her arms like a sack of rubbish, amongst the parked cars and onto the sidewalk before the fixer appeared on his side of the car and started toward him.

"Stop," he yelled, holding Ginny up, the

hypodermic in her throat, thumb on the plunger. "Another dose of pentothal and she'll never wake up again, and I'm betting I can still push it even with one of those star things in my neck, before I die. What do you think?"

"Let her go," the fixer said coldly. "Her life makes the difference of how much you suffer when you die, fucker."

"Does it?" Gannery said. "You kill me, now or later, her life isn't worth shit. Do you hear me? Vinnie, in there, and his cronies have strict orders. Anything happens to me, and she becomes their number one target. She's the one they will hunt to the exclusion of all else until they get her. And they don't have to kill her with a bullet. They can poison her food in a restaurant, a scorpion in her bed, a passing car when she's jaywalking. It doesn't matter how many of them you kill, it will only give them more of a reason to track her ass down and do her in. Get me? It will be your fault, because you ignored me and killed me anyway."

Vinnie crawled out of the limo and fell to the blacktop, bleeding from his hand and one ear, moaning. Palmer stood on the far side of the limo watching, not moving.

The fixer stood fuming.

Finally he said, "Let her go, Gannery."

"Do we have a deal?"

He could almost hear the fixer's teeth grinding from here. Finally, the man said, "Yes."

"No more contract," Gannery said.

"No more contract," the fixer repeated.

"Man of your word?" Gannery asked.

"Unlike some," the fixer said.

"Don't get insulting," Gannery said sarcastically. "And don't sulk. I don't mind saying, you had us on the ropes. But it's like I always say, an honorable man is the weakest of them all. Shed your scruples, fixer, and maybe you'll win next time."

"Shut the hell up and let Ginny go," the fixer snapped.

Gannery hesitated, then lowered Ginny to the ground. He looked up, then quickly pulled the needle from the girl's neck. The fixer took a step toward him, reaching for something under his long coat.

"Ah-ah-ah," Gannery said, backing up against the wall in fear. "I have your word of honor."

The fixer drew out a throwing star and flipped it expertly back and forth between his fingers like a coin. "What good is a word of honor given to a man without honor?" he asked, giving Gannery a cold, crooked smile.

Gannery swallowed. "You throw that thing against your word, and you're no better than me. I would throw it, if I were you. You'd be just like me."

The fixer's smile snuffed out like the flame of a candle. The star vanished back under his coat again. Holding out his hands, palms forward, the fixer moved to one side, away from the limo. Gannery slunk away from the fixer and slipped between bumpers, then rushed to the limo. He bent over Vinnie and felt for the man's gun, then remembered it had fallen out of the car.

He glanced over and saw the fixer picking Ginny up in his arms and carefully laying her over his shoulder. Gannery dove into the car and whispered, "A gun! Someone give me a gun!"

One of the moaning, bleeding men pressed a gun into Gannery's hand. He turned and leapt out of the limo again and scanned the street, bringing the gun to bear. The fixer, and Ginny, were nowhere to be seen.

CHAPTER 25

"You should go home," Gregory said to her. "You look tired."

Patricia lay curled up at the foot of the reclined bed by Gregory's feet, one pillow from the couch under her head and another clutched between her knees. She was comfortable, and they could still look at each other while they talked.

"Don't want to," she said. "I like it here. And I want to wait till Jet comes back to see if Ginny's all right."

"I'm sure she is," Gregory said. "You spend more time between here and work than you do at home. What about Monster?"

"Oh Monster doesn't live here in town," she said. "He's back home with Mom and Dad, helping them run the Bed and Breakfast. I miss him, but he wouldn't be happy here in the city. He's got a doggy door there and he can..."

"Give me a pillow," Jet demanded as he rushed into the room, Ginny cradled in his arms.

Patricia leapt to the floor and rushed over to the couch where Jet was headed and propped the pillows she had taken from there against one of the arms. "What's wrong with her?" she asked as Jet laid the girl carefully on the couch, placing her head gingerly on the pillows. He was surprisingly gentle.

"Drugged," he said. "I think she'll be okay."

"You should take her to the hospital," Patricia said.

"She'll be fine," Jet said firmly, smoothing the girl's hair out of her eyes. "We'll let Margie have a look at her when she gets in, in the morning."

"What happened?" Gregory asked from across the room.

Jet walked over and, with one last look at Ginny, Patricia followed him.

"Was it Gannery?" Gregory asked.

Jet nodded. Even Patricia, who didn't know the man all that well, could tell he was struggling with something. "He got to her at Bergdorf's. He was carrying her out when I got there. God knows what he told them to get her out of there. He took her just to get at me. I chased them down and got her back."

"Thank God," Patricia said. "Are you all right?"

Jet nodded impatiently, as if that didn't matter, then looked long and hard at Gregory. Finally, he said, "The contract's off."

Gregory said nothing, but his eyes widened.

Jet nodded again. "But that doesn't mean we can't

bring him down. Go ahead and give Jurgens the papers. Wait a few days, let Gannery get comfortable again. Then take the papers to Jurgens and tell him to tell the cops he found them in a filing cabinet he and Dr. Gannery shared, so it will be perfectly logical and legal for him to have taken them. They'll take it from there."

Patricia put a hand on Jet's arm, but felt only hard, unyielding steel there. Still, she said, "It's better this way, Jet. You'll see."

He didn't look at her, but turned away. He seemed to hesitate, as if about to turn back and say something else, then he just walked silently out of the room, head down, shoulders sagging, as if defeated.

*

Patricia stayed the night, sleeping in Margie's easy chair, and was relieved to wake up around three, by the Snoopy clock on top of Margie's TV, to find Ginny standing in the middle of the room stretching and yawning expansively. They went to the kitchen and shared a pot of coffee while Ginny told her what happened, growing increasingly angry as her story went on. She was glad to hear that Jet had consented to turning the papers over to Paul Jurgens. When Margie got in she looked into Ginny's eyes and used a stethoscope to listen to her heart. The nurse gave Ginny some pills for the migraine that had developed at the back of her skull and sent her to bed.

The next two days were odd for Patricia. Gannery was subdued, when he was in the office, and yet more irritable than usual. But, as irritable as he seemed, he didn't lash out like he used to, instead he seemed as impatient with himself as anyone or anything else. Patricia was left to her own devices as often as not and spent a lot of time chatting with Gregory over the computer.

She was given occasion to wonder what would happen to her job when Gannery was arrested. Would she need to find another one, or would Paul Jurgens keep her on out of gratitude? She had never put so much effort into making her own job superfluous, but she felt the strongest of convictions that it was the right thing to do.

So days she spent in the office or running minor errands for Gannery or accompanying him to interviews and meetings, evenings she spent at Gregory and Jet's house, and nights back to her lonely apartment. Jet came and went, as usual, only now she didn't have to duck him. He kept to himself and barely spoke to anyone. Gregory said Jet was struggling with memories and to leave it at that, so she did.

But Ginny didn't.

Once, as Patricia was slipping out of Gregory's room after having talked him to sleep, as they often did, she ran into Ginny stalking up the hall toward her own room, a tremendous pout on her lips and a furrow in her brow, grumbling.

"What?" Patricia whispered.

Ginny glared at her and whispered back. "The least he could do is say no thanks. Girl comes to his bed, makes herself clear, y'now, gratitude and stuff, you know what I mean. He takes me by the arm, walks me out and shuts the door on me."

"I'm sorry," Patricia said sympathetically. "Didn't he say anything?"

"He said, 'That's not what you're here for.' What the hell does that mean?"

*

"Jacqueline," Salomé Johnson screamed at the top

of her lungs. "Get the goddamn door, will you?"

She lay in bed amid copious covers and a seemingly endless array of pillows that often made it hard to extricate oneself from the bedding, but given that she often slept past noon she liked it that way. Her head was splitting again, as it did every morning, and right now all she wanted to do was re-gather the shrouds of death-like slumber around her.

The knock came again, as insistent as before, followed by a heavy-handed ringing of the doorbell, and it was clear that Jacqueline, the housekeeper, was not about to obey her employer and answer the goddamn door. Cursing colorfully, Salomé fought the pillows and covers for air and to get to the edge of the bed, where she pulled herself upright and slipped her feet into her fuzzy slippers.

With a murderous cast to her bloodshot eyes, she snatched the security system remote control from her nightstand and stuffed it into the pocket of her nightgown, marched to the hallway and headed down the stairs. "Jacqueline," she screeched one last time before reaching the door and yanking it open so hard that the chain made a loud bang, like a gunshot. Wincing at the sound, Salomé peered out through her soiled bangs at the rough-looking man outside her door.

"What the fuck do you want?"

"Salomé Johnson?"

"Yeah. What the fuck do you want?"

"I'd like to talk to you for a minute," he said. He smelled acridly of traffic and leather, and the smell made her nauseous. Pushing the door enough to undo the chain, she flung the door open and turned away to stumble toward the kitchen.

"Jacqueline," she screamed again as she went, then held her throat and coughed. In the kitchen she found some Alka Seltzer in the cabinet where it belonged. She went to the refrigerator and fetched a bottle of water. She tried to put one of the tablets into the bottle, but the neck was too narrow. "Shit!" She turned and fetched a tumbler, which she filled and added the tablets.

"Jacqueline," she cried miserably. "Where the fuck are you!"

"It looks like she's given her notice," a male voice said.

The stranger from the door had followed her into the kitchen and was leaning against her dishwasher. In his hand he held an envelope and a folded stationary card. He held it out to her.

"I found it right here…" pointing to the counter "…with a key that I presume goes to the front door."

Salomé snatched the letter from him, but she couldn't seem to bring the thin, elegant writing into focus.

"It says she has found another position and can't work for you anymore," he offered. "Then it gives an address to forward her final check."

"Shit," she said without verve and took too big a gulp from the tumbler. She choked on the fizzing liquid, stumbled into him and dropped the tumbler to shatter on the kitchen tiles. "Shit," she said again.

"Don't move," he said, holding her shoulders. "Where's your broom?"

"The fuck should I know," she mumbled at him.

He let her shoulders go and she teetered, but stood. He returned with a broom and a dustpan and cleaned up around her feet. Disposing of the glass shards and returning the broom to wherever he'd gotten it, led her by the shoulder to the dining room and sat her in a chair.

She held her throbbing head in her hands and tried not to puke. She heard hissing, smelled coffee, then he took her wrist and forced a cup into her hand. "Mmm...sugar..." she mumbled.

"Black," he said firmly, sitting around the corner of the table from her.

"Cream," she whined.

"Black," he said, pushing up on the bottom of the cup until she was forced to put it to her lips and drink. There was something in the coffee...vodka. Greedily she took another gulp that nearly scorched her tongue.

"Hair of the dog," he said. "I found a fifth in the cupboard, almost gone. Took a chance."

"Good guess," she said, drinking and feeling a little better. "Who are you again?"

"Someone who needs a favor," he said. "Drink. Plenty of time to talk."

She finished two laced cups and started on a third, unlaced and this time with her precious cream and sugar, before she began to feel human again. He was polite and solicitous. He would make a great replacement for Jacqueline, but he'd have to take a bath and get rid of that ratty old leather hat. Finally, he got down to business.

"You used to work for Dr. Gerald Gannery," he said. It wasn't a question. "You should know that he's going to jail soon. So the well is drying up."

Salomé squinted at him. "I don't know what you're talking about."

"Fifty thousand a month," he said. "On the first of each month. Like clockwork. For over twenty-five years."

"You must have me confused with..."

"You already answered to the name, Salomé," he said dryly. "Can't be two Salomé Johnsons in the five boroughs, much less the state of New York."

She sighed. "What'd he do?"

"Everything," the stranger said. "His private records have been found and will be handed over to the authorities soon, if they haven't been already. Everything over the last two and a half decades. Everything."

Salomé closed her eyes and sighed again.

"You'll be called to testify, of course," he said. "And I'm guessing Gannery is going to offer you a lot of money not to testify."

She opened her eyes again and licked her lips. "You think so?"

The stranger frowned at her. "You've been living off his dole your entire life. Living pretty well. What I want you to do is to turn down his offer, whatever it is. I want you to testify, no matter what the offer is."

She made a rude noise.

He wiped her spittle off his face and glared at her. "If for nothing than your own pride," he said.

"Pride," she mimicked him. "Pride? What pride? Look at me. You see any pride?"

"I see a drunk," he said. He pulled her arm out. "And a junkie," he added and nodded at the crook of her elbow where old red scars and fresh black needle-pricks dotted the flesh.

She yanked her arm away from him and pulled her loose sleeve back down over it defensively. "Fuck you."

"No thanks," he said. "You are going to testify."

"Fuck you," she said again, vehemently.

"You know why?"

"Fuck you," she screamed at him.

"Because your supply is going to dry up," he said coldly.

"F-fu-hu..." her expletive ran out of steam as what he said sunk in.

"No matter how much he gives you," he drove on relentlessly, "it'll be the last. He'll be in jail and you'll run out of money, eventually. What then?"

"Fuck you," she said again, but it lacked conviction.

"You're going to testify," he said. "Because I want you to. And in exchange for testifying, for telling the truth about what you know, I'm going to get you into a rehab. Free of charge."

"Rehab," she said, incredulously. "What the fu...rehab? Fuck that. I don't need rehab. I'll quit. I just won't use any more."

He looked at her doubtfully.

"I can do it," she screamed at him. "I can quit any time I want. You and my dad. Neither one of you has any clue whatsoever what I'm capable of. I'm not some weak piece of shit. I can quit any time I want. And I will."

"Stronger people than you have tried and failed," the stranger said.

"Get out," she screamed. She stood up and kicked his shin so hard he jumped back out of his chair and raised a fist as if to backhand her. "Get out," she screamed again, "or I hit the panic button." She pulled a security remote out of her pocket and pointed with it to the security control pad on the wall by the door.

The stranger looked at his own fist, lowered it and turned to leave. She followed on his heels and when he turned at the door to say something else she slammed it in his face.

Where the fuck did he get off, calling her a junk and a drunkie, or whatever, the point was he didn't know her. No one knew her. Not even Jacqueline, who left only a note behind and abandoned Salomé. No one knew what she could do and what she couldn't do. She could quit any time she wanted.

She turned and padded back up the stairs to her bedroom. From the vanity she pulled out her kit and opened it. Inside were a surgical stainless steel reusable hypo, a rubber tourniquet, a tarnished spoon, lighter and four caramel-colored crystals of meth. She could quit any time.

She went to her bed and climbed in, holding the kit steady, then placed it in front of her. In order, she applied the tourniquet to her left arm, placed a crystal in the spoon and turned to heating it with the lighter.

Quit any time she wants. She'd show them. She'll quit. Just as soon as she used up these last four crystals.

CHAPTER 26

"What are you thinking?" Gregory asked.

Patricia smiled at him. "I don't know."

"You have to be thinking something."

Patricia, once more perched on the foot of Gregory's hospital-style bed, pulled her knees up and clasped her hands around them. "Okay. I suppose I was wondering if you remember anything about the accident."

"No," he said. "I actually don't remember anything clearly for about a week afterwards. They kept me pretty doped, and when they didn't it was so they could do tests and stuff, and those times I was in so much pain that it's all a blur."

She winced. "Sorry. Didn't mean to bring it up."

"The pain was actually a blessing, really," he said.

"How so?"

217

"Because I was so focused on it that they had to tell me several times that I was paralyzed. It sunk in so slowly that by the time the pain was receding I was already pretty much used to the idea. No real trauma or shock. Just relief that the pain was going away."

"How does that work?"

"What?"

She pointed to the array of tubes in front of his face. "That."

"Come here," he said. "I'll show you. You can see the screen better from here."

Turning around, Patricia lay down next to Gregory and put her head on the pillow next to his. From here she could hear the soft blowing and sucking sound he made as he operated the tubes, and see one of the screens in from of him flicker. It showed what he was saying as he said it.

"See," he said, or the computer said for him, "you select from a set of predetermined sentence templates, then you select nouns, verbs, adjectives, and voila."

"Seems complicated," she said. "Can't you just do it word by word?"

"Yes. But it really is faster this way."

"Wow." She shook her head.

"Want to try it?" he asked.

"Really?"

"Sure."

"Well, okay."

"Take the yoke."

"The what?" she asked.

"The thing that holds the tubes," he said.

The apparatus he was referring to was a simple affair, really, that strapped around the back of his neck and rested on his chest with a rigid bar in front into which each individual tube snapped. She was able to remove it from his neck and wrap it around her own.

She placed her lips on the tube she had observed him use for speaking and felt the slightest of suction there. The better to keep the tube free of saliva, she presumed. The screen that controlled his speech presented a series of options to choose from.

Simple statement, fact.
Simple statement, fact, imperative.
Simple statement, fact, authoritative.
And so on.

She blew into the tube and the highlight bar that colored the current option bright yellow cascaded down the list so precipitously that she stopped and cried out. She heard a wheezing noise and looked at Gregory in concern.

He was laughing at her.

"Shut up," she said, laughing with him. "It's more sensitive than I thought."

He struggled to nod with only partially functioning neck muscles and continued to laugh.

She put the thing in her mouth again and sucked in. The currently selected option disappeared and she was prompted for a noun, given a list to choose from. With no idea what sentence template she'd selected, she blew again. Once more the highlight shot down the list so fast that she sucked in just to stop it. She was prompted for another noun. She blew very softly and though the highlight bar descended more slowly it was still faster than she could see and she sucked in again at random.

Gregory's voice came out of the computer. "My henhouse is perplexed."

She heard the wheezing of his laughter again and she joined him, re-fastening the yoke around his neck. "That's harder than it looks."

When able to reach the tube again, he said though his computer, "That was too funny."

"It's so hard," she said again. "And you do it so fast and so seamlessly. How do you do it?"

"Ten years of practice. Plus, since I rewrote the program, it has an element of artificial intelligence, so it remembers the most common sentences you use and puts them at the top of the list. It builds a vocabulary for you based on the words you use most often."

"You rewrote the program?"

"Sure."

"You should sell it," she said admiringly.

"I have."

"What else can you do with this stuff?" She gestured with her finger, an arc that encompassed all of the equipment surrounding them.

"I do electronic schemas and computer programming. I have forty-two patents and about a hundred programs out there being used by the disabled community."

"No shit." Patricia smiled at him.

"No shit," he said, turning his eyes to her.

"I'm impressed"

"Good."

They looked into each other's eyes for a moment.

He stopped smiling.

She stopped smiling.

"Patricia..." he said, but she slipped a hand up and pinched off the tube he spoke with.

"Shh."

She leaned up and kissed him.

He sighed and looked at her.

"Could you feel that?" she asked.

His eyes told her, "Yes."

"Can I do it again?"

His eyes said, "Please."

She kissed him again.

And again.

*

"Why?" he asked her when she had settled back on the pillow again.

"Don't ask why," Patricia sighed. "Never ask why."

They lay in silence for a while.

"Patricia," Gregory said, "I can't do certain things."

"Oh God." She laughed and put her hands up to her face in embarrassment.

"I'm sorry," he said. "It's just that you should know this can't go anywhere."

She hoisted herself up on an elbow and looked straight down into his eyes. "For such a smart guy you sure are stupid." And she kissed him again. "I love you, Gregory....Gregory...um... what the hell is your last name, anyway?"

"Gatling," he said.

"What's your middle name?" she asked.

"John. Did you just say you love me?"

"Hush," she said, and kissed him again.

"How can you love a quadriplegic?" he demanded.

"Whoah," she said, looking at him, feigning a cross frown. "Don't tell me you're prejudiced."

221

"Answer the question," he said.

"I can love a quadriplegic," she said in the same tone one used when reciting an answer for a teacher or parent, "because I met one who's funny, and smart, and sensitive, and kind, and ethical, with more character than any man I've met in a long, long time. Now are you going to shut up?"

"But..."

"Look," Patricia said, sitting back on her haunches on the bed, fists on hips, and staring at him firmly. "It may be a cliché but I mean it when I say I like who I am when I'm around you. I don't care that you can't have sex. I don't care if you can't feel it when I hold your hand, like this. You've gotten in here, Gregory John Gatling." She was pointing to her head, then she pointed to her heart. "And here. I can't help it. You're the one, man. Get used to it."

They looked at each other long and hard.

Finally, he said, "Kiss me."

And she did.

CHAPTER 27

Harold Bloom sat hunched at his desk, his elbows on the edge, his hands folded and his chin on his knuckles. From this level, the tall chrome trophy for Manhattan Regional ProAm Darts Champion, Singles, Adult Division looked like a statue on a pedestal outside any major museum or art gallery. The pedestal was a royal blue holographic diamond design and on it stood the graceful, gleaming shape of a man stretched up and out in the very last arc of throwing the miniature dart in his hand. To either side of the pedestal were little upright silver laurel wreaths with small shields inside their horseshoe-like shape.

It was the most beautiful thing Harold Bloom had ever seen.

"Mr. Bloom?" Dora's voice came over the intercom.

Bloom sighed wistfully, then sat up. "Yes, Dora."

"A Mr. Steven Lancaster to see you."

"Well, does he have an appointment?"

"No sir, but..."

"Then tell him to make one," Bloom said irritably. "Jesus, Dora."

"Sir, it's about the Gannery project," Dora said in a tone that told him not to take that tone with her.

"What about it?"

"Ask me in and I'll tell you," a distant male voice came over the thin intercom.

Bloom picked up the trophy and looked around him for a place to put it. "Fine, send him in, Dora."

As Bloom walked over to his filing cabinet and placed the trophy on top of it along with some other plaques and a plant, the door to his office opened. "Take a seat, Mr. Lancaster."

When he turned the man was standing a pace behind him admiring the trophy. The guy was taller than Bloom, which wasn't unusual, most men could beat Bloom's five feet and six inches by half a foot or more. This guy was a good foot taller. He wore a shapeless Fedora and one of those ankle-length coats, jeans and cowboy boots, a rodeo buckle on his belt and a face like James Arness from Gunsmoke. Bloom summarily concluded the visitor was in the entertainment industry, the guy was just too kooky not to be.

"What can I do for you, Mr. Lancaster?" Even the name was probably borrowed from the famous movie star.

"Steven," Lancaster, said. "Darts. Champion no less. Impressive. I used to be pretty decent myself."

"Really?" Bloom said, intrigued.

"Years ago," Lancaster said. "Not sure how I'd do now."

Bloom was no dummy. He knew when he was being hustled into a challenge. But that was okay. He enjoyed challenges, hustle or no. "Care for a game?" he said, pointing to the darts cabinet on the far wall.

"Oh, I don't know," Lancaster said. "Couldn't hurt, I guess."

You sly devil you.

Bloom went over, opened the cabinet and took down six of the twelve darts racked therein, his favorite set and three others which he handed to Lancaster. The key was, hustle or no, to never underestimate your opponent.

"You first," Bloom said. "Visiting team, and all."

"Five-oh-one?" Lancaster asked. "Tourney rules?"

"Why not?" Bloom said gamely. "If you think you can keep up."

Lancaster gave a slight bow, toed the duct tape on the carpet and took his stance.

"So what's this about some Gannery project?" Bloom asked casually. "Can't say that I recognize the name."

"No?" Lancaster said. He threw. A triple nineteen on his first throw. Not bad. "You don't recognize the name 'Steven'?" Another triple nineteen on his second throw. This guy was good. "Steven the intern?"

Bloom started, then recovered and watched Lancaster's third throw, a triple nineteen. One hundred seventy-one on his first turn. Not bad at all, in fact damned good. "You don't work for Rontell. I checked. So tell me another one."

Lancaster retrieved his darts. "Like I said, name's

Steven Lancaster. And no, I don't work for Rontell. But he owes me and I intend to collect. By stealing away this show."

Bloom raised his eyebrows, then took his position and threw his first dart. A thirteen. Not only was it an unquestionably sucky first throw, but the metaphysically unlucky number was not an auspicious start to the match.

"Steal it how?" he asked.

Second dart, a triple twenty, by God, now that was more like it.

"By offering you and Gannery more money," Lancaster said.

Bloom's third dart was a triple twelve. Opening with a hundred and nine was why he took home that trophy and a check for five thousand dollars while others went home with only stories. He'd consider going pro if it paid better. But Lancaster had a stronger lead.

"How much," Bloom asked.

"I'll double what Rontell offers, whatever he offers."

"Bullshit," Bloom said, rounding on Lancaster after plucking his last dart out of the board. "You'd have to have a studio lined up and ready to go at that price."

Lancaster raised an eyebrow at him.

"Really?"

Lancaster nodded, then threw the first dart of his second turn. A triple twenty. "How does Fox grab you?" His second dart yielded another triple twenty. "Call them and verify if you don't believe me." His third dart scored yet another triple twenty, the three darts clustered together in the tiny slot. One eighty for the turn, three hundred fifty-one match so far. Controlling what showed on his face during negotiations was Bloom's strong suit, but the deal Lancaster was offering combined with his unbelievable dart-playing was proving to be Bloom's greatest challenge ever.

Lancaster took out a cell phone, flipped it open and dialed. He then set it on the corner of Bloom's desk. A ring tone emitted from the phone's speaker.

Bloom took the board with a treble seventeen, a double ten, and a direct bull for fifty points. One hundred twenty-one, for a total of two hundred thirty match so far. A very respectable score after six darts, yet not even close to Lancaster's.

"Norsted," came a blustery voice from the cell phone on the desk. "Talk fast."

"Mr. Norsted? Steven. Here's Mr. Bloom."

"Bloom! I was expecting your call. How's it going, Steven?"

"Don't know yet, sir," Lancaster called out. "But I think he's intrigued by the idea." Lancaster looked at Bloom with a question in his eyes.

Bloom gave a non-committal shrug. "You serious, Norsted?" he called out to the speaker phone.

"Serious as my triple bypass," the voice on the line said. "Let Steven tell you all about it. I gotta get back to this golf game, finish kicking Woods' ass."

"Is that Tiger Woods?" Bloom asked.

"Who do you think it is?" Norsted said. "Natalie Wood? Now that'd be an easy match, her bein' six feet under and all." Norsted laughed boisterously. "Later, Bloom!"

Bloom hung up the speaker phone.

"Well?" Lancaster said.

"I'll need to talk to Gannery," Bloom said.

"How soon can that happen?"

"Don't know. Depends. He's been a bit jittery lately. But this will be good news. I'll call you and let you know, okay?"

"Well don't be too long about it," Lancaster said, taking careful aim and throwing two darts of his next turn. "We want to get this one on by next fall. That's a lot of work to do between now and then." He threw his third dart while looking over at Bloom. "The sooner we get started the better. And that's three hundred one."

Bloom looked, added up the score, including the required final double. Lancaster had thrown a treble twenty, a direct bull and a double twenty. He'd won handily. Even with three perfect treble twenties Bloom couldn't tie him. He looked at Lancaster with slack jaw as the tall, lanky stranger snapped the phone closed and smiled darkly back at him.

*

"Really?" Ginny whispered to Margie, shocked. "How does that work? I mean..."

"Hush, child," Margie scolded in the same subdued tone. "It ain't our business. It's a beautiful thing, is all."

Margie sat in her easy chair, the small TV in front of her currently on commercial break between gavel-falls on the faux court program. Ginny sat on the arm of Margie's chair with a bag of roasted pumpkin seeds in her hand, munching them whole and not bothering to spit out the shells. She watched across the room as Patricia sat cross-legged next to Gregory on his bed spoon-feeding him that muck he ate. It didn't smell bad, and probably tasted fine, but it looked evil.

"I don't get it," she said, shaking her head. "I mean he can't...y'know...can he? I mean, a girl has needs."

"Sometimes, all you need is love," Margie said.

"Well thank you, Paul McCartney." Ginny laughed quietly. "I don't know. I don't see it. I couldn't do it."

Margie patted the girl's knee in a distracted way. "To each her own, dear, to each her own. Now hush and go play. My stories are back on."

Jet walked into the room and headed for Gregory's bed. Ginny hopped down off the arm of Margie's chair and followed him more for something to do than anything else. She was beginning to get restless here, and Jet hadn't told her yet what more he wanted from her. She was glad to do it in exchange for a free place to live, but she wished he'd get to it.

Patricia was just wiping Gregory's chin when the two of them walked up. Ginny wondered if Jet knew about what was going on with these two and if he approved. It was like something out of the Twilight Zone to Ginny. Sure it was sweet, but it still came out of the realm of definite weirdness.

"Thanks, Mr. Norsted," Jet said to Gregory.

"Who's Mr. Norsted?" Ginny asked, confused.

"You're welcome son, you're welcome." A hearty, blustery voice came out of Gregory's speaker.

"Oh," Ginny said. "That's Mr. Norsted, whoever that is."

"How did you match his voice?" Jet asked.

"He was interviewed on Good Morning America," Gregory's regular voice came out this time. "I was able to synthesize his voice off the TV. Not perfect sound, but good enough for over the phone."

"My genius," Patricia said, taking one last swipe at Gregory's chin with her napkin.

Jet did a double take and Ginny wanted to pitch over with laughter, but she contained herself. She saw Patricia catch Jet's glare and flinch.

After a beat, Patricia said, "Ginny, why don't you come help me get the papers together."

Ginny wanted to stay and see the fireworks, but Patricia took her sleeve and led her firmly across the room to the couch where a bunch of papers were stacked on the coffee table. Patricia produced a stack of file folders and showed them to Ginny. "One stack per folder, got it?"

"I got it," Ginny said.

As the two women worked, stuffing each stack into its own folder and slipping it into a larger cardboard filing box, they each stole glances over to the two men speaking in subdued tones. Jet had his back to them, head down, so Ginny couldn't read his lips, and of course no one could read Gregory's. The whole thing was all just so infuriating.

After a time, Jet turned and looked long and hard at Patricia, who busied herself with the files and was clearly trying not to notice. Jet walked stiffly over and stood towering over them.

"I haven't seen him this happy in a long time," he said.

Patricia looked up and Ginny saw the moisture in her eyes.

"Even if it doesn't last, thanks for that, at least," he concluded.

Patricia stood and went over and hugged him. Jet stood awkwardly for a minute, then put one arm around her in return, more a mechanical gesture than a natural one. Ginny couldn't help but notice, his eyes were dry.

Dead and dry.

Finally he pulled away.

Patricia wiped her eyes, then knelt back down and returned to helping Ginny stuff folders. She paused and held up a stack of check stubs paper-clipped together. "So no luck with Salomé Johnson?" she asked, and Ginny could tell it was as much to change the subject and gloss over the awkwardness than anything else.

"No," Jet said. "She won't testify. She's a complete mess. I couldn't get through to her."

Patricia stuffed the stubs in a folder and dropped it in the box. "That's all right, there's enough here to put Gannery away for a very, very long time, even without her."

Jet excused himself and left.

Once Patricia and Ginny were done filling the box Patricia left it on the table and went to sit with Gregory some more. The two were inseparable these days. Boringly so.

Making sure no one was looking, Ginny surreptitiously slipped a hand into the Salomé Johnson file and pulled out a check carbon. On it was the name and address of the payee, the kind of check that went into an envelope with a little cellophane window for mailing. When deposited, the original, endorsed, was returned to the signee. She memorized the address and put the stub back in the file.

She walked casually around the table, brushing a hand over a plant, scuffing her shoes. Finally she called out to no one in particular, "I'm going for a walk."

"Stay close, dear," Margie said without taking her eyes off the TV screen. "You know how Jet worries."

Patricia waved goodbye.

Ginny walked out of the room and up to the front hallway. Taking her sweater off the coat rack there she stepped outside. Jet let Patricia and even crippled old Gregory help, but ever since Gannery had tried to snatch her Jet kept Ginny locked up like a princess in a tower.

Well, she had a stake in taking Gannery down, too, and she wanted to help. So if Jet wouldn't tell her how she could help, she'd have to find her own way.

Flagging down a taxi, she gave him Salomé Johnson's address and got in the back seat.

CHAPTER 28

After the face-off with the fixer, Gannery didn't feel as victorious as he expected to feel. In point of fact, it was a dirty, sordid little victory, if victory it really was. He used Ginny as a shield, and when the fixer drew that star, apparently ready to throw it in spite of his word, Gannery nearly pissed himself, because he had no basis on which to trust that the fixer was a man of his word. That the fixer was such a man made him the nobler combatant in the end, and Gannery the smaller man for hiding behind a girl only just out of her teens, an unconscious one at that.

So as the days progressed Gannery became more disgruntled, not less so. He had released Vinnie and his men from their duties as his bodyguards with thanks and a hefty paycheck, relatively sure he was safe now. But being safe at the cost of dignity galled him. Not a man accustomed to self-recriminations, the usually arrogant and self-assured Gannery became sullen and even depressed.

Now, three days after that encounter, Gannery sat in his office after everyone had gone, and stewed in the juices of his own self-loathing. He won the game, broke the King's Gambit. But he did it with an endgame that left the metaphorical judges in his imagination hissing and booing, a thing once called a *jade's trick* which was, strictly speaking, within the rules but considered an underhanded way to win. Such as declaring *check mate* without having first declared *check*. The entire purpose of declaring check in the game was to draw your opponent's attention to his danger, thus winning strictly by contest of skill alone and not by the mistake of an opponent.

Now Gannery hated what he was thinking. Because what he was thinking was that the only way to redeem his victory was to restart the game, to call the fixer out once more and achieve victory by honorable means, thus erasing his earlier disgrace. He hated that, because the game had grown tiresome, and it meant once more placing his HBO project in jeopardy.

But how could he live with himself unless he did it?

But to do so was to reactivate the danger that the fixer could use the papers he stole against Gannery. In that, the fixer currently had the upper hand. Should Gannery restart the game, he would first have to put them back on equal footing. And that meant somehow getting those stolen documents back.

Which he just plain couldn't see any way to do.

Would that he had hid them better.

Would that he had made copies of them.

As Salomé had.

Salomé Johnson had copies of those documents. Copies Gannery could use to alter their appearance, to make them contradict those that the fixer had, re-implicating Paul Jurgens. If well-forged, such duplicate documents would muddle any investigation and subsequent hearing and might well end in a mistrial. Failing that, they would certainly delay proceedings long enough for Gannery to get his affairs in order and flee the country.

Gannery rose from his chair, grabbed his jacket and headed for Salomé Johnson's apartment.

*

To Ginny's knock Salomé Johnson opened the door and said, "Come in," without even looking at Ginny. Ginny obeyed her and walked in. The woman wore jeans and a sweater, much like Ginny herself.

"Here's what I expect," Salomé, closing the door behind Ginny. "You *will* be on time. You *will* work from 6 AM to 6 PM, straight hourly wage, no time-and-a-half or bullshit like that. You *will* do windows, dishes, bathrooms and floors, as well as any other damn thing I ask you to do without back-talk. You don't like that, get the fuck out now."

"Excuse me," Ginny said, "but who do you think I am?"

"You're not the new maid?" Salomé looked Ginny up and down for the first time.

"I'm not the new maid," Ginny confirmed.

"The fuck are you, then?" Salomé sneered.

"Never mind my name," Ginny said. "I know you, Salomé Johnson. We have something in common that I think you might find interesting."

Salomé snorted. "Aside from bra size, what could we possibly have in common?"

Ginny bit her lip to keep from snorting herself. She was a good two bust sizes bigger, at least a cup size bigger and hers didn't sag like Salomé's did. Instead she said, "Can I come in and sit down."

"Suit yourself," Salomé said and nodded toward the living room to the right of the entry way.

Ginny went into the tastefully decorated room, clearly done by a decorator by the way everything matched, blended and contrasted so precisely. Only training rendered such starchy, museum-worthy results. She perched on the edge of the couch and waited until Salomé sat on a chair opposite her and lit a cigarette.

"I used to work for Dr. Gannery as well," Ginny said.

Salomé peered from squinted eyes through the plume of smoke rising out of her pursed lips. "That so?"

"Yes, it is."

"The fuck do I care?"

"Because he's paying me to keep quiet like he is you."

Salomé paused to snap the ash off her butt into an ashtray with a sculpture of a young boy in knickers playing a flute perched on it. Then she sat back again and said, "Don't know what you're talking about."

"Fifty thousand a month for more than twenty years," Ginny said, then clucked her tongue. "Very short-sighted of you, Salomé."

This seemed to catch the older woman's attention. "How so?"

"You didn't factor a cost of living increase into your agreement," Ginny said. "I did. I've only been taking money from him for five years, but with the annual increase built in I'm already making a hundred grand a month."

"Bull shit," Salomé spat, but no longer seeming so sure of herself.

"It goes up to fifteen grand per month the first of the year," Ginny shrugged, pretending to smooth out a crease in the front of her sweater.

Salomé was grimacing. "Mother fucker," she said, looking past Ginny's left ear, clearly speaking of Gannery. Then she asked, "So why're you telling me this? What do you care?"

"Because I got the same visit yesterday that you got this afternoon," Ginny said. "Tall drink of water with cowboy boots and a leather hat? I'm going to testify. I think you should to."

"Why?"

"Because he's ripping you off: Gannery."

"Why are you testifying?" Salomé asked.

"To save my own skin," Ginny said. "Comes out I've been blackmailing Gannery, I got my own world of shit to worry about. But I testify, and the prosecutor conveniently forgets to come after me."

"Y..." Salomé started to say when a loud knock came at the door.

"Shit," Salomé said. "Regular Grand Central here today. That'll be the maid. Wait here."

She went to answer the door.

"Dr. Gerald Gannery," Ginny heard Salome call out in mock surprise from the entry way, loud enough as warning to Ginny. "What are you doing here?"

Ginny froze like a rabbit in a spotlight. For a moment her fear wouldn't let her think, wouldn't let her move.

"We need to talk," the familiar voice came, and sounding none too happy. She heard heavy footsteps on the hardwood of the entryway, coming this way. She stood but still couldn't lift her feet from the floor, as if they were set in cement.

"Well let's talk in the kitchen," Salomé said quickly. "I need me some coffee."

The steps paused, then receded the other direction, as did the voices. Ginny breathed, but still heard the beat of her own heart in her ears. She had to get out of there. She moved as quietly as she could out into the foyer and toward the front door.

"All I want is copies."

"And I said no," Salomé's voice echoed from the kitchen opposite the living room. "I said no then and I say no now. We have our agreement. Let's leave it at that."

"Where are they, Salomé," Gannery asked, danger ringing off his voice like a death knell.

"Not here," Salomé said, her voice quavering. She clearly heard it too, that tone in Gannery's voice that preceded what he called the 'lessons'.

"Where?"

Ginny thought she should do something. She didn't have a cellular phone and she didn't see a landline when she was in the living room.

"I'm not fooling around here."

Who would she call even if there was a phone?

"Calm down, Gerald."

She didn't know how to get hold of Jet.

"Give me those goddamn documents."

911?

She heard Salomé cry out in pain, followed by the crash of something shattering on the tile. Ginny put a hand to her own mouth to stifle a scream. She turned around in place trembling in the entryway. She spotted the stairs. Surely a phone in a bedroom somewhere. Could she make it up there quietly, call someone in time?

A slap, one with a solid thump behind it, preceded another cry of pain from the woman in the kitchen and Ginny's eyes filled. She remembered having her hair pulled in the hotel room, the helplessness, the humiliation. Part of her wanted to rush in, find a knife and fight Gannery back, but she knew that only risked both she and Salomé.

"I don't have any," she heard Salomé scream.

"You don't..." Gannery's perplexed voice followed. "Any what?"

"Any copies," Salomé said. "It was a bluff. I only knew what I saw, suspected the rest and I...I lied."

"A bluff?" Gannery bellowed. "All these years, all that money, on a bluff?"

"Y-yes," Salomé cried. "L-let go. You're hurting me."

"Jesus Christ," Gannery growled. "A bluff. So I could have killed you years ago and no one would have found anything at all."

"N-no, Gerald," Salomé pleaded. "I'm sorry. I'll do anything. D-don't kill me."

Ginny was arrested by the drama she was overhearing in the kitchen and made no move toward the stairs.

"I'm not going to kill you," Gannery said with disgust. "You're a sorry bitch. You aren't worth the cost of the bullet."

239

A thud and a crash and Salomé cried out again. The footsteps began crossing the tile back toward the foyer. Again Ginny cast about for somewhere to run when the loudest explosion Ginny had ever heard shattered the air. There was another crash and this time it was Gannery who cried out.

"You...you bitch," he said.

"Fuck you, you son of a bitch," Salomé bellowed and another gunshot sounded out.

This was followed by much crashing about, things breaking and falling. Ginny's curiosity overcame her fear and she crept forward, peered around the archway, through the dining room. Beyond, in the kitchen, she could see Gannery and Salomé in a clinch, rolling to and fro on the floor. They were struggling for control of a gun. There was a lot of blood on both of them, but it was hard to tell whose.

The gun went off again and a chunk of wall three inches from Ginny's head exploded and she nearly cried out, ducking lower, almost all of the way to the floor. She watched the struggle with rapt fascination, as if she were watching a TV show or motion picture.

The gun went off again, this time muffled, and the two on the floor in the kitchen suddenly froze. They remained clenched, but didn't move for what seemed a very long time. Finally Ginny saw Salomé's arms go limp and fall to the floor. Her head lolled against Gannery's shoulder and a drool of blood poured from her mouth and down the back of his pinstriped shirt.

"Fuck," Gannery said. With a sudden surge of movement he leapt up and backed away. "Fuck fuck," he said again, his voice shaken.

He backed into a chair at the dining room table

and turned to notice his jacket draped over the back of it. Picking this up, he donned it mechanically, not taking his eyes off of Salomé's body.

"You stupid bitch," he whispered almost reverently.

He held one arm carefully out away from his body, as if injured, the hand of which was completely crimson and bleeding. At first Ginny thought he was going to run out of the apartment, in which case she was prepared to hide again. Instead he sat down in the chair and ran his clean hand, trembling, through his hair.

"Think," she heard him mumble. "My blood, everywhere. They'll know. Can't leave. Think."

Ginny watched the man consciously calm himself and strategize, murmuring to himself.

"She's a junkie, called me, as an old friend, shook me down. I said no, she shot me, we struggled. Her gun, that's true...yes, that should do it. No mention of anything else, no reason to."

He stood, stumbled over to a phone on the wall, dialed three numbers and waited.

"Yes," he said. "I want to report an accidental shooting. Yes." He gave the address, then just before he hung up he said, "I did. It was self-defense. Yes, she's dead. Yes, I'm sure."

Ginny backed away at a crawl. Shaken herself, she stood and slipped out of the apartment, unheard and unnoticed.

*

Ginny mentioned nothing about the shooting to anyone when she got back to the house. She murmured some innocuous response to Margie's query about her walk, went straight to the guest room and went to bed.

241

She determined not to ever tell anyone about her botched attempt to manipulate Salomé into testifying, as a way to help Jet bring Gannery down.

She didn't sleep well, so when Patricia came to her room – "Are you okay, Ginny? You seem upset." – Ginny wept uncontrollably and the entire story came out in a series of coughing, jerking spasms and drool on the back of Patricia's shoulder as the two women held each other.

CHAPTER 29

Although she looked worried and tired, the woman who answered to Patricia's knock was the same one she'd seen on several occasions before, but only formally introduced to once. Her concern about whether or not the woman would recognize her was answered as the woman's face first widened in surprise and then narrowed into dark resentment and suspicion.

"What do you want?"

"Good morning, Mrs. Jurgens, I'm Patricia Duf..."

"I know who you are," Gloria Jurgens said. "You're Gannery's flunky. I said, what do you want?"

"May I came in?" Patricia asked, using her knee to help her get a better grip on the box she carried. It didn't seem heavy at first, until she carried it across a once

243

manicured lawn now gone almost wild and stood on someone's stoop holding it. "This is heavy, and I need to speak to Dr. Jurgens. Is he here?"

Gloria looked Patricia from head to toe, then backed away from the door without a word of welcome. The house smelled stuffy and close, as if a window hadn't been opened in days, and there were clothes and children's toys in the hall and on the stairs. Gloria was dressed in jeans and a sweatshirt, with her hair up in a clip and no makeup. Patricia knew Gloria did pro-bono legal work for a charitable organization, though she couldn't remember which offhand, but the woman looked as if she hadn't reported to work in quite some time.

Patricia cast about her, then walked awkwardly into a parlor to the left. She slipped the box onto a coffee table, trying not to knock off any of the dirty dishes there but did pitch over a family portrait. As she righted it she saw a beautiful family smiling, one boy, two younger twin girls. Another picture nearby of just the boy had a shattered glass.

Patricia looked at Gloria and smiled in embarrassment. The woman narrowed her eyes at Patricia, then, "I'll wake Paul. But if he doesn't want to see you – he hasn't been taking company these days – you'll have to leave."

"Tell him it's me," Patricia said. "I'm sure he'll come." She hoped she was right.

Gloria eyed her again. "Have a seat," she said, then turned to go up the stairs, picking things up as she went. Patricia looked around, then decided to greet Dr. Jurgens standing.

She heard murmuring upstairs, what started subdued and grew into a bit of a tiff, though she couldn't make out what was being said. Then the stairs creaked and she saw a pair of hairy legs in slippers descend, followed by Dr. Paul Jurgens in a robe, unshaven and looking haggard.

"Patricia," he said groggily. Passing his left hand through unruly, thinning hair, he shook her hand with the other.

"How are you, Dr. Jurgens?" Patricia asked in genuine concern.

"Heavily medicated," he said. "Antidepressants. Haven't quite got the dosage right yet. Please, have a seat. Gloria will bring us out some tea in a minute."

"Like hell I will," his wife called down.

"Oh none for me," Patricia said as if she hadn't heard. She turned and cleared a settee of magazines and was about to sit down when Paul stopped her.

"Not there," he said. "That's Gloria's thro...seat. Here, sit on the couch."

Patricia did as bid and Paul sat in a chair, holding the bottom of his robe closed in self-conscious modesty. "I really am fine," he said. "If that's why you came. Not suicidal. Any more." He tried a weak laugh, which fell flat. "Just waiting for that knock on the door. Y'know, men in suits. 'Can you come with us, Dr. Jurgens?' That sort of thing."

"Paul, I..."

"And don't apologize," he said, hurriedly. "It isn't your fault. I know that. It's really my fault. I didn't know because I didn't want to know. I should have paid more attention. It's like he said, I was a dupe."

A disgusted noise came from the hall and Patricia looked up in time to see Gloria headed toward the kitchen.

"Dr. Jurgens," Patricia said.

"Call me Paul," Jurgens said.

"Paul, I'm really sorry. I swear, I had no idea. If I'd known, I would have told you. I hope you believe that."

"Hardly matters, really, anymore," he shrugged. "But I don't blame you Patricia, even if you did know. Don't worry."

"But I didn't," Patricia said.

"'Kay," he said.

"Well maybe this will prove it," she said, placing a hand on the lidded file box.

Paul barely looked at the box, registered no curiosity at all. Gloria appeared with a tray and tea service, which she placed on an end table and began serving them with a put upon air. She also poured herself a cup and took a position on the settee with a stern attitude as if she dared anyone to ask her why she'd served tea when she said she wasn't going to, or to leave them alone.

Neither Paul nor Patricia did either one.

"This is for you," Patricia said, drawing their attention to the box once more.

Gloria did show interest. "What's in there?"

"Before I show you," Patricia said, "I need to tell you that a lot of time and effort went into this, some of it not so legal. So you'll have to cover your tracks on how you got it, or we might both go to jail."

"What?" Gloria asked indignantly. "As if we don't have enough..."

But Paul was leaning forward slowly and both women watched him silently. For the first time his eyes showed a brightness as he reached for the box, as if he knew what was in it. Pulling it over onto his lap he rested his hands on it reverently for a moment, then flipped the lid off and onto the floor at his feet.

As he leafed through the files, taking some out to read them more thoroughly, Patricia sat back and sipped from the cup Gloria had given her. She watched as he grew more and more animated, and watched Gloria as he handed her files and she perused them herself.

"I'm not going to ask you where you got this," Paul whispered.

"Others deserve credit, too," Patricia said. "The one you call the fixer, and another. I can't tell you their names, but they came through for you, Paul. With these files you can clear your name, and put Gerald Gannery away for a good long time. It's him who will be unable to practice for the rest of his life. As it should be."

"My God," Gloria whispered. Patricia could see she was perusing one of the malpractice files. Gloria looked at Patricia with wide eyes.

"Why?" she asked. "I mean...why?"

"Just setting the wrong things right," Patricia said proudly, privately quoting Jet. "Just setting the wrong things right."

"Fixing things," Paul said, looking at her, a vague smile on his face.

"You could say that," she nodded, "sure."

Paul's face darkened again. "And the fixer, is he going to, y'know...?"

Patricia shook her head. "That contract is null and void, in view of this. But I don't think you'll mind if he keeps the money paid."

Paul shook his head vigorously, "Absolutely not. He earned it. Tell him...tell him thank you. From me."

"And me," Gloria said, holding a file in each hand

and looking from one to the other.

"I will," Patricia said. "Now here's what you need to tell the police about how you got hold of these files, to keep yourself and the rest of us in the clear..."

CHAPTER 30

A nationally prominent doctor against an obvious alcoholic and drug addict who used to work for him until he fired her for pilfering from the office pharmacy? Of course the police believed him. Still, the number of times he had to repeat his story and the amount of paperwork he had to sit through had grown tiresome by the time the police let Gannery go with a reminder that there might be some follow-up in the investigation, but an assurance that the whole thing seemed open and shut self-defense.

Gannery slept, uncharacteristically, until 11 AM that Saturday morning and awoke with a migraine so accurately and viciously splitting his skull right at the part on the left side of his hair that he immediately regretted waking at all. His left arm was stiff where it had been wrapped with bandages. The bullet had gone right through his bicep, lacerating muscle and veins but thankfully missing any bone. He'd have to keep it wrapped, changing the dressing twice daily until the stitches could be removed. Meanwhile the arm was virtually useless to him.

"Bitch," he murmured again, thinking of Salomé Johnson.

He'd been walking away from her. Four or five inches to the right and the bullet would have gone right through his heart. Ironic that one went right through hers, and purely by accident, in the struggle for the gun. Gannery had never deliberately killed anyone in his entire life, though two had died on his operating table, but he didn't regret this accident, not one bit. She'd lied to him, taken his money for years. With the copies she claimed to have she was a credible witness. Without them she was nothing but a disgruntled employee with a drug habit. He could have gotten away with not paying her.

And now Gannery didn't have anything to balance the scales in order to re-start the game with the fixer and recover his honor. He needed something else, something to put them on a level playing field once more, start fresh, start anew, man against man, as it should be.

His cell phone rang and he snatched it off the end table. The screen said it was Harold Bloom calling once more. The man had been calling repeatedly for several days. Gannery knew what he wanted, but Gannery had nothing new to tell him about the dissolution of the partnership with Paul Jurgens. He had given the IRS and the Justice Department more than enough ammo against Paul without being too obvious about it and still they stalled. He didn't know what else he could do.

On the other hand, he couldn't go on ducking

Bloom's calls forever.

Sighing, Gannery thumbed the button and said, "Gannery."

"Ger, it's Harry," Bloom said excitedly. "Harry Bloom. Where ya been, buddy? Been trying to get hold of you for two days."

"My assistant's been sick," Gannery lied. "This is a new phone and she didn't show me how to pick up voicemails on it yet. What's up?"

"Good news, Ger. Really good news. There's another player in the mix."

"A what?"

"Another player in the mix," Bloom repeated.

"Speak English, will you?" Gannery demanded, holding his head and trying to keep still so as not to aggravate the migraine.

"Had a visit from Steven Lancaster the other day."

"Who?"

"I'm not surprised you don't know him," Bloom said. "But he's a major player. Producer with Fox already in his pocket on a deal twice as good as the one we're cooking with HBO. Did you hear what I said, Ger? *Twice* as good. As in twice the dough."

Gannery couldn't believe his ears. It paid to answer calls, even when you didn't think you wanted to. "Are you serious? They'll put up two for one?"

"Yup," Bloom said. "Two dollars for every one you put up."

Gannery stood. He wanted to whoop, but mindful of his headache he settled for an understated, "That *is* good news, Harry. Tell him he has a deal."

"Not so fast," Bloom said. "He said they'll double

anything HBO offers. That's a blank check, that kind of open-ended statement. What we gotta do, we gotta get HBO to counter. Doesn't matter which way we go now, buddy, the deal is done, only a matter now of who buys in highest, who bids more. You got your show, Gerry, the rest is just gravy."

Gannery was beaming in spite of the pain. "I trust you to do the negotiations, Harry," he said. "That's your job."

"A job I do very well, thank you," Bloom gloated. "I hope your other shit is taking care of itself...?"

"Only a matter of time, Harry," Gannery said, his enthusiasm only slightly dampened. "Trust me."

"Shame if it got in the way of this," Bloom said. "A sweeter deal you're never going to get, not twice in a lifetime, my friend."

"Trust me," Gannery repeated.

"Okay, Ger," Bloom said. "Take care. Enjoy your weekend."

"I will now," Gannery said. "Thanks," and hung up.

That was it, he thought. That was it. He had to conclude this business with the fixer and now. He wanted nothing distracting, no old business to attend to when this new chapter in his life opened. This one last piece of business, recovery of his honor, his integrity, was paramount even more now than ever. Only now it was also urgent.

He went to the bathroom to wet his face and find more of the Oxycodone he'd grabbed from his own pharmacy – stronger than the Percocet the doctor had given him. He only grabbed a sample, enough to get by on for the night, and would write himself a prescription for more if he needed it. There were only two more pills left in the bubble-pack, and it occurred to him he'd already taken too much for a single night. He took the remaining pills, chased them with a cupped handful of water, then went back to his bedroom to get dressed.

What to level the playing field? What to put them on equal footing again?

He chose some Chino slacks and a black shirt.

Leverage. Like Ginny, but not in the way, like he put her in the way. Just something to bring the fixer out to play. Just something to draw him out. Something to force him to play one more match, winner take all. Gannery was certain he would win this match. Worthy opponent though he was, the fixer was still just a mechanic, not an evolved thinker like Gannery himself.

Tying his sneakers – a task, given he could only extend one arm - Gannery wracked his brain for some way to leverage the fixer. Something he cared about, like Ginny. Something he'd come to rescue like Ginny. But what? Whom?

Gannery rolled his eyes when the name came to mind. It was so simple, so obvious he was nearly impatient with himself for not having thought of it before. But the glow of his own brilliance burned any self-resentment out as he set his mind to plot and strategize. Timing would be critical. He would need Vinnie and his men again, strictly controlled this time.

"It could work," he murmured to himself.

Reaching for his phone again, he dialed Vinnie Testarosa's number.

CHAPTER 31

Paul sat in the interrogation room with his box on the table in front of him and his arms folded across his chest, completely unaware of how much he looked like a young boy impatiently waiting to show off the box of snails he'd collected. He was showered, clean shaven, wearing his best black Armani suit, black shirt and gold tie shot through with a single metallic-red ribbon of color.

Of course he was nervous, he reflected. Who wouldn't be? He fully expected to be hauled into this room under other circumstances long before this. To come here voluntarily was a little like throwing oneself to the lions. He understood and approved of the story the fixer relayed through Patricia, but he didn't fool himself into believing that the authorities would buy it for a second. The question was, would they take it anyway, because it got them what they wanted.

After an hour's wait the door finally opened and no less than six people entered the room, all wearing the proverbial dark suits, all with deadpan expressions and some with bulges under one armpit of their jackets, some the right, most on the left. Among them was Agent Gloucer, the one who had shown him to this room on his arrival and request to talk to someone about the investigation into Gannery & Jurgens, MDs.

Gloucer didn't bother to introduce the other men and women, but they arranged themselves around the room like vultures circling a corpse, all looking at him with dead but hungry eyes, as if expecting him to confess and expose a jugular for them to feed on.

"What's in the box, Doctor?" Gloucer asked.

Paul cleared his throat and scooted forward in his chair, which scraped loudly on scarred linoleum tile. "What would you say if I told you I have proof that my partner is guilty of the fraud for which you are investigating me?" he asked. "What would you say if I told you that?"

"Is that what's in the box, Doctor?" another man asked to his right, a man with an incongruously cheerful purple tie.

Paul looked at him and licked his lips. "May I?" he asked Gloucer, motioning to his box.

"Please," Gloucer gestured expansively.

More than one of them put their hands on their belt buckles, ready to reach for their weapons if need be. The box had passed through the metal detectors at the entrance to the US Customs House where they now were without a peep, but Paul supposed these men were trained to be overly careful, especially in post 9-11 New

York.

He stood and, clearing his throat again, removed the lid of the box and set it on the seat of the chair he just vacated. Removing one of the files, he opened it long enough to identify which one it was. He and his wife had spent hours going over the stuff in this box, amazed at how much was here, how completely it implicated Gannery in everything.

"These are signed deposit slips for one account in the Cayman Islands in the name of Gerald Robert Gannery," he said, offering the file to Gloucer. "These," he said, pulling out another file and glancing at its contents, "are duplicate registers contradicting those seized by your office showing the real routing of invested funds into slush funds and ghost accounts."

He went through the files one by one and Gloucer passed them around as they were handed to him. By the end the men and women were all gathered around the table perusing files and documents, consulting one another, dipping into the box themselves and riddling Paul with questions. There were smiles and heads that shook with wonder and even exclamations of triumph and glee.

At one point Gloucer looked at the man in the purple tie and said aloud, "I knew it. Didn't I tell you?" The man in the purple tie, grinning, nodded.

As the other five men busied themselves Gloucer pulled Paul aside. "I have to ask you where you got these," he said, then held up a hand hurriedly to hush Paul. "Before you answer, I need you to think long and hard about what you are going to say. If these documents were gathered by any means illegal, you will most likely be opening yourself up to prosecution for theft.

"On the other hand," he went on, watching Paul closely to make sure he was getting the point, "if you got these papers out of the public domain, or they were, say, left lying out in the open or something, then you did nothing illegal by picking them up and looking at them. You were shocked by what you found in them and thought it your civic duty, not to mention self-preservation, to bring them to our attention."

"I was, indeed, shocked," Paul said, "when I found them in a filing cabinet shared by both Dr. Gannery and myself."

Gloucer's smile was slow but broad. "And there's no reason anyone can contradict this? No way for a sharp Park Avenue lawyer to shake you off this story?"

"None," Paul assured him.

"Good," Gloucer clapped him on the shoulder.

They turned and watched the others for a moment, then Gloucer said, "I don't mind telling you this is a relief. I knew there was more to this. Something didn't smell right, everything was too neat, like someone was handing it to us on a silver platter. Life is never that neat and packaged. Life is messy and unplanned and chaos. That's why we were holding out. I wanted to give you, someone, time to find the mess. And you did."

"Yes," Paul said, silently tipping an imaginary hat to the fixer. "Yes, I...or someone...did."

"Do me another favor?" Gloucer said. "Although you may be tempted to, don't tell Dr. Gannery. He may be tempted to make himself scarce, and we don't want that, do we?"

CHAPTER 32

Daniel Rontell reclined on the terrace of his palatial Beverly Hills mansion, his robe hanging wide open, his naked wife snuggled up against him sharing the chaise on which they lay. She dozed, snoring softly and adorably. After nearly twenty years of marriage he still found her, at the age of fifty, just as cute as a bunny and as mysterious as the surf at Big Sur.

Few who saw his movies and TV series would expect the poetic side of Rontell, nor, given the money most projects he had written and produced had raked in, would much care. That was a frustration with which Rontell long since came to terms. His dream had been to be a renowned and respected literary genius, as his Masters in Liberal Arts attested. But life had taken him in an unexpected direction, making of him instead a renowned and envied mass media genius for whom anything he touched instantly turned to twenty-four karat box office gold.

So Daniel Rontell remained in the closet, poetically speaking, writing poetry only for his own pleasure and for that of his biggest fan, the woman whose exquisitely soft and sensual body warmed half of his body now.

Julie stirred and moved her hand down his chest and into the front of his boxers, cupping his masculinity. Not so asleep anymore, she moaned suggestively, "Up for a Southern Good Morning?" she asked.

"Always," he mumbled into her hair.

At which inopportune time the telephone rang.

Rontell sighed.

"Don't," she said in her affected little-girl voice, the one reserved for wrapping him around her little finger.

"I have to," he said, working himself out from under her. "This might be one of about twenty calls I can't afford to miss."

"Come back," she said, reaching out to him plaintively as he padded back through the French doors and into the bedroom.

"I will, Nell," he said in his affected Dudley Doright voice. "I promise." He doubted anyone, those not in their mid-fifties at least, would even know who Dudley Doright was, but the voice always made Julie laugh, as it did now.

"Y'hello," he said into the floor-standing princess phone that his wife loved so much. For himself, the heavy brass thing was more of a burden than a fantasy.

"Mr. Rontell, this is Gabby," his secretary said on

the other end of the line.

"What's the matter, Gabby?" he asked, concerned by the distress in her voice.

"I'm really sorry to bother you on a Sunday morning," she said. "But the gentleman said it was urgent and, well, after he told me what it was about...I really think you ought to take this call."

"What are you doing in the office this morning?" he asked.

"I'm not," she said. "I'm at home. He tracked me down here looking for you. He's very determined, which makes what he has to say even more disturbing."

"Well what is it, Hon?" Rontell asked.

"I really think you ought to hear it from him," she said. "Can I give him your home number?"

"If you think it's that urgent," Rontell said. "Sure, go ahead."

He hung up, chewing his lip and staring at the phone, then turned and went into the hall. The phone was ringing again as he trotted to his office, closing and tying his robe in case any of the house staff were up and about. He sat behind his desk and picked up the lighter plastic phone thereon.

"Rontell."

"Mr. Rontell, you don't know me, and I'm not going to give you my name." The voice sounded firm, confident, authoritative. "I'm going to give you some free information and some free advice. You're going to take my advice because after we hang up you're going to make a call and find out that the information I'm about to give you is one hundred percent absolutely accurate. What I get out of it is that a friend of mine, a good man who deserves it, will be helped out by the favor you do me.

What you get out of it is a much more reliable and honest business partner on a particular business deal we are about to discuss. Are you following me so far?"

"Yes," Rontell said, sitting back. There didn't seem to be anything else to say. The man had anticipated all of his questions thus far: why should I take your advice? What do you get out of it? What do I get out of it?

"Dr. Gerald Gannery is talking to another producer about the same project he discussed with you. His plan is to either drag you into a bidding war, or to undercut you and go to production and air before you with another, similar deal on another network."

Rontell was sitting forward again. He could feel the familiar heat in his face and knew it was turning red, which is what Julie told him happened when his anger rose. "How do you know this?"

"Never mind," the caller said. "The call you are going to make to confirm this is to Harold Blood in New York."

"Of course," Rontell said. "Who are you? No, never mind, you aren't going to tell me, are you? What's the favor you want from me in return?"

"Simple," the stranger said. "I want you to offer the exact same deal you were negotiating with Gannery to a friend of mine. A Dr. Paul Jurgens."

"Never heard of him," Rontell said.

"True, he's not as famous as Dr. Gannery," the voice said. "But I guarantee you he's ten times the surgeon Gannery ever was. And more importantly, for you anyway, is he's an honest man."

"There's no such thing," Rontell said sarcastically.

"Yes there is," the caller averred. "I've done some

checking up on you, Rontell. You're one."

Rontell was speechless.

"Don't' worry," the stranger chuckled on the phone, "I won't tell anyone and spoil your reputation. But if you do the deal with Jurgens instead, you'll have a much more entertaining show, because you'll actually be able to film him doing the surgeries himself."

Rontell blinked. Gannery had insisted on one condition of the show, that no cameras be allowed into the operating room itself. Rontell fought that one but Gannery had been absolutely intractable there, which was a complete mystery to Rontell. He didn't buy Gannery's assertion that it was for the privacy of the patient, who was a guest on a national televised reality show anyway, but he had finally given in.

"If I find out that what you're telling me is the truth," Rontell said, "then I'll give your friend a call. That's all I can promise."

"That's all I ask."

"What's his number, this Dr. Jurgens?" Rontell wrote it down and recited it back for confirmation, and then the line was dead, without so much as a goodbye.

"Everything all right, Dan?" Julie stood at the doorway in her robe.

"Don't know yet," he said distractedly. "I'll be down for breakfast in a few. Go ahead and start without me, I have some calls to make."

He picked up the phone again and dialed Harold Bloom's personal cell number.

"Bloomy," Harry's voice came over the line. "Who may I say is calling?"

"It's Daniel Rontell," Rontell said.

"Rontell," Bloom greeted him jovially. "I was just

thinking about you! I was going to give you a call from the office on Monday. You must be psychic."

"Yeah," Rontell said levelly, "must be. Listen, I just got wind of something kind of upsetting. I'm hoping it's a bad wind. You know, the kind that isn't true at all."

There was a beat, then Bloom said, "Depending on what it is, Daniel, I'm afraid it just might be."

"You're not even going to try to deny it?" Rontell struggled to keep his temper under control.

"Depends on what *it* is," Bloom said cagily.

"You know damn good and well what *it* is, Bloomy." Rontell used the name snidely. "How could you do this to me? We've done business a long time."

"Hey, it's nothing personal," Bloom said earnestly. "It's business. It's just business. I still love you, baby."

"Stow that shit," Rontell said between clenched teeth. "So this is why all the delay, so you could work this other deal in and cause a bidding war."

"I'm not at liberty to say, actually," Bloom said.

"Or were you stalling me while you went to production somewhere else ahead of me?"

"Wait, now," Bloom said. "Let's not get paranoid. I don't do that kind of underhanded shit, you know that. I wish you wouldn't get so sore, Dan. This sort of thing is done all the time. It's competition. It's the way this business is done."

"We shook hands on our deal," Rontell said. "Figuratively speaking. That used to mean something."

"It does," Bloom said. "It means I like you, and I'm going to give you preference over this other guy. But you gotta give me something to go back to Gannery with or it's kind of outa my hands. Y'know?"

263

"Well, Bloomy, here's what you take back to Gannery for me," Rontell said, realizing that this would have been his decision even if it weren't the advice of some anonymous voice over the phone. "Tell him the deal's off."

"Now, Daniel," Bloom said hurriedly. "There's no need to go off all angry and shit. Take some time and think about it. Relax, enjoy your weekend. Sleep on it. Let's talk in the morning."

"No, Harry," Rontell said. "Deal's off. I mean it. Go with your other deal. I'm out."

"Well if that's how you feel," Bloom said. "I'm sorry to hear it of course. No hard feelings?"

"Good luck," Rontell said.

"Don't," Bloom said in a sympathetic voice. "Don't say it like 'goodbye.'"

"Good luck," Rontell said again. "Good luck *and* goodbye."

He hung up.

Rontell chewed his thumbnail vigorously for a moment.

"Dan," his wife called from downstairs. "You coming to breakfast? Sheba's picked wild strawberries from the garden. They're scrumptious, absolutely scrumptious."

"In a minute, dear heart," he called back. He was looking at the blotter on which he had jotted the name *Dr. Paul Jurgens* and a telephone number with a New York area code. He slowed the chewing of his nail until he stopped. Rolling his chair forward he picked up the phone again and dialed the number on the blotter.

CHAPTER 33

Gannery walked into the office late Monday afternoon, having spent the morning once more with his editor and the lunch hour standing outside Vinnie's house, because for some inexplicable reason Mrs. Testerosa wouldn't let him inside, explaining to his childhood friend what he wanted from him this one last time. Vinnie had turned out to be understandably eager to redeem himself and take one more shot at the fixer and this promised to be a much more successful shot than any prior attempt.

When Gannery walked in the front door of the practice he was nonplused to see Dr. Paul Jurgens coming through the inner door escorting a woman, smiling and talking to her in reassuring tones.

"You'll go to sleep here in my office Wednesday afternoon," Paul was saying cheerfully, "and wake up two hours later to a much younger-looking you. I promise."

"Thank you, Doctor," the woman nodded and left.

The waiting room was teaming with patients once again.

"Paul," Gannery said.

"Gerry," Paul greeted him heartily, reaching out and shaking his hand vigorously. The dark circles around his eyes were gone, as was the haunted expression and the stoop. Paul Jurgens stood tall once again and was smiling, no, grinning broadly.

"Feeling better, are we?" Gannery asked, trying to hide his perplexity.

"You know," Paul said, as if even surprised himself, "I think I am. Thank you so much for asking. Hey, what the hell happened to your arm? It's in a sling."

"Oh, um, hyper extended rotator," Gannery heard himself say, "tennis."

"Ooh, too bad," Paul said. "Well, would love to stay and chat, but I have a patient in examination room nine. Good to see you again, Gerry. Really."

And he was off, back through the swinging doors that led to the examination rooms once more.

Shaking his head slowly, Gannery pushed through them himself once the doors had stopped swinging so wildly and made his way back to his office. He was amazed that the office was a-buzz with activity again, and there was more than one examination room occupied at the moment.

Something had changed. Something had caused a genuine transformation in his partner and revitalized the practice Gannery had been gleefully throttling to death just days before. And whatever had changed Gannery had a steadily growing horrified feeling that he wasn't going to like it.

He stopped by his office to drop off his briefcase and jacket, then turned and entered Patricia's office. Patricia bent over a plant on the floor, testing the soil in the pot with one hand and splashing water into it with a spouted pitcher in the other hand.

As he looked down at the pot, he spotted something else, the corner of a piece of paper protruding from underneath Patricia's desk behind her that she clearly hadn't seen. Gannery liked a tidy office, and bent himself to pick it up.

"Patricia," he said.

She stood and turned. "Dr. Gannery, you're back."

"So, clearly, is Dr. Jurgens."

"Yes," Patricia beamed. "Isn't it wonderful? Isn't it amazing what a change almost a week off will do? He's like a new person. It's like he's got a new lease on life. And I can tell you it's contagious. I even caught Nurse Crone smiling a few minutes ago."

"Has he said anything." Gannery frowned. "Anything about what was bothering him? Anything about why it isn't bothering him anymore?"

"No," Patricia said. "But I can probably guess."

"You can," Gannery, narrowing his eyes.

"Sure," she said. "Man works the kind of hours he's been working, Gloria was probably on him about not being home more, missing kids' band performances and plays and such. So I'm guessing he and Gloria went away somewhere really romantic for the week. Or maybe they took the kids with them. Anyway, whatever it was, it's done him wonders, don't you think?"

"Wonders," Gannery said from behind clenched teeth. He had hired Patricia for her gullibility, but sometimes her very obtuseness could be infuriating. She was utterly useless to him as an office spy. "Whatever. See if you can find out, will you?"

"Why don't you just ask him?" Patricia said cheerfully.

"Because I don't have time, all right," he snapped at her. All this cheerfulness in his office was making him irritable. "Just do it, Patricia."

"Fine," she said, with not quite a sullen tone.

He turned and returned to his own office. Before he sat down he realized he still had the paper he'd picked up from under Patricia's desk in his hand. Turning back, intending to return it to her, he glanced down at it and froze.

This wasn't hers. This was his. It was a page from the middle of an arbitration transcript, and by the names on the paper he could identify it as arbitration of one of the malpractice suits he'd settled out of court many, many years ago, before Paul had joined the practice and taken over the surgeries. This paper didn't belong in any file Patricia had access to. In point of fact this belonged with the rest of his secret stash of papers, in the locking hidden drawer at the back of his filing cabinet.

This was one of many documents Gannery discovered stolen from him a week ago, the day Paul Jurgens left.

One by one, like puzzle-pieces dropped from a great height, things slowly fell into place and Gannery ground his teeth like never before, so hard he could hear his laboring heart through them, through the bone in his skull, like an amplifier in his head.

Patricia had somehow tricked Gannery into giving her that day off. He didn't know how, but she had. She knew somehow that Paul was leaving and why. Maybe he told her everything, and in some misguided attempt to help him, she searched Gannery's office and found his hidden drawer, and stole his papers.

How had she guessed the combination? It was not the most expensive lock in the world, he hadn't thought it needed to be, so well hidden was it. But it was a sturdy lock. She had to have the combination, there was no way she could have guessed six digits so quickly. Which meant in spite of all his efforts to keep them apart she and Ginny had somehow gotten together. But how?

Ginny with the fixer at the banquet.

Of course. The fixer recruited Ginny to his side, and he did the same with Patricia. All this time, behind his back. He'd been a fool. The King's Gambit had been so much more subtle and insidious than he could ever have imagined. The fixer was not just good, he may well be better than Gannery himself, a fact Gannery found no pleasure in admitting.

Now, Paul back in the office, smiling, cheerful, treating patients again. That could only mean one thing. The dark specter of possible arrest had been removed, and Paul knew it. The papers had been turned over to Paul Jurgens and Gannery's partner and former friend had turned them into the authorities. Which meant it was only a matter of time before Gannery himself heard that proverbial knock on the door.

Gannery galvanized. Grabbing his coat and his briefcase, he left his office and headed toward the front waiting room. He would have loved the opportunity to deal with Patricia, but that would have to come later.

Right now he had to get away before...

"Dr. Gannery," Nurse MacDenna addressed him as she came the other direction down the hall. "There are some men in the waiting room, a lot of them. They say they need to see you on an urgent matter."

Gannery blanched. Pressing his back against the wall, he whispered hurriedly, "Yes, um, of course. I know what this is all about. Please tell them I'll be right out."

Nurse MacDenna nodded, looking at him in confusion at his behavior. She turned and went back toward the front waiting room. Gannery turned and power-walked the opposite direction. He passed examination room 9 as Paul stepped out of it.

"Gerry?" Paul called after him. "Is there something wrong?"

Gannery just brushed past him and picked up his pace, heading for the back hall, turning and diving for the back exit. Just outside of this he turned left and ducked into the stairwell. It was a long way down but Gannery prided himself on the shape he was in, even at his age, and he rushed as fast as he dared down endless flights to the ground floor.

He peered out of the stairwell door and, seeing no one in the street level lobby, crossed the big tiled floor and headed for the revolving doors at the front of the building. Rushing through, he turned left and ran to the parking garage where Palmer would be waiting for him in the town car. Slipping into the garage, he sprinted, the jacket over his arm flapping in the wind, and came to the car. Palmer was in the back watching a soap opera on the television that dropped down from the ceiling. Gannery took him completely by surprise.

"Palmer," Gannery snapped.

Palmer slapped the TV screen shut and jumped out of the car. "I'm sorry, boss. I didn't expect you so soon. Why didn't you call for me to bring the car around?"

"There's no time," Gannery huffed, out of breath.

"Well, I need to ask you about something," Palmer began.

"It'll have to wait," Gannery said as he climbed in the back seat. "You need to take me to my bank, now."

Palmer got into the driver's seat and pulled out of the slot, heading for the exit. "Is there a problem, Boss?" Palmer asked, looking at Gannery via the rearview mirror.

"Yes," Gannery said. "Well, no. Well, yes and no."

"Does it have something to do with the credit card, sir?" Palmer asked, pulling out into the street.

"What credit card?" Gannery snapped.

"The credit card," Palmer said. "The one you give me for gas and stuff for the cars. I went to get gas just now while you was upstairs and the damn pump took my card and he wouldn't give it back, and he wouldn't give me no gas, neither."

Gannery inhaled and held it, counting slowly to ten.

"So all I'm wondering is," Palmer went on, "is everything all right?"

Gannery let his breath out. "Stop the car," he said angrily. "Pull over, right here."

Palmer did as instructed.

Gannery took out his cell phone and dialed. At least it still worked.

"First National Bank," came the woman's voice on the other end.

"Yes, let me talk to Stan Hunt," Gannery said. "He's a Vice President there."

"Just one moment," the woman said, and canned music replaced her voice in Gannery's ear.

From where they sat Gannery could see the front of the building where his and Paul's practice held offices. From the entrance emerged six men in dark suits. Some of them Gannery recognized as those he'd spoken to when guiding them to the evidence he had so carefully planted implicating Paul Jurgens in embezzlement and fraud. Now they were looking up and down the street urgently.

Gannery slouched in the seat in spite of the darkly tinted windows and worked on steadying his breathing.

"This is Hunt," a voice said on the phone.

"Hunt," Gannery said. His voice sounded to his own ears desperate, stalked. He cleared his throat and said, in a voice more approaching normal, "Stan. Hi. This is Gerry. Gerald Gannery?"

"Gerry, man." Stan's voice had dropped precipitously into a whisper. "What the hell's going on, man? Feds were here. All your accounts here are frozen. All your assets. Locked up tighter than a virgin's..."

"Shit," Gannery said and disconnected the line. He sat slouched down and chewed his lip, trying to think clearly. He didn't have enough cash on him to get out of the city, much less the state, never mind the country. It was safe to assume all of his stateside accounts were similarly frozen, and since those papers also had account numbers for several offshore accounts it was reasonable to assume that they were being watched as well, if not also frozen. He needed money.

He now saw the folly in keeping all of his secrets

in one place like that, no matter how well hidden and secure he thought them to be.

He watched as the men in suits got into a row of cars parked along the curb several car-lengths ahead of his town car.

"Boss?" Palmer ventured.

"Shut up, you big idiot," Gannery snapped.

Two of the three cars pulled away. One stayed, clearly staking out the building.

"Shit."

From the entrance now came Patricia and Dr. Paul Jurgens, arm in arm. They were smiling and laughing as they paused at the curb and talked to each other. Gannery watched with interest. After a brief exchange, Patricia accepted a peck on her cheek from Paul and they went their separate ways, Paul toward the garage Gannery had just left where his reserved parking space waited, Patricia to the curb where she hailed a cab.

As the taxi pulled away, Gannery sat up straight.

"Follow that cab," he told Palmer. "If you loose her, I'll personally kick your balls up into your throat."

Palmer glanced at Gannery in the mirror, eyes hooded, but pulled away from the curb and followed the bright yellow taxi in silence. Gannery stared as they passed the stake-out car, at two men drinking coffee and talking, clearly socked in for the long haul.

Once past, Gannery faced forward, opened his cell phone again and dialed without looking.

"Vinnie? Slight change of plans. No, you go on ahead like we talked about, but I'm not going to be there. Not right away, anyway. I have a stop to make, I don't know how long it's going to take me. I'll call you and we'll hook up later. You know what to do. Don't fuck it up this time."

He hung up and locked his gaze onto the taxi three cars in front of them.

CHAPTER 34

Paul Jurgens pulled into the driveway of his house, got out of his car after turning it off and danced a little to the radio until it faded away gradually, as it had been designed to do. Then he leaned in and pulled out his briefcase and the bouquet of flowers he picked up for Gloria on the way home. In his case were three CD's, one of Maroon 5 for his son and two different Taylor Swift ones for the twins.

As he walked up the sidewalk he admired the maticulously manicured lawn that he worked on all day the day before after returning from the US Customs House in the city. The lawn needed a haircut for a long time and he'd finally felt in the mood to do it.

"Glo," he called, letting himself into his own house, "kids." Everything was spic and span and just as organized as it always was. He left his briefcase on the small mail table by the door and shifted the flowers from one hand to the other as he doffed his coat and hung it on one of the hooks nearby.

"Where is everyone?" he called out.

He stepped out into the foyer and looked from left to right.

"There you are," he said, walking in to the family room on the right. Gloria sat in a dining room chair directly in the center of the room with her arms behind her. Why she held her scarf in her mouth he couldn't figure.

"What's going on," he said jovially, expecting the kids to jump out and yell *surprise* any second. He stepped into the room and saw to the left two large, muscular men were holding his kids. His son was struggling as one man held him with a hand over the boy's mouth. The girls merely stood with wide eyes while the other man had each of his hands around their heads and covering their mouths.

"What the..." Paul said, before his skull split open and all of his thoughts seemed to spill out onto the floor behind him as his legs gave out and he felt himself pitching over to the side. *I've been hit*, he thought in a very war movie kind of way before darkness took him.

*

"Pookie-pie," Patricia called out as Gregory spotted her coming into his room.

"Oh god," Jet said, turning away from Gregory's bed and looking at her ruefully. "I'm leaving if you guys are going to start talking like that."

"That was the general idea," Patricia said, brushing past him and giving Gregory a kiss on his nose.

276

"Hello, Patricia," Margie called out.

"Hey, Margery," Patricia returned the greeting. "Where's Ginny."

"Out," Jet said. "No one knows where. As usual. How is she, y'know, after...?"

"She has nightmares," Patricia said. "She's handling it as well as can be expected."

"It would be nice if we could get Gannery on a murder rap," Gregory said.

"Ginny's still adamant that though Dr. Gannery seemed willing to beat Salome up, she doesn't think the shooting was on purpose," Patricia said. "Salome shot him first, after he hit her, they struggled for the gun, it went off. Pretty much what Ginny heard him tell the police on the phone before she snuck out. We'd all like to put Dr. Gannery away for a long time, but asking Ginny to spin what she saw is something he would do. Not us."

"I didn't mean..."

"I know that's not what you meant," Patricia said, leaning over to kiss his nose.

"Besides," Jet said, heading for the door, "when Dr. Jurgens hands over the papers and the authorities see those checks written to Salome Johnson, they're going to take a good hard second look at her quote-unquote accidental shooting."

"You don't have to go, Bro," Gregory said to Jet. "Patricia was just kidding."

"No, I do have some errands to run, anyway," Jet said. "You two have fun. Don't wait up."

"Bye, Jet," Patricia said, raising up to her tiptoes to kiss his craggy cheek in spite of his attempt to pull away. "I don't care how uncomfortable it makes you," she scolded him, "I'm going to keep doing it until you get used to it. Or at least until you stop ducking me."

Jet said nothing, but turned and left the room.

"Jet's going to have his hands full with my Patricia," Gregory said when Jet was gone. "How was work today?"

"Wonderful," Patricia said. "Paul was back and he was his old self again. Old sour-puss showed up and it was almost too funny to see his reaction. He didn't know what the hell was going on. Oh, and something awesome. The Feds showed up and Dr. Gannery split ahead of them. Probably went out the back way. They were still looking for him when we left."

"They didn't get him?" Gregory asked.

"Don't look so worried," Patricia said, "they will. He won't get far."

"What if he goes after Dr. Jurgens?" Gregory asked.

"He'll be too busy ducking Feds to go after anyone for a long time," Patricia said. "My God, you're such a worrier."

"Now that you're here, Patricia Dear," Margie called out, "I'm heading home."

"Thanks, as always, Margie," Gregory said as Patricia crossed the room to hug his nurse and send her on her way.

Patricia returned to his bedside. "Have you eaten?"

"Not hungry," he said.

"Me either," Patricia said, climbing in next to Gregory and sharing his pillow as she was wont to do lately. "Let's watch TV."

"Okay," Gregory said, and switched his lips to the television control.

"Well ain't this cozy," a familiar, chilling voice intruded.

They both turned their heads to see Dr. Gerald Gannery walk into the room with a negligent air, hands clasped behind his back.

*

The fixer pulled the motorcycle over, slipped into neutral while he fished the vibrating cell phone out of the breast pocket of his coat and put it to his ear, saying nothing.

"M-Mr. Fixer?" came the timid voice. "Y-you there?"

Jet had already checked and recognized the number.

"What's up, Dr. Jurgens?"

"I'm supposed to tell you I'm fine," he said. "I'm supposed to tell you we're all fine, my family and me. I'm supposed to tell you that we won't be for long if you don't do exactly what you're told."

"Get that, Mr. Fixer?"

Vinnie Testarosa.

"Bad move, Vinnie," Jet said. "Didn't you get the memo? Contract's off. Talk to your boss, he'll tell you."

"You'n me," Vinnie said. "We got a score to settle."

Jet rolled his eyes.

"Let them go, Vinnie," he said. "Otherwise, I might be forced to kill you this time."

The squeal of a little girl came over the line and the fixer's face stormed over immediately.

"Tasty morsel," Vinnie said. "Think if me and the boys take a turn she might end up splittin' like a wishbone. What do you think?"

Jet took a moment to keep from crushing the phone in his grip.

"What do you want?" he said.

"You," Vinnie said. "In exchange for them. We're at the house now. You come and turn yourself over to my men, the Doc and his family go free. That simple."

Jet switched off and re-stowed the phone. Revving the engine to an ear-splitting scream, he popped the clutch and the rear wheel left a skid as black as Satan's heart before the bike leapt forward and sped down the avenue reared back on only one wheel in a streak.

*

Gregory heard Patricia cry out as he watched Gannery give her arm, which he held behind her back, a little extra twist and push. "What did you think you were going to do, coming at me like that," Gannery asked her, his other arm around her neck. She tried to kick back at him but he clearly found that easy to evade.

"What are you, quad?" Gannery turned himself and Patricia to face Gregory's bed.

The kind of man who called a quadriplegic a 'quad', Gregory thought, was the same kind of man who called African Americans 'niggers.' Gregory was infuriated at his helplessness. He didn't know who the man was until Patricia tried to attack him and by then it was too late. Gannery twisted Patricia's arm behind her back and snatched Gregory's yoke away even as he was trying to activate his silent alarm to Jet and the police. On the screen now was the final prompt, unanswered, to trip that alarm.

"How did you get in?" Patricia hissed through her teeth. "There's a security lock."

"Interesting the comings and goings in this

place," Gannery said. "First I follow you here, then who do I see leave but that fixer asshole. I was looking for a way in when I heard someone else coming out. It was a simple matter to hide below the stoop as that black lady left, then leap the rail and stop the door before it closed. Who was she, your nurse?"

This last, directed at Gregory, was a question of course he no longer had the power to answer. Gregory looked into Patricia's eyes and the pain he saw there made him want to cry out. He didn't know he was working his jaw until Gannery laughed.

"Look, Patricia, he's trying to raise an alarm."

"Leave us alone," Patricia screamed, struggling again.

"Why?" Gannery asked. "Leave you alone when you wouldn't leave me alone? I must admit, you people did get the better of me. I always knew my biggest danger was when a group of my enemies joined forces. Until now no one had the guts or foresight to try it. Kudos to Paul Jurgens for putting together a real crack team of con artists.

"Oh, but then it really wasn't Paul, was it? I mean he hired the fixer, but he was really out of the loop until just recently, wasn't he? So really my compliments should go to this fixer guy. What's his real name?"

Patricia didn't say anything. Gannery twisted her arm cruelly and she cried out.

"Jet," she snapped. "His name is Jet. Not that it'll do you any good. He's only going to be gone a second and then he's coming right back. He'll deal with you once and for all."

"Jet, hmmm," Gannery said. "Such an appropriately macho name for such a theatrical guy. Who does he think he is, Clint Eastwood or something? I don't think he'll be coming back any time soon. He's got other matters to tend to right now."

Gregory noticed a bloodstain on the sleeve of Gannery's left arm, and it was spreading. It must be the wound where Salome shot him. It would make that arm weaker. If only he had a way to tell Patricia, if she could somehow throw her weight that direction, break Gannery's grasp...

"How did you find out," Patricia asked, "about everything?"

"You were sloppy," Gannery said. "You dropped one of my very special papers under your desk. The ones hidden in the back of the filing cabinet? I found it this afternoon."

Gregory looked down at his yoke hanging uselessly by the side of the bed. He glared at his hand and willed it to move, to grab the yoke and replace it in front of his mouth. But the hand, as it had for ten years before this, refused to move. He looked up into Patricia's face and tried to convey his shame for being so useless to her.

"It's okay, baby," Patricia said. "I know." Tears quite suddenly flooded her cheeks. "I know you would if you could."

"Baby?" Gannery laughed. "Baby! Are you two f-fuh...?"

He finished the thought with a sudden intake of breath and a whimper. His face drained of color and he sucked his lips in to bite them until they, too, turned white.

Gregory couldn't see what caused such a reaction.

"Now let...me...go," Patricia demanded harshly.

Gannery released her and she turned away from

him, but her other hand, the one that had remained free, was now twisted into the fabric of Gannery's pants, right at his crotch.

"Try anything and I'll rip it off," Patricia said, "you son of a bitch."

Gannery stood with both hands raised as if to protest his helplessness, then suddenly one hand swept down and hit hers away from his crotch with such force that she was not only impelled to let go, but she spun away and Gregory found her facing him once more.

She scrabbled at the bed as Gannery grabbed her from behind and pulled. She twisted her fists into the sheets and Gregory felt his bed tilt. Patricia screamed and Gannery hauled on her hair. Gregory saw the world around him wobble and tilt. The bed spilled over and his head smacked the floor, hard, his vision clouding.

He blinked his eyes, trying to clear his vision while foggy shapes struggled in front of him. He could hear them both grunting with the exertion. As his vision cleared he saw them over by Margie's supply station. They were knocking things over as they fought.

Something moved in his peripheral view, below his head, and he strained his eyes. A pool of blood was spreading out from under him. He was hurt in the fall. How badly he couldn't tell, his entire body numb. He strained his eyes up again and tried to see who was gaining in the struggle.

"Damn it," he heard Gannery yell and he saw their feet separate as Gannery backed away.

"Get out of here," Patricia yelled as Gregory watched her feet advance on Gannery's and the intruder's feet retreat again.

"Give me that," Gannery said. "Little girls

shouldn't play with sharp things."

Sharp? Gregory tried to think of what Margie had at her disposal that might be sharp. He couldn't think of a thing. Even the scissors that she used had blunt tips that could double as a clamp.

There was another rush of movement and now Patricia was on her knees in front of Gannery facing away from her attacker, leaning out, looking directly into Gregory's eyes. She struggled to pull at the rubber tourniquet that Gannery now held around her throat, from which she dangled. Her cheeks were puffing out and her face turning red.

Gregory wept openly, in rage, in helplessness, in hatred.

"This is for disloyalty," Gannery said.

Gregory saw the doctor's hand sweep down in front of Patricia's face, something silver gleaming in his fist. A scalpel, one that Margie kept in case Gregory ever choked on anything and needed an emergency tracheotomy.

He watched as Patricia's face went slack and blank of expression. Her arms fell to the floor before her as if boneless. She looked back into Gregory's eyes as a thin red line formed across her throat, the line traced by the swipe of Gannery's scalpel. The line became a gash and blood cascaded to the floor between them, rushing over to join the spreading pool of blood under Gregory.

Gannery let her drop like a bag of rubbish. Gregory heard footsteps, and then the man leaned way over so that he was looking directly into Gregory's face, his own mostly upside down.

"I don't suppose I need to give you the same treatment," Gannery said, breathing hard from his exertions but smiling. "Looks like you aren't long for this world anyway. Happy death. See you on the other side."

Gannery's face went away, then the scalpel fell, between Gregory and Patricia, bounced high, then clattered to the ground once again. But Gregory wasn't watching the dancing scalpel. Gregory only had eyes for Patricia.

Her eyes, on him, were fading fast.

A hand appeared and slapped down into the blood with a sticky sound, startling him. It was Patricia's. Using it, she dragged herself forward, toward him. Gregory was sobbing openly as his love worked her way to within inches of his face, blood now pouring from her mouth and down her chin.

"Love you..." she bubbled.

Gregory tried to convey through his own eyes all the love in his heart that was dying with her. He watched as her once bright eyes dulled, went glassy.

Then Gregory prayed for his own death to come soon.

CHAPTER 35

Vinnie held his gun to Gloria Jurgens' head as his cousin Jocko let the fixer in the front door, his gun drawn, and they moved out into the middle of the foyer so the fixer could see. Vinnie sneered at the man and screwed the gun into Gloria's ear until she cried out.

"Any bullshit," Vinnie warned him, "and she gets ventilated. Got it. Search him, Jocko."

Jocko did and came up empty handed.

"No fancy ninja weapons today, huh," Vinnie taunted. "Put the cuffs on him."

The fixer put his fists behind his back cooperatively and allowed Jocko to cuff him. Meanwhile he looked around the room, seeing where the kids and the doctor were tied up in a chair and on the couch.

"I'm sorry," Jurgens said to the fixer miserably.

"Thanks for coming. I'm sorry." He was quite beaten and bloody, attesting to the fight he'd put out before they could tie him down.

Vinnie allowed himself a low, satisfied laugh before he walked away from Mrs. Jurgens and stepped up to the fixer, his face inches away from the man.

"I had my way," Vinnie told him, his wet whisper dripping like menace, "we'd do ya right here, right now. But that ain't how Ger wants it. So we're going to do it Ger's way. See, my friend Ger, he's got more imagination than me. Me, I'd as soon kill a guy than deal with his shit anymore. But my friend Ger, he likes to come up with all kinds of creative ways to make a guy suffer 'fore he lets us do him. That might just be worth seeing, don't you agree?"

"You said you'd let the family go," the fixer hissed back at him. "Better do it before we go."

Vinnie searched the fixer's face for any sign of fear. Finding none, he turned away.

"Untie them," he said. "Keep the gun on them until we leave. Hey you, Doc? You call any cops, you speed up this guy's death. Then maybe we come after you. You lucky, you smart and don't call the cops, maybe you never see us again. Sound like a deal?"

Jurgens rubbed his wrists and eyed the gun in his face. "I'm sorry," he said again to the fixer. "I don't know what to say."

"It isn't over yet," the fixer said behind Vinnie.

"Anyone here hear a fat lady singing?" Vinnie cried out jovially.

"No," Jocko said behind him. "But I hear her warmin' up."

Vinnie joined his friends and relatives in laughing

heartily at the old joke. "All right, lets beat feet," he ordered and they all filed out, Jocko leading the fixer ahead of him. They all piled into Jocko's van, Vinnie behind the wheel.

"Jeez," someone complained. "It still smells like Tommy the Fish's brains in here. Wassa matter, Jocko, you don't clean up your van ever?"

"I wouldn't have to," Jocko answered back, "you stop shootin' guys in here."

"All right, all right," Vinnie called back. "Shut up and keep your eyes on the prisoner. He's a tricky one."

"He don't do nothin' but just sit there," Jocko said.

"Yeah," someone else agreed. "He don't do nothin' but just sit there."

Vinnie steered the van in a U-turn, back toward town when his cell phone rang. Driving with one hand, he pressed the talk button and put the phone to his ear. "Yeah, Ger, you get done what you hadda get done?"

"I did," Gannery said on the other end. "Where are you now?"

"We're in the van, on our way back to town," Vinnie said.

"You have him, then?"

"Yeah, we got him," Vinnie said. "So far he's coming all peaceful-like."

"Well don't let your guard down for a minute," Gannery said. "I'll be at the warehouse shortly after you get there, okay. You know what to do, so start without me."

"You got it, Ger," Vinnie said and hung up, returning the phone to the breast pocket of his suit.

*

Gannery heard the screaming the moment he got out of his car and looked quickly around to be sure no one else was within earshot. He was in an abandoned junk yard from which most of the junk had been pirated or removed. What was left was a large slab of broken concrete like at an airport surrounded by a chain link fence. He could smell the salty-sour scent of Long Island Sound nearby.

He was alone, having sent Palmer home early. The driver would find himself minus an employer in the morning, but that was no longer Gannery's concern. By then, with luck, he'd be on a plane more than half-way to Brazil.

The only structure here was a single corrugated metal shed or warehouse about the size of a small house. Vinnie's van was parked halfway nose-in at the entrance, probably using the headlights to see by, as it was growing dark outside and undoubtedly dark inside. It was from this building that the screaming came.

Gannery made his way to the building, squeezed between the van and the edge of the entrance and walked into the room. In the center of the high beams sat the fixer in the disenfranchised bucket seat of some sports model car, resting on the floor on its metal tracks. He was surrounded by men. He was bleeding from several contusions in his face.

"You saved the best for me, right," Gannery said.

"Hey, Ger," Vinnie came over and greeted him warmly. "Sure we did. We was just softening him up. He's all yours."

The men slowly stepped back as Gannery approached the fixer in his seat. His hands were still cuffed behind him and he was bound to the chair with several bands of bungee cords that cut into his arms, chest and stomach cruelly. The fixer didn't look up at Gannery as he approached, so Gannery veered and walked completely around the man before stopping in front of him once again.

Finally, the fixer looked up at him through eyes already closing from bruises.

"You've been quite a burr in my side, my friend," Gannery said. "I don't mind telling you, you played the game much better than I gave you credit for. Way better than I expected. Way better than anyone else before you has ever played it. You got the upper hand on me. I applaud your effort."

At that he started a one-man slow-clap, the sound of which fell dead in the air. When he stopped he put his hands on his hips. "Problem is, you quit when you thought the game was over. But it was only check, my friend, not check mate."

"We had an agree..." the fixer tried to say through swollen lips, then gave up.

"An agreement," Gannery finished for him. "We had an agreement? Is that what you were about to say?" Gannery tsked. "I found I couldn't live with that agreement. You see, that agreement left me without my honor. And that is just something I can't live without. So I need it back, and you're going to give it to me."

"H...h...h..." the fixer tried. Clearly marshaling his breath, the fixer finally blurted, "How?"

"You see, your endgame has left me without any liquid assets," Gannery said. "Either the IRS or the Treasury Department has frozen all my accounts. I need money if I'm going to skip out of the country and escape this ridiculous bind you put me in. And since you put me in this bind, I figure what better, more poetic way to get the money I need than to take it from you. I figure you got it. Paul told me he paid you half a million. I about fell over. But as busy as you've been, I don't think you've had time to spend it all. So I'll take whatever you've got left. Just tell me where it is, and this stops here. We all go our separate ways."

The fixer's head lolled, then he seemed to nod. He began to whisper quietly.

"What? I can't hear you?" Gannery said, moving closer. "Speak up."

He could hear whispering coming from between those bleeding, misshapen lips, but couldn't make out the words. He moved a little closer.

The fixer reared back and head-butted Gannery just above his eyebrow so suddenly that Gannery didn't have time to pull away. Gannery found himself sitting on his rump near the bumper of the van, shaking his head and blinking through the pain encompassing his entire skull, but centering on the one single spot just to the left of center in his forehead.

When he cleared his vision he saw that Vinnie's men had gone back to work on the fixer once more. It took two shouted orders to make them stop. Gannery stumbled to his feet and walked back toward the fixer, who now lolled even more limp in his bonds.

"That's your answer?" Gannery said groggily. "Fine. Vinnie, bring me the black valise in the back seat of my car."

"Valise," Vinnie said.

"Valise," Gannery snapped. "The black bag, the black doctor's bag."

After just minutes Vinnie appeared from behind

the van with a black case, which he carried over and placed at Gannery's feet. Bending over, Gannery flipped the latches and the lid of the bag. He rummaged around until he came up with what he was looking for. He lifted the items and showed them to the fixer, not even sure if the man could still see through his beaten eye sockets.

"See these," Gannery said. "Do you know what they are? This" – holding up a flat length of steel with a raised thumb-rest on it – "is an Osteotone. And this" - holding up the second of three implements – "is quite obviously a hard rubber mallet, more specifically a rhinoplasty hammer. With these I break a subject's nose prior to reshaping it to a more pleasing profile. Have you ever had your nose broken deliberately, without anesthesia? Quite painful, or so I've been told. And this is the least I can do to you."

Gannery held up the third tool, what looked at first glance to be a pair of forceps but with teardrop-shaped loops at the end, turning it slowly for both he and the fixer to get a good look, opening them so the prisoner could see the striations on the insides of the loops for better traction.

"Do you know the term Enucleation," Gannery said. "Removal of the ocular organ, or in laymen's terms, the eye, is also done under anesthetic. The muscle tissue and nerves are cut away and the eye *popped* out like a wet, peeled grape. It can also be ripped out by the roots using this beauty here without anesthetic. This is plan B. I really hope we get to plan B.

"These instruments are going to ask my questions for me," Gannery went on. "I think you might answer them. Hold his head."

One of the men came behind the fixer and tried

to put his head in a hold between two palms, but the prisoner was too violent in writhing and resisting. In the end it took three men to hold him still, two alone to hold his head. Gannery enjoyed watching this worthy enemy squirm.

"Tip his head back." Gannery placed the concave end of the osteotone under the bridge of the fixer's nose, holding it firmly there. "The money," he said.

The fixer's bloodshot eyes focused on Gannery's own with sudden, piercing clarity. There was nothing but refusal in that glare.

Gannery clucked his tongue and shook his head. Hefting the hammer, he tapped the end of the osteotone once. The fixer's eyes shot wide and his scream was low and filled with pain. Gannery could see that pain swimming in his erstwhile patient's eyes like drowning sparks struggling to stay alight.

"Well?" Gannery said over the fixer's yell. At no answer, Gannery flicked the end of the osteotone with a finger and listened to the redoubled screaming. "How about now?" he demanded.

No answer, just more screaming and sobbing.

He lifted the cartilage-breaker.

"Your nose isn't broken yet," Gannery said in a reasonable tone. "That was just a tap, but you see how painful that was. You see, one thing I know about pain, being a doctor, is that the sensation recedes after an extended period. The brain comes to realize that such a concentrated source of pain in one area of the body is overwhelming sensations from all over the body. So as a matter of self-preservation it tends to begin isolating or ignoring the pain in the one area, closing it off, so that it can remain aware of the other extremities as well. The key to get past this is to step back and wait until sensation starts to return to the nerves again."

Gannery slipped the implement up under the fixer's columella, the column of cartilage that formed the central nasal structure, relishing the fear he saw in the fixer's eyes. "Do you want to answer the osteotone's question yet?" Gannery asked, moving his ear close.

The fixer's face was distorted in pain, but he refused to answer.

"Hmm? No?" Gannery asked. He moved the hammer to the osteotone and aimed. Rearing back, he tapped very hard this time. The accompanying crack was loud enough to echo in the warehouse.

The fixer was now openly screaming and crying at the same time, bellowing like a bull caught in a bear trap. In among all of those sobs, Gannery thought he heard the words, "Fuck you."

He released the osteotone and pulled back, leaning over to look into the fixer's eyes inquisitively. "Hmm? Did you say something?"

"I'm not telling you dick," the fixer said.

"C'mon," Gannery said, smiling. "It's only money."

"Not about the money," the fixer huffed behind his pain. "Sp...spite."

"Hmm," Gannery said. "Pride." He raised the loop forceps and considered them. "I believe a person's pride is stored behind their right eye. Shall we have a look?"

The fixer eyeballed him and Gannery smiled back. "Agreed," he said, then placed the forceps on the fixer's cheek, prying the eye open with the fingers of his other hand. Tilting the forceps up, he placed this inside the fixer's eyelids. Spreading them he forced his enemy's eye open wide. As he pushed in at the borders of the orbital socket he heard the fixer whimper something.

"Hmmm," he said. "Did you say something again?"

"Please," the fixer sobbed. "No more."

"And, um, the money?" Gannery pressed, speaking politely, as if to a child.

"Yes," the fixer said. "Key. Lining of my coat."

Gannery pulled the forceps away and rocked back on his heels, regarding the fixer like a specimen in a Petri dish. He stood, went around behind the fixer and looked down at the dirty coat spread around him with distaste. "In here?"

The fixer nodded as well as he could, still held by three men, even though he could no longer see Gannery behind him.

Sighing, Gannery bent and reached in between the men holding the prisoner still, fingered the lower hem of the fixer's coat. Starting in the middle he worked his way to the left edge and found nothing. Clucking his tongue, he checked the other side...and felt something.

"Get me a knife," he said to no one in particular.

Instantly he was surrounded by five hands, each holding out knives of various sizes and designs. Gannery shook his head in an *I should have known* way and selected one of the knives that seemed the sharpest. The canvas was not easy to cut, but cut it he finally did. Into Gannery's hand dropped a key on a fob. He read the fob and smiled.

Gannery moved back around to face the fixer and squatted down to catch his eye. He said. "You've earned yourself a quick and easy death."

Gannery stood and turned to Vinnie. "Leave him alone for now. Wait for my call, just to be sure he isn't lying. Then kill him quickly. I mean it Vinnie, a single bullet between the eyes, quick and clean. A worthy opponent such as him deserves no less."

"You got it, Ger," Vinnie said.

Gannery marched toward the door. Before squeezing back out between the doorway and the van he turned back to the fixer. "Thanks, Jet," he said. "I appreciate it."

The sudden intake of breath would have been satisfying enough to Gannery as the fixer clearly came to the realization of the only people from whom Gannery could have gotten his real name, but the sudden lift of his head and dagger-glare from the suddenly wide-open eyes was even more precious to him.

"I'm afraid both Patricia and that paralyzed fellow are quite dead," Gannery said sadly. "But on the bright side, you'll see them soon."

"Gannery!" the fixer bellowed as Gannery squeezed past the gap and walked toward his car. "You're a dead man, Gannery! You hear me? A dead man!"

Gannery paused by his car to remark to himself, "That would sound so much more threatening if it didn't come from a dead man himself."

He let himself into his car and drove away.

CHAPTER 36

Vinnie watched the fixer strain against his bonds as he screamed his last breath at Gannery's departing back. He clucked his tongue and shook his head, but couldn't bring himself to laugh. Somehow, the sight left him nauseous. There was another reason he didn't torture men before he killed them that he didn't tell anyone. Shooting a man outright, sometimes in the back of the head when he was least expecting it, left a man his dignity. This, this was just too sordid and demeaning for Vinnie. He was already eager for Gannery's call telling him to finish the fixer off. It would now almost be a relief to do so.

Then he saw something that defied all logic and description. First, not only did the fixer stop yelling as soon as Gannery was out of earshot, but suddenly all signs of pain and defeat — bowed head, sagging shoulders, labored breathing - left him. Instead the fixer's face became serene, almost Zen, as he seemed to concentrate.

Then Vinnie saw clearly as the prisoner's own hand in the cuffs, well, the only way to describe it is the hand collapsed. Vinnie stood slightly behind the fixer looking down at him, watching in disbelief as the man's right hand seemed to collapse on itself, become a sort of elongated flipper instead of a hand. He had never seen a man deliberately dislocate his own fingers in that way, and the rapid-fire cracking of knuckles sounded like breaking twigs.

It allowed the hand to slip right out of the cuff.

Vinnie watched fascinated as the knuckles of the fixer crackled once more and the hand returned to its original shape. Too engrossed to raise the alarm, Vinnie watched the fixer work the hand into a fist, and then grip the one now loose cuff and clap it on to the wrist still bound to keep it from dangling.

It was actually Jocko who finally yelled the alert, "Hey, he's out of the cuffs."

This woke Vinnie up and he scrabbled at the small of his back for his gun. The men rushed forward but the fixer was already making good use of his freed hands to spring the bungee cords. As Jocko and another came at the fixer from the front, his feet lashed out and caught each in the shin, kicking them back a step. By the time Vinnie leveled his weapon there were men between he and the fixer, one of them reaching around to pin the prisoner from behind. Vinnie sidestepped around the struggle when the fixer reached up and grabbed the man behind him, pulling him overhead and throwing him, just missing Vinnie but sending the man into the two front attackers and knocking them all back into the grill of the van.

When Vinnie had a clear shot, he raised the gun and fired. Moving faster than an encumbered man had a right to, a man supposedly beaten and tortured to the limits of his endurance, the fixer rolled to his right, pulling the entire bucket seat assembly over on top of him and Vinnie's two bullets ricocheted off of the steel runners welded to the bottom of the seat instead.

The seat flew right at Vinnie, launched directly at him from where it once lay on top of the fixer. Vinnie tried to duck away but one of the lower tracks on which the seat was made to slide when mounted, clipped his shoulder and sent him spinning one way while the gun, released from his stunned and numbed hand, went skidding God knew where.

All Vinnie could think as he sprawled and fought to regain his feet was that if the fixer could do that, why didn't he escape earlier? Why put up with the pain and torture if he could have escaped at any time?

He and his men converged on the pool of light illuminated by the van's headlights, looking everywhere, but the fixer was nowhere among them. Night had fallen outside and the warehouse was virtually lightless beyond the edges of the halogen light beams. Then something flew out of the darkness beyond the light, a six inch surgical steel bone saw with finely serrated edge and handles on both ends, and smacked into Jocko's head so hard that Vinnie heard the hollow thud. Jocko went down like a felled oak, blood drooling from a long gash in his scalp. The blade clanged away into the darkness.

"The lights," Vinnie shouted, backing quickly out of the range of the headlights. "Someone turn off the van's lights."

There was a cry of pain as a scalpel seemed to spring from another man's throat, felled him right at Vinnie's feet. The man squirmed in pain, grabbing at Vinnie's pant leg for help. Vinnie pulled away and moved.

Finally, someone turned the headlights off and they were cast into utter darkness.

"The case," someone yelled out. "He's got the doctor's medicine bag."

Vinnie heard a scuffle, a cry and assumed that whoever had called out, giving away his position, was now a corpse at the hands of the fixer. That left only him and one other guy.

The only answer to why the fixer waited to escape when he clearly could have any time he wished, was that he was waiting for Gannery to put in an appearance. The only logical reason he would have put up with Gannery's torture was that he wanted Gannery to believe he was telling the truth about the key. So either the key led nowhere, or it was a setup.

Vinnie had to get out of here alive and warn Gannery.

There was another scuffle nearby to Vinnie's right and he moved away rapidly. That would be the last of his men going down. Vinnie's only hope was to make it to the van and get the hell out of there. He worked his way to the passenger side, tried to open the door quietly and got a loud metallic *kathunk* for his trouble, but the door opened for him.

His position now given away, all caution to the wind, Vinnie jumped in and slammed the door. He would have slid over into the driver's seat, but the fixer was already there, his teeth gleaming in the moonlight as he grinned at Vinnie.

"I spent years being tortured in a Chinese prison camp," the fixer said conversationally.

Vinnie swung his left fist back-hand at the fixer's face, but the man caught it and held it.

"Those guys were experts," he said in the same casual tone.

Vinnie brought the gun in his right hand to bear but the fixer released his left arm and snatched the gun, slipping his finger inside the trigger guard, behind the trigger, blocking Vinnie from pulling it.

"Compared to them, you guys tickle," the fixer said calmly.

Vinnie let go of his gun and tried to jump out, but his door was suddenly locked, probably by the automatic control on the fixer's side of the console.

The last thing Vinnie Testarosa ever thought was that he recognized that key from somewhere. The last thing he ever saw was the fixer's forked fingers coming at his eyeballs.

CHAPTER 37

Jet left the van rolling as he jumped out and sprinted up the steps of the house. The front door was still open and he ran inside, taking the interior steps three at a time. He hesitated just outside the door of Gregory's room as he saw the two bodies lying in a pool of blood, then rushed forward again.

The spill of deep red had spread so far and so wide that it seemed more a lake, an ocean of crimson life force to Jet. In it lay Patricia and Gregory, nearly face to face. Patricia still clutched Gregory's hand in hers, and it seemed somehow more tragic to Jet that his brother would never have felt that contact in the waning moments of his life.

Jet didn't cry.

He squatted in the doorway wearily and hung his

head. Whatever happened now, Gannery had won. There was no way Jet could kill the man enough to atone for the pain he had caused Jet's heart by killing his brother, his only remaining family, his one last tenuous link to sanity.

Jet pressed clenched fists to his temples and rocked in place, unable to cry and unable to let go.

Jet threw himself out across the floor, careless of the blood, and rolled Gregory over. Those blue eyes, so like his, once more alive than Jet's could ever be again, looked up at him dull, devoid of any spark.

The sound was so soft that Jet nearly missed it in his state of silent, helpless grief. When it came again he looked up. He watched and waited...and heard the sound again. The blood directly in front of Patricia's face rippled ever so slightly.

"Patricia," Jet said, turning to her and bringing his face close to hers. Her eyes fluttered like the dying throes of a butterfly, then opened to slits. She looked at him. "Don't move," he whispered.

A scream split the air and Jet looked up to see Ginny on her knees in the doorway, a sack from Bergdorf Goodman spilling shoes and accessories around her. She had gloved hands to her mouth trembling as she looked around at all the blood.

"What ha...ha...happened?" she cried.

"Call 911," Jet hissed. "She's still alive."

Ginny knelt where she was, looking at the blood and making small little mini-screams into her hands.

"Ginny," Jet snapped loudly.

Her head jolted up, her eyes meeting his.

"Call 911. Patricia's still alive."

Ginny nodded, slowly at first, then more vigorously. Averting her eyes, she used the doorjamb to steady her as she stood and sprinted up the hall to the phone in her room.

Jet looked down at his brother, but now Patricia's lips were moving. She was trying to speak through what remained of vocal cords lacerated and torn. Jet watched those lips, and though there was no breath or sound behind them to make so much as a child's whisper, there was no mistaking what they said.

"Kill him."

*

Harry bloom sat at the computer on his desk with his contact database open to Dr. Gerald Gannery, MD's information. He glowered at the screen and chewed his lip. As Gannery's agent, it was his job to tell Gannery that both deals had soured. Rontell had refused to bid and backed out completely, and when Bloom tried to contact Steven Lancaster he got a 'number disconnected' recording. On calling Norsted from Fox he learned that not only had Norsted never heard of a Steven Lancaster, but he had never heard of Dr. Gerald Gannery nor, for that matter, of Harold Bloom himself.

Something had gone horribly wrong. Someone had played a despicable trick and Bloom, savvy and street-smart Park Avenue Talent Agent, had fallen for it. Now, it was his duty to call his client and tell him that they no longer had any deal on the table anywhere, and it was all Bloom's fault, because he'd let himself be played.

Or there was the other alternative.

Bloom tapped the *delete* key. At the prompt to confirm, Bloom moved the mouse pointer over the button labeled OK and clicked. Dr. Gerald Gannery was permanently deleted from Bloom's contact database. And as far as Bloom would be concerned in the future, he'd never heard of the man, had never dealt with him as a client, much less presided over the utter and complete botching of not one, but two possible very lucrative television deals.

Bloom powered down his computer, donned his jacket and headed home.

*

Jet watched from a darkened recess across the street as Gerald Gannery paced the sidewalk. A careful man, Gannery was hesitating. The fixer could sense him working through it in his head, trying to decide whether it was a setup or the real article.

He watched for fifteen minutes while the doctor, dressed in jeans, a flannel shirt and a windbreaker, vacillated. He wore a knit cap as further disguise and as he deliberated, he watched the street for any sign of pursuit.

Clearly coming to a decision, he clutched something in his hand, turned and went inside.

Jet waited and checked his watch every few seconds.

At nine thirty-four and twenty-two seconds, the window to room 29 of the Excelsior Hotel exploded outward, releasing a plume of yellow-orange flame that lit the entire street and heated the buildings across the way before rising into the air and becoming black with soot and smoke. The entire hotel would not likely burn down, though the whole second floor was liable to be completely gutted. Still, most of the surrounding structures would surely be saved.

As Jet hoped, it had clearly taken Gannery some time to track down the hotel whose name was embossed, with the room number, on the key fob. Enough time for the fixer to make it here and witness the fruits if his revenge. He hoped Gannery burned to death cursing the fixer's name.

Jet turned and walked back up the street, hands deep in the pockets of his duster, the canvas stained and soiled, with one very large rust-colored stain now in front, still damp but drying. He kept his head down and made sure not to make eye contact with any of the people now coming cautiously out of the surrounding buildings and peering back up the street at the merrily dancing orange flames.

There would be an investigation into the cause of the fire, and residue of high explosives would be found. Of particular note would be a phone call made several minutes before the explosion instructing the desk clerk to evacuate the building.

Jet turned at a well-lighted intersection, hailed a taxi and instructed the driver where to take him next.

*

Trying to be as quiet as he could, the fixer unlocked the handlebars of his motorcycle and kicked the kickstand back up into place. Straddling the machine, he kicked the pavement and coasted down the hill, away from the peaceful, sleeping suburban neighborhood.

But as stealthy as he could be, he was unable to hide from eyes watching all night long, expecting him and relieved to see him. Before he got far, Dr. Paul Jurgens ran out of his house, still dressed in robe and slippers, and stepped in front of the silent bike, forcing the fixer to apply the front brake and stop.

"You don't know how glad I am you got away from those men," Paul said to him. "I can't believe you traded yourself for my family. Who would do such a thing? You certainly aren't what I thought you were."

The fixer said, "They will never bother you or your family ever again."

"Really?" Paul said in relief. Then, "I...I wanted to say thank you," Dr. Jurgens said. "For...for everything."

The fixer nodded and started to kick his bike forward again, but Paul didn't move.

"I got a call yesterday," he said. "Producer in California. Wants me to do a reality show. Gloria was born in LA and has always been after me to go back for a visit. Looks like we'll be moving there. After...well, earlier...the kids could use a change of scenery, too."

"Nice enough place," the fixer said. Again he started to move forward and again Paul refused to move.

"Is there any way I can show you just how grateful I am?" he asked. "I mean, you were well paid. Still..."

The fixer regarded him for a moment.

"There is one thing."

"Name it," Paul said.

"I believe that show of yours will need a host," the fixer said. "I want you to give a friend of mine an audition."

"Audition hell," Paul said. "Your friend has the part, I don't care how many strings I have to pull."

"No," the fixer shook his head. "She wouldn't want the job like that. Just an audition. Let her prove herself to you. Then she'll earn it, and she'll know she earned it. Her name is Virginia Smith. Ginny. This is her number."

The fixer handed Paul a small card with a name and number on it.

Paul flicked the card between his fingers and

shook his head, smiling. "You knew I'd see you. You knew I'd offer a favor. You had the card ready. How do you do that?"

"I have to go now," the fixer said.

"Of course," Paul said, stepping out of the way.

The fixer got the bike rolling down the hill, then picked up his feet and put them on the pegs. Once he'd rolled far enough away from the darkened house and gained enough speed, he turned the key. The headlight came on. He popped the clutch and the engine roared to life.

He sped away, his long coat stretching behind him like the wings of a bat.

*

Gregory's grave was among others on the side of a gentle slope over which a giant weeping willow stood sentry. His funeral was held on a bright Texas Saturday afternoon, family and childhood friends gathered so densely around the oblong hole in the ground that two figures standing some distance away couldn't even see the casket itself as it was slowly lowered into the ground.

Jet took Patricia's hand and placed it in the crook of his arm. She was still quite weak and took baby steps, especially here over uneven grassy terrain. They'd chosen not to join the mourning party, avoiding inevitable questions for which the answers would be, well, awkward.

They moved away, and Patricia issued a husky, "Yes."

"No," Jet said firmly.

"Yes."

"No."

"Set the wrong things right," she said.

"No,' Jet repeated himself.

This time she stopped and turned to face him. Eyes now deeper caverns of hurt than they ever ought to have been, surrounded as they were by the scars of grief and rage. They bored into his. "Yes," she said.

He sighed and looked around them, but in the end he had to return to meet those eyes squarely. He owed her that much. "The wrong things right," Jet agreed.

"And you'll let me help," Patricia pressed. "From now on?"

"From now on," Jet said. "I promise."

The two toddled on toward the rental car, the passenger side of which opened and Margie got out, ready to help Patricia in and see her well healed before moving on to other employment. Together, Patricia and the fixer moved toward her, their backs to Gregory's grave.

ABOUT THE AUTHOR

Kevin Paul Tracy has published countless fiction and non-fiction pieces over the years. He has travelled extensively spanning half the globe and both sides of the equator, and has held just about every odd job you can think of, from cave spelunking guide, wildlife photographer, interstate courier. He has SCUBA-dived under ice and snow, caves, and craters deep underground. He currently lives in Colorado with two very charismatic St. Bernards.

You can follow Kevin at:
www.KevinPaulTracy.com